Rent a Bridesmaid

HAVE YOU READ THEM ALL?

WHERE TO START
THE DINOSAUR'S PACKED LUNCH
THE MONSTER STORY-TELLER

FOR YOUNGER READERS
BURIED ALIVE!
THE CAT MUMMY
CLIFFHANGER
GLUBBSLYME
LIZZIE ZIPMOUTH
THE MUM-MINDER
SLEEPOVERS
THE WORRY WEBSITE

FIRST-CLASS FRIENDS
BAD GIRLS
BEST FRIENDS
RENT A BRIDESMAID
SECRETS
VICKY ANGEL

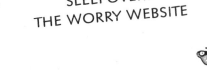

HISTORICAL ADVENTURES
THE LOTTIE PROJECT
OPAL PLUMSTEAD
QUEENIE

ALL ABOUT JACQUELINE WILSON
JACKY DAYDREAM
MY SECRET DIARY

FAMILY DRAMAS

THE BED AND BREAKFAST STAR
CANDYFLOSS
CLEAN BREAK
COOKIE
FOUR CHILDREN AND IT
THE ILLUSTRATED MUM
KATY
LILY ALONE
LITTLE DARLINGS
LOLA ROSE
THE LONGEST WHALE SONG
MIDNIGHT
THE SUITCASE KID

MOST POPULAR CHARACTERS
HETTY FEATHER
SAPPHIRE BATTERSEA
EMERALD STAR
DIAMOND
LITTLE STARS
THE STORY OF TRACY BEAKER
THE DARE GAME
STARRING TRACY BEAKER

STORIES ABOUT SISTERS
THE BUTTERFLY CLUB
THE DIAMOND GIRLS
DOUBLE ACT
THE WORST THING
ABOUT MY SISTER

FOR OLDER READERS
DUSTBIN BABY
GIRLS IN LOVE
GIRLS IN TEARS
GIRLS OUT LATE
GIRLS UNDER PRESSURE
KISS
LOVE LESSONS
MY SISTER JODIE

ALSO AVAILABLE
PAWS AND WHISKERS
THE JACQUELINE WILSON
CHRISTMAS CRACKER
THE JACQUELINE WILSON TREASURY

✯ ABOUT THE AUTHOR ✯

Jacqueline Wilson is one of Britain's bestselling
authors, with more than 38 million books sold
in the UK alone. She has been honoured with
many prizes for her work, including the Guardian
Children's Fiction Award and the Children's Book
of the Year. Jacqueline is a former Children's
Laureate, a professor of children's literature,
and in 2008 she was appointed a Dame for
services to children's literature.

Visit Jacqueline's fantastic website at
www.jacquelinewilson.co.uk

Jacqueline Wilson

Illustrated by Nick Sharratt

Rent a Bridesmaid

DOUBLEDAY

DOUBLEDAY

UK | USA | Canada | Ireland | Australia
India | New Zealand | South Africa

Doubleday is part of the Penguin Random House group of companies
whose addresses can be found at global.penguinrandomhouse.com.

www.penguin.co.uk
www.puffin.co.uk
www.ladybird.co.uk

First published 2016

001

Set in 13/17.25pt New Century Schoolbook by Falcon Oast Graphic Art Ltd
Printed and bound in Great Britain by Clays Ltd, St Ives plc

A CIP catalogue record for this book is available from the British Library

Hardback ISBN: 978–0–857–53272–5
Trade Paperback ISBN: 978–0–857–53271–8

All correspondence to:
Doubleday
Penguin Random House Children's
80 Strand, London WC2R 0RL

Penguin Random House is committed to a sustainable future
for our business, our readers and our planet. This book is made
from Forest Stewardship Council® certified paper.

To Sian Tolfree
with love

Chapter One

This story starts with a dress. Not any old dress. Not a checked school dress or a pinafore dress or a party dress or a princess dress. This is a bridesmaid's dress. The most beautiful bridesmaid's dress in the world.

It's pink. It's not a sickly bright stick-of-rock pink. It's a very soft and subtle pink. I don't think I've ever had raspberry ice cream but it's that colour: vanilla ice cream mixed with just a few red raspberries, all swirled together to make this beautiful shade of pink. It's made of silk, so smooth you want to keep stroking it. It has puff sleeves and a collar, both edged with a tiny piece of lace,

1

a tight waist, and a very flared skirt with three ruffles. It has its own petticoat too, a slightly darker pink, and the hem is trimmed with the same lace as the dress.

It's not my dress. It's my best friend Matty's bridesmaid's dress. We're both called Matilda, only no one ever calls us that, apart from Miss Hope at school, particularly when she's cross with one or other of us. It's usually Matty. She's very naughty and very cheeky but everyone likes her a lot, even Miss Hope.

I like her ever so ever so ever so much. I'm enormously happy that she's my best friend in all the world. I didn't have a best friend before Matty. I had *friends*. I mostly went round with Cathy and Amanda. They were always very nice to me. It's just that I knew Cathy liked Amanda best, and Amanda liked Cathy best too. It's a bit depressing being second-best with everyone.

Dad says it's because I started at this school in Year Three, when everyone had already made their best friends. But Matty only came to Heathfield in Year Four and I think practically the whole class wanted to be her best friend, even Cathy and Amanda. But Matty picked me!

It was right on the very first day, straight after Register. She came up to me and said, 'Hey, you. Matilda! Guess what, I'm Matilda too.'

Well, of course I knew that, because I'd just heard Miss Hope call it out, but I pretended to be surprised, just to be polite.

'Really? Wow!' I said, though it wasn't really such a coincidence. There are two girls called Ayesha in Year Four, two girls called Eleanor in Year Five and there are actually *three* girls called Jasmine in Year Six.

I worried that I sounded silly. I felt very shy of Matty then. She had bright red curly hair, a great mop of it, and lovely green eyes, and a funny turned-up nose sprinkled with freckles. She wore an ordinary Heathfield blue-and-white checked dress, but she'd pinned different badges all over her front and she wore amazing emerald-green trainers, all sparkly with sequins.

'I love your badges and your shoes,' I said.

Matty grinned. 'They're cool, aren't they? Miss Hope told me we're not supposed to wear stuff like this, but she didn't get cross because I'm a new girl. So, what do you think about being called Matilda?'

I shrugged, not really knowing what to say. I liked my name. I especially liked it that there was a great story about a girl called Matilda who loved reading. I love reading too. I have six copies of the *Matilda* book at home because people think it's a great idea to give it to me for a Christmas or birthday present.

'It's a totally rubbish name, isn't it?' said Matty. 'But everyone calls me Matty. Do they call you that too?'

'They call me Tilly,' I said.

'Yeah, some of the kids at my old school tried calling me that. Silly Tilly. But I soon put a stop to it. Don't you mind being called Tilly?'

'Not really.'

'OK then. It might have got a bit muddly if we were both Matty. So shall we sit next to each other in class?'

'Well, I'd love that, but Miss Hope usually says where we have to sit.'

'That's OK. I'll tell her I'm shy because I'm new and I need to sit next to someone nice,' said Matty.

I was thrilled that she thought I was nice – though Matty was the least shy girl I'd ever met. Somehow she got her way. Miss Hope let her sit next to me, and by the end of that first day I felt I'd known Matty all her life.

When the bell went for home time she said, 'Can you come to tea?'

'That would be great, but won't your mum mind?'

'She'll be pleased I've got a new best friend,' said Matty.

She said it so casually, but for me it was the most amazing sentence I'd ever heard. She'd actually said I was her best friend. I must have looked a bit stunned because she gave me a nudge.

'We *are* best friends, aren't we?' she said.

'Yes! Yes, of course we are,' I said.

It wasn't hard to pick Matty's mum out from all the other mums waiting at the school gate. She had a mop of bright red curls, and so did Matty's little brother. I liked their clothes too. Matty's mum had a long green dress and a black velvet coat and purple wedge shoes. She looked very arty, reminding me a little bit of my own mum. Matty's little brother had six old loom band bracelets on one wrist and a brown bobble hat with a pompom at either side, like ears.

'Hey, Mum!' Matty called, and took hold of my arm. 'This is my best friend Tilly. She's coming to tea!'

'That's great,' said Matty's mum. She smiled at me. 'I'm Angie. Where's your mum, Tilly? Shall we check it's OK for you to come to tea?'

'My mum's . . . not here,' I said. 'Aunty Sue picks me up from school. She's that lady over there, the one with the beige jacket.'

Aunty Sue also had beige trousers, and a beige jumper, and beige lace-up shoes. She had beige hair too. The only bright thing about her was her lipstick. I did my best not to get too near her because I didn't want red smudges all over me. She was the exact opposite of

Sylvie, Mum's friend from when they were at art school together. Sylvie had collected me from my old school. She always wore black and lots of big bangles and she had hair down to her waist, *blue* hair. I missed Sylvie now.

'Let's go and ask your aunty then,' said Angie.

'She's not my real aunty – she's just a lady who looks after me,' I said quickly.

'Hi, Sue,' said Angie, as if she'd known her all her life.

Aunty Sue looked surprised. She's old, the sort of lady who likes to be called Mrs Brown.

Angie chatted away without realizing this.

'You want Tilly to come to tea *now*?' said Aunty Sue. 'Well, it's not quite convenient today, not at such short notice. Perhaps another time.'

'Oh please, Aunty Sue,' I begged. Perhaps there wouldn't be another time. Perhaps Matty would choose some other girl to be her best friend and go to tea with her tomorrow.

'Well, we'd have to ask your dad, dear,' said Aunty Sue.

'Can we phone him?' I asked.

'I don't think we should bother him at work.'

'He said I can phone him any time I want,' I said.

'Yes, but only if it's something very important,' said Aunty Sue.

'Oh, but it *is*!' said Matty. 'Please let's phone Tilly's dad. I'm sure he won't mind. Go on, Aunty Sue. Be a sport. Please, please, please.' She clasped Aunty Sue's beige arm and looked up at her pleadingly.

Aunty Sue isn't exactly strict, but I always have to do what she says. I can't ever get her to change her mind. But Matty worked wonders.

'All right then,' she said, smiling at Matty.

She has one of those ages-old phones and she always forgets to charge it. She often forgets how to *work* it. I held my breath as she fumbled away, but at last she got through to Dad and explained.

Then she handed the phone over to me.

'Hi, Dad, I've got this new best friend called Matty – she's a Matilda like me – and please can I go to tea with her now?' I gabbled.

Dad asked to speak to Matty's mum, and then he said yes.

'You go and have a lovely time, chickie,' he said.

So I did! I'll never forget that first wonderful tea time. The tea itself was fantastic. Aunty Sue gives me a glass of milk and a chocolate teacake first of all. I don't mind milk and I like chocolate teacakes, but it gets a bit boring having them day after day after day. Then, if Dad ever has to work overtime and won't be back in time to give me supper, Aunty Sue microwaves a pizza for me.

'I know pizza's your favourite, Tilly,' she always says.

I love going to Pizza Express with Dad for a treat. Aunty Sue's little frozen pizzas aren't the same at all.

Angie didn't give us milk or chocolate teacakes or pizza. When we got back to their house she gave us fizzy water with a slice of orange in it and a quarter of a peanut-butter sandwich and a raw carrot and a doll's-house plastic saucer of blueberries. Matty's little brother Lewis put his mouth to the saucer and gobbled down more than his fair share of the blueberries.

'Lewis! Don't get your nasty slurp all over our berries!' Matty complained.

'I'm not Lewis. I'm a big brown bear,' said Lewis, patting his bobble hat. 'You shush or I'll eat you all up, Matty!'

'I'm not Matty – I'm a bear hunter. Watch out or I'll go and fetch my gun,' said Matty.

She wanted Lewis to stay in the kitchen with their mum while we went off to her bedroom to play.

'I'm coming too,' said Lewis.

'No, we want to be private,' said Matty.

'Don't be mean,' said Lewis. '*You* want me to come and play too, don't you, Tilly?'

I hesitated. He was looking up at me pleadingly with his big brown eyes. I wanted to say yes, but I also didn't want to annoy Matty.

'It's my bedroom too,' said Lewis. 'So I can go there whenever I want and you can't stop me.'

Matty sighed. 'Worst luck. I wish I didn't have to share with you,' she said. 'You don't half get on my nerves sometimes.'

I wished I *did* have someone to share with. I liked my bedroom. Dad decorated it specially for me, pale blue with white curtains patterned with hyacinths and a duvet to match. He even bought me a cuddly blue bunny, to lounge on my pillow during the day. I like the bunny, but after Dad's kissed me goodnight I tip it out on the floor and cuddle Stripy. He's an old bedraggled teddy I've had ever since I was a baby. He used to have a stripy jumper but he lost it ages ago.

It's a lovely bedroom but it's a bit lonely in there. I've got my books in the bookcase and my china dogs walking along the top of my chest of drawers and my photo of Mum on the bedside table, but that's about it. I used to have all my dolls sitting on the windowsill, and they would jump down and play with me, but Cathy and Amanda seemed astonished that I still played with dolls. I felt very babyish so I put them in two carrier bags at the bottom of my wardrobe. I got them out weeks later because I missed them so much, but they wouldn't play any more. They just lay there like dead things. I felt terrible. I sometimes leave my drawing book out and spill my felt tips all over the floor just to make it look as if someone actually uses the room.

There was no doubt whatsoever that Matty and Lewis used their room. They'd only just moved to their new house but their bedroom was already ankle deep in soft toys and Lego and scribbled drawings and old dolls with weird felt-pen make-up and little ponies and tiny trolls and plastic

11

dinosaurs and books and all sorts of clothes and trainers and boots. There was clutter all over their beds too, and it was hard to tell what colour their wall was because it had so many pictures and posters pinned up on it.

'Excuse the mess,' said Matty, kicking a space for us to sit in.

'Mum says she's going to chuck out all our stuff if we don't tidy up – but she doesn't mean it,' said Lewis, climbing to the top bunk bed and sitting there, swinging his legs.

'Does your mum fuss about being tidy?' Matty asked me.

I took a deep breath. 'Not really,' I said, which was sort of true.

'Soooo – what do you want to play?'

I fidgeted, not knowing what to suggest. When I went to tea with Cathy or Amanda we usually played games on their iPads or dressed up in their mums' high heels or watched pop videos and tried to copy the dances. I didn't know which Matty would prefer.

'Let's play the Warrior Princess game!' said Lewis.

'That's babyish,' Matty said quickly.

'No it's not. It's our best game ever. Go on,' said Lewis. 'You want to play it too, don't you, Tilly?'

'If Matty does,' I said.

'Well, we could play it just for a bit. To stop Lewis pestering. But don't blame me if you think it's a stupid game,' said Matty.

It wasn't a stupid game at all. Lewis was right. The Warrior Princess game *was* the best ever. It was exactly the sort of game I liked to play. I didn't know anyone else played like that, especially girls of our age.

I thought there would just be one warrior princess – Matty. But Matty said we could each be a Warrior Princess, with our own kingdom.

'This is Princess Powerful,' Matty said, picking up a doll with a green face and scribbled tattoos up and down her arms. 'She rules over Monster Kingdom. This is her private army.' She set up all the dinosaurs and trolls rambling over the rugged terrain of assorted books.

Lewis picked up a doll whose eyes were jammed shut. 'This is my dolly,' he declared. 'She's Princess Go-to-Sleep who rules over Pillow Kingdom. And these are her army people.' He gathered up all the soft toys and tucked them up carefully on two pillows and a duvet.

Then Matty and Lewis looked at me expectantly. I stirred the little pile of dolls. There was one who had a purple face and purple hair too, tied in a ponytail. I picked her up.

'This is Princess Pony and she's the Warrior Princess of Magical Horse Kingdom,' I said. I gathered a little herd of toy horses, and set them to graze on a green dressing gown. 'My doll has invisible wings and so have all the horses in her kingdom, so they can flap their wings and fly through the air whenever they want.'

'Hey, you know how to play!' said Lewis.

'Brilliant, Princess Pony,' said Matty, looking relieved. 'None of my friends at my old school had a clue how to play. So, let battle commence!'

Princess Powerful led her dinosaurs up and down the rocky terrain of her kingdom, ready to attack Princess Go-to-Sleep. The dinosaurs and trolls all growled and gnashed their teeth, ready to rip the soft toys to shreds as they slumbered. But Princess Go-to-Sleep awoke as the first dinosaur pounced and waved her arms in the air while singing a lullaby, and immediately Princess Powerful fell into a deep sleep, snoring very loudly, and all the dinosaurs and trolls became comatose, their plastic feet in the air.

'Attack them!' Princess Powerful hissed, between snores.

So Princess Pony mounted her biggest steed, and all the horses started attacking Princess Go-to-Sleep from the rear. When she whirled round and tried to wave and sing them to sleep, they all rose in the air out of her reach, though I let a couple of the smallest ponies fall to earth and start snoring too.

Then Princess Powerful woke up and there was a prolonged battle, the dinosaurs and trolls against the ponies, while Princess Go-to-Sleep started building a Lego defence wall all round Pillow Kingdom to protect her soft toys.

We played Warrior Princesses for ages, until Angie called us for supper. That was lovely too. She'd made real pasta with a cheesy sauce and we had a salad too, and then raspberries and ice cream.

'Thank you very much, Mrs Davies,' I said. 'That was yummy.'

'I'm glad you liked it, Tilly. Call me Angie – it's much more friendly than Mrs Davies.'

Not *Aunty* Angie, like Aunty Sue.

Matty's dad, Tom, came home from work in time for supper. He made a bit of a fuss of Matty and Lewis, romping with them in the hall. I watched, wishing my dad acted silly like that. Then I felt bad and wanted my own dad. All the old feelings came rushing back. What if my dad had had an accident? What if he suddenly decided he needed to have time to himself? What if he simply lost his memory and went wandering off, forgetting all about me? What would I do without a dad? What would happen to me?

When Dad came to collect me at half past seven, I rushed up to him too and hugged him hard. After we'd both said our thank-yous and goodbyes and were in the car, Dad turned to me.

'What's up, Tilly? Didn't you like it there? Isn't this Matty as nice as you thought she was?' he asked anxiously.

'I *loved* it there. And Matty's fantastic and the best friend ever,' I said.

'So why did you come rushing up to me like that?' he asked. 'You seemed desperate.'

'I – I was just happy to see you,' I mumbled.

16

'Oh, Tilly,' Dad said.

His face screwed up. I couldn't work out whether he was happy or sad. His hand reached out and he squeezed mine, but then he had to use both his hands for driving.

The house seemed extra quiet and tidy when we got home.

I was really looking forward to going to school the next day, and yet I was a bit scared too. Maybe Matty had changed her mind and decided she didn't want me as a best friend any more. She didn't go to breakfast club, so I just sat eating my cornflakes by myself as usual and then read my book. But when it was time to go out into the playground, Matty came haring through the gate, yelling my name.

'Hey, Tilly! Didn't we have a great time yesterday? You're so good at playing. You're brilliant at making things up. Promise you'll come again soon? Mum says you can come any time you like.'

'Great!' I said. I *felt* great. I wasn't that little shy quiet mousy girl with a secret any more. I was Matty's best friend, Tilly, and I was suddenly a great big bouncy funny girl who was *brilliant at making things up.*

Matty asked me back to tea that very day and I so wanted to, but Aunty Sue said it was too soon. She wouldn't even let me phone Dad this time.

I wished Aunty Sue wasn't so strict and bossy. I'd never really liked her. Dad had put an advert in the local newsagent's when we moved to our new house and I was about to start going to my new school.

> # WANTED
> Kind reliable lady to collect
> my daughter from junior school
> on a daily basis and give her
> tea occasionally. Fair wage paid.

Sid the newsagent read the advert and sucked his teeth.

'Funny how times have changed. Kids used to walk themselves home from school and get their own tea. Ah well. I don't expect you'll get many replies, but here's hoping.'

We didn't get *any* replies the first week. Then an old lady answered – a really ancient lady who rode a buggy and had a hearing aid and very thick glasses. Dad didn't think she was suitable even before she accidentally drove over his foot. He wanted someone younger to look after me, but the next person was almost too young, a girl of fourteen called Shelley.

I was in awe of Shelley, with her bright blonde hair and her perfect eyebrows and her very short school skirt. Dad wasn't at all sure, but decided to try her out for a week. I had to wait a good half-hour for Shelley to pick me up because the Seniors finished school later than the Juniors, but I didn't mind. I sat on the school wall and read my book, and sometimes drew extra little scribbly pictures of Matilda in the margins. But on Friday Shelley's boyfriend met her after school, and they went up to the park and forgot all about me. The school secretary had to phone Dad to come and collect me when I'd been waiting more than an hour. That was the end of Shelley.

'I think you're going to have to go to after-school club,' said Dad.

I'd been to after-school club at my old school, after Mum left. I'd hated it because a boy called Jeremy kept breaking all my pencils and crayons and saying hateful things about my mum. I knew Jeremy wouldn't be at this new school and no one there knew about Mum, but I was still sure I'd hate it. Breakfast club was bad enough. After-school club was longer and much worse.

I couldn't see why I couldn't do what Sid said children did long ago. I rather fancied the idea of walking myself home and I could easily make myself a sandwich for tea. I was good at cheese on toast too, and I knew how to use a can opener if necessary. I begged and pleaded, but Dad said I couldn't – and then Mrs Brown the beige woman knocked on the door and said she was answering our advert. She was quite old but not so old she used a buggy, and she certainly wasn't going to go to the park with her boyfriend.

'I'm sure we'll get along fine and dandy,' she said, giving me her best bright smile and patting me on the shoulder. 'You must call me Aunty Sue.'

Dad said Aunty Sue was a godsend. If that was so, I wasn't surprised. God was probably happy to have got rid of her. I felt truly fed up now when I had to go home with her instead of going back to Matty's house.

When we lived at our old house and Sylvie sometimes collected me from school when Mum couldn't, she let me do painting with her, proper painting with big tubes of colour. Sylvie didn't care if I dripped paint on the floor or got it all over my school clothes. She just laughed when I tried painting my hair blue to copy hers.

Painting was out of the question at Aunty Sue's, though she didn't mind if I did drawing or colouring. I kept some spare paper and my second-best set of felt tips at Aunty Sue's house, so I drew a picture of the three Warrior Princesses and their tribes having a gigantic battle.

'Is that homework, Tilly?' asked Aunty Sue.

'No, just a picture,' I said.

'You've been working on it for ages, dear. What are you drawing?'

'Princesses,' I said.

'Oh, lovely,' said Aunty Sue. 'I liked drawing princesses when I was a little girl.'

But then she came to peer over my shoulder, which was very annoying. I tried to cover my picture with my hands, but the paper was too big and my hands too small.

'My goodness,' said Aunty Sue. 'Why have you coloured their faces such strange colours? Don't you have a pink felt tip? And what are all these other monster things?

21

And why are they biting and hurting each other?' She sounded really bothered about it.

'It's just a picture,' I said, and I shut my drawing book quickly. 'Can I watch television now?'

Aunty Sue and I watched *Pointless* together. It was her favourite programme. She tried to get me to join in and guess the answers. I hardly knew any of them. Aunty Sue didn't either, but she still loved watching. She talked about Alexander and Richard as if they were her best friends.

When Dad came to collect me, Aunty Sue murmured to him when she thought I wasn't listening. I heard her say, 'Very strange . . . violent . . . disturbing.'

Dad didn't say anything to me in the car or when we got home. He didn't ask to see my picture. But when he came to tuck me up in bed, he sat beside me and said, ever so casually, 'So how are you feeling, Tilly?'

'Fine,' I said.

'You're still getting along with Matty?'

'Yes. She asked me to go to tea with her again! Mean old Aunty Sue wouldn't let me.'

'You can't keep going to Matty's house day after day.'

'She says I can!'

'Yes, but it wouldn't be polite. And I think Aunty Sue might be getting worried that she'll lose her job. I pay her to look after you.'

'I wish you'd pay Angie, Matty's mum!'

'So you haven't had any fights with anyone?'

'What? Dad! I don't fight!'

'No one's picking on you?'

'No. Well, Cathy and Amanda said I was stupid wanting to be friends with old Carrot-Top, but they're just jealous because I'm Matty's best friend now.'

'Miss Hope hasn't been cross with you?'

'No. In D and T she said my purse was very good. I sewed a cat on it. She said . . .'

'Yes? What did she say?'

'She said it would make a lovely present for my mum.'

'Oh. Well, you can save it to give to Mum when you next see her,' said Dad.

I didn't say anything. Dad didn't either. We just stayed still in my very quiet bedroom. Then Dad gave me a kiss on the cheek and went downstairs. I threw Blue Bunny out of bed and clutched Stripy.

I couldn't go to sleep for a while so I played my own favourite game inside my head. It wasn't a wildly exciting game like Warrior Princesses. It was a pretend game called Wedding.

My mum and my dad were getting married. Mum wore a long white dress that showed off her slim waist. She had her long fair hair coiled up and held in place with her pearl slide. She let me play with her pearl slide once when I was watching her put on her make-up. I ran my thumb up and down the pearls. I liked feeling the little bobbles. I thought they were real pearls once but they were only pretend. She had a veil too, very white and lacy. I wanted this wedding to be as traditional as possible.

Dad wore a very smart suit, with a long black jacket and grey pinstripe trousers. He had a waistcoat too, black silk with gold embroidery. Dad never wore fancy clothes. It was hard work imagining him in anything but jeans or his suit for work, but it was his wedding after all and I wanted him to look wonderful. I made sure he was wearing a shirt as crisp and white as royal icing, and I polished his shoes until they were like black mirrors.

Then I had to dress myself up too, because I was the bridesmaid of course. My bridesmaid's dress varied. Sometimes it was very pale pink, sometimes hyacinth blue, sometimes delicate apricot. If it was winter I wore a red velvet dress with white fur round the hem, though I was worried I might look too much like Santa Claus. I never thought of dressing myself in raspberry pink, the best colour of all.

We went to the church in a white limo. All the neighbours in Willow Road, where we used to live, came to their garden gates to have a good look at us. We gave them a wave and then we drove off to the church. I knew brides were meant to drive separately but we were a family, so it made sense for us all to go together.

The limo had blackened windows. We could see out perfectly but no one could see in. Dad laughed and said, 'Close your eyes, Tilly,' and then he put his arms round Mum, careful not to crease her dress, and gave her a big film-star kiss. If I tried to draw this scene I'd have a fat little cherub flying above Mum and Dad's head and a ring of little hearts above their heads like haloes.

Then we drew up at the church. Dad sprang out first and then helped Mum. I gathered up all the skirts of her dress and made sure they didn't get stuck in the car. Then we walked solemnly into church, Dad and Mum together, me walking behind, holding my bridesmaid's posy.

The church was crowded out with all our guests. Most of them were people we knew before, and children from my old school. But sometimes I added Aunty Sue, wearing a beige dress and a funny hat, and Miss Hope in the suit she wears on parents' night, and Cathy and Amanda in ordinary clothes looking enviously at my beautiful bridesmaid's dress. I added Matty and Lewis and Angie as special guests of honour, in the very front row.

Then Mum and Dad promised to love and honour each other for ever and never ever part.

Chapter Two

I made myself a special chart in my drawing book. I divided the page into seven sections, carefully pencilling down the page using my ruler, and then I ruled across the page from the top to the bottom, so I had lots of squares. I wrote a title at the top, using a different colour for every letter:

IS MATTY STILL MY
BEST FRIEND?

I labelled each of the seven columns for the days of the week, and then, with my favourite green pen, did a big tick in the first box.

I went on ticking day after day, week after week. It was very satisfying. I drew other pictures in my drawing book too, but decided not to attempt any further Princess Warrior scenes because I was worried about Aunty Sue having a sneaky peep and telling Dad. Sometimes, when I wanted to try out a scenario in my head before going to tea with Matty, I'd sketch out scenes in the back of my school jotter book. Soon dinosaurs crept along the bottom of most pages, jaws wide open, while soft animals screamed and ponies were savaged. I showed Matty and she was very impressed. She tried to invent a Warrior Princess scenario in her own jotter, but her dinosaurs looked like big pussycats and she tore out the page impatiently.

Then, one day, we did a spelling test in our jotters. We all swopped our books at the end of the test. I marked Matty's and she marked mine. She wasn't actually a very good speller, so sometimes I squinted so I didn't see the word properly and marked it with a tick. I often made a few mistakes too, but Matty was even kinder and marked me ten out of ten most times.

But then Miss Hope got suspicious and asked to see the spellings in our jotters for herself. She gave Matty her jotter back with a telling off, but she kept mine, flicking through the pages. My heart started thumping. I knew what she was looking at.

She asked me to wait behind at the end of the lesson. Matty stayed too, but Miss Hope told her to go out into the playground. I hopped uncomfortably from one foot to the other.

'I've been looking at all these drawings in your jotter, Tilly,' said Miss Hope.

'I'm sorry, Miss Hope. I know we're not really supposed to draw in our jotters. I won't do it again,' I gabbled. 'Can I go and play now?'

'Just a minute. These drawings are very . . . violent,' said Miss Hope.

'Well. They're dinosaurs. They *are* violent,' I said.

'Not necessarily. Many dinosaurs were vegetarian, totally placid creatures who lived in harmony with other creatures.'

'Yes, but mine are the *Tyrannosaurus rex* kind,' I said.

'I didn't know you were especially interested in dinosaurs, Tilly,' said Miss Hope.

'Oh yes, I am. That's why I draw them lots,' I said.

'So what is this grey one called? And this one here with the spiky mane? And the one with big teeth carrying the pony in its mouth?'

Matty simply called them Greyboy and Spiky and Toothache.

'I can't remember their proper names,' I admitted.

'Have you been to the Natural History Museum in Kensington to see the dinosaur exhibition there?' asked Miss Hope.

I shook my head.

Dad once took me to the Victoria and Albert Museum in Kensington and I'd quite liked some very old wooden dolls with a whole cabinet of beautifully made little clothes. Then we went to Harrods and I liked the dolls there even more.

'Have you been watching any dinosaur films?' Miss Hope persisted.

I shook my head again.

She leaned nearer, not at all cross now.

'Do you sometimes have nightmares about dinosaurs?'

I had lots of nightmares. Sometimes they were

about Mum. Sometimes they were about Dad disappearing. Nowadays they were mostly about Matty breaking friends with me, though I still ticked a box on my chart every night.

Miss Hope was surprisingly close to me. I suddenly saw her as a person, not just a teacher. I liked the way she tied her hair up, showing her ears. She wore tiny silver earrings in the shape of a crescent moons. I wished I had pierced ears and could wear moon earrings. I wondered about saying all my secrets into her ear. Just for a moment it seemed possible.

Then I changed my mind.

'I don't have nightmares about dinosaurs,' I said truthfully.

Miss Hope looked at me for a long moment. Then she just nodded and patted my arm.

'All right. Off you go,' she said.

I thought she'd forgotten all about it, but one morning the next week she was in the playground when Dad dropped me off at school for breakfast club.

'Can I have a word, Mr Andrews?' she called.

I hovered nearby. This time I couldn't hear

properly, but I saw Dad frowning. He glanced at me, looking worried. I stopped being scared and got furious instead. How dare Miss Hope tell tales and worry my dad!

I flashed Dad a big cheesy grin. I was trying to reassure him, but he looked even more anxious. Perhaps he thought I was baring my teeth at him like one of my dinosaur drawings.

I wanted to rush up and tell him that he mustn't worry, that stupid Miss Hope and hopeless Aunty Sue were getting in a silly state about nothing. But I didn't get the chance. Dad just waved to me when Miss Hope was done and started hurrying away, pointing at his watch. I knew he was already late for work.

Miss Hope tried to smile at me reassuringly. I didn't quite dare say what I thought, but I glared at her and stamped off to breakfast club. I poured my cornflakes into a bowl and then bashed them into little golden crumbs with my spoon.

I was still in a bad mood at the start of school. It turned out that Matty was in a bad mood too.

'You'll never ever guess what!' she said.

'What?'

'Mum's insisting I've got to be a *bridesmaid!*' Matty groaned. She mimed despair, her eyes screwed up, her mouth an O of anguish.

'A bridesmaid,' I repeated. 'But that's lovely, isn't it?' All my different dresses for my Mum-and-Dad-Wedding game flashed before my eyes as if they were hanging on a washing line.

'No! It's the absolute opposite of lovely. It's totally foul. I absolutely can't stand the idea of being a bridesmaid and looking a right idiot. I've told Mum I won't but she says I have to, because it's my Aunt Rachel getting married – she's Mum's younger sister, so I'm her niece, so I *have* to be a bridesmaid. And I'm going to look soooo stupid, because Aunt Rachel wants a pink-and-white theme. She's wearing a white dress but she wants pink roses in her hair and a pink rose bouquet, and me and my cousin have to wear pink dresses. *Pink*, when I've got red hair!' Matty chuntered on and on about it, before lessons, at playtime, and during lessons too.

We were supposed to be working together, making up a poem about a feeling. It could be love or hate or fear. We had to list all the things we loved or hated or feared to help us get inspired.

I usually liked our Literacy lessons, but I couldn't stand writing about feelings. I put *Writing stupid poems* in our Hate column.

'Yeah, it's rubbish, isn't it,' said Matty. She added *Being a Bridesmaid* underneath.

She mumbled to herself and then she snapped her fingers. 'Got it! Listen!' She recited her poem proudly.

'I can't
Be a bridesmaid for my aunt
I'll look silly
In a daft dress with a frilly
Bit at the bottom
In finest pink cotton.'

'There! It's great, isn't it?' she said.

'Aren't bridesmaid's dresses usually silk or satin? Not cotton?'

'Yeah, but then it wouldn't rhyme.'

'It's a bit short, isn't it?' I said.

'Well, you add a bit,' said Matty.

So I wrote:

I'll add a second verse
Because it could be worse.

34

I'll eat lots of cake and drink lots of Coke
And have a laugh at every single joke
And I might even spill
Down my silly pink frill.

'Cool! Draw a picture of me doing just that!' said Matty. 'Then draw all my dinosaurs attacking my Aunt Rachel.'

'I can't. I'll get into trouble. Miss Hope told Dad about my dinosaur drawings this morning,' I said, starting to draw Matty.

'What, she told on you to your dad just for scribbling in your jotter? Everyone does it!'

'Yes, I know. But she got fussed about them being dinosaurs. And so did Aunty Sue. She told Dad too. It's because they're violent. If you draw very violent things, then they think you've gone a bit weird and send you to see a lady in a clinic,' I said.

'No they don't!'

'They do too,' I told her.

'How do you know?' asked Matty.

I hesitated. I'd said too much. I didn't want to tell Matty everything, even though she was my best friend in all the world.

'I just do,' I said lamely.

35

'Well, they're not your dinosaurs, they're mine, Princess Powerful's very own pets. I invented them. Tell your dad and Miss Hope and that Aunty Sue lady that it's all my fault,' said Matty.

'No, because then you'd maybe get into trouble too. And what if Dad said I couldn't play with you any more?' I could feel my face getting very red. 'I couldn't bear that.'

'Me neither,' said Matty. 'But don't worry. I don't think anything will happen. They're not going to cart you off to any scary clinic. I won't let them!'

I felt incredibly comforted, even though I knew Matty couldn't possibly defend me against three adults. When I was at Aunty Sue's after school, I drew the most normal picture in the world, a house with a garden with lots of carefully coloured flowers, and two girls holding hands standing on the very green grass. I gave one girl orange hair, and each had a very smiley mouth. Then I took my yellow felt tip and drew a big sun at the top of the page with rays all around. The sun had a smiley mouth too. I even gave the blue front door a curved letter box so it looked as if the house was smiling as well. Aunty Sue hovered above me. 'Oh, that's a lovely picture, dear,' she said, and she offered me another teacake.

When Dad came to collect me, Aunty Sue said, 'Show Daddy your lovely picture, Tilly.'

I showed Dad and he smiled. When he came to tuck me up in bed that night, he was a bit fidgety, roaming around my room, running his finger along the top of all my paperbacks and turning my china dogs the other way round. He didn't look at the photo of Mum. He never did.

He finally sat down on the edge of my bed with Blue Bunny on his lap. 'I really liked your picture of the house and the little girls,' he said, 'but Miss Hope says you've been drawing all those monster things in your school books.'

'It's only my jotter. We're *allowed* to draw stuff in our jotters,' I said.

'Yes, I'm sure you are. Miss Hope isn't cross. She's just a little worried that you might be a bit upset about something,' said Dad.

'Well, I'm not,' I said. 'Not any more.'

After the whole Mum thing I *had* gone a bit weird. I cried a lot at first, especially at home. I sometimes went and sat in Mum's wardrobe just because the few clothes hanging there still smelled of her. But after a while I got angry. One day I got so really red roaring angry that I got the scissors out of the kitchen drawer and cut Mum's clothes up into little bits. I kept drawing Mum too, taking great care, doing every curl separately and drawing all the numbers on her watch, but then I'd take my big black wax crayon and I'd scribble all over her until you could only glimpse bits of her through the black.

I'd had to go to a clinic once a week and talk to the lady there. She wanted me to play with all the little dolls in the doll's house and the plastic toys in the sandpit, though I felt stupid playing games in front of her. She especially liked it if I did lots of pictures. She didn't tell me off if I scribbled with black crayon. She just talked about it with me. Talked about Mum.

I didn't like talking to her, especially about Mum. My pictures got darker and darker. Sometimes I used powder paints and a big brush and coloured a whole page black. I was in the toilets at the clinic one day trying to wash all the black off my hands when an older, very thin girl came out of a cubicle and shook her head at me.

'You'll be stuck coming

here for ever if you paint a lot of black things,' she said, washing her own hands. 'They think that means you're angry and fed up. The trick is to paint happy things. Smiley faces and suns and cute bunnies and kittens. They think that shows you've worked through your problems.'

I went on washing my hands thoughtfully. 'Do you do that?'

'Course I do.'

'So why do you still have to come here then?' I asked.

'Because I won't eat,' she said.

'Why?'

'Because I don't want to. Quit asking me questions. You're worse than they are,' she said, and she splashed me.

I splashed her back. We started to look as if we'd been for a swim.

'Hey, better stop now. They're so nuts they'll think we tried to drown ourselves in the wash basins,' said the thin girl.

I took her advice on my next visit. I painted a very sunny, smiley picture of the countryside. It was a pretty awful painting, because I did it too quickly and the blue sky trickled down the page and flooded the green grass, and all the black and

white cows in my meadow turned muddy grey —
but their pink mouths still smiled.

My lady smiled too, and said she thought it was
a *lovely* picture. I was careful to play sunny, smiley
games after that too. I made the family in the doll's
house all kiss each other and have a plasticine feast
from the tiny tea set on the miniature table. I
arranged all the plastic clutter in the sandpit into a
pretty pattern, taking care not to bury anything.
Quite soon the lady and Dad had a discussion, and
I didn't have to go to the clinic after that.

I desperately didn't want to go back there. It
made me think about Mum too much.

'Tilly,' said Dad, putting his arm round me.
'Tilly, do you still miss Mum a lot?'

His voice sounded very strained. I knew he
didn't like to talk about Mum either.

'I don't miss her at all,' I said.

We both knew I was fibbing, but Dad decided to
let it go. He tucked me up and kissed me goodnight.
I played my wedding game until I went to sleep.
This time I pictured myself in a pink bridesmaid's
dress. It was the wrong shade of pink. I hadn't
seen Matty's raspberry-pink dress. It hadn't even
been made yet. But the next morning at school
Matty showed me a little square of silk.

'What is it? A little handkerchief?' I said, puzzled.

'No, you nutcase! It's a sample of my new bridesmaid's dress. Isn't it the yuckiest colour ever?'

'I think it's beautiful,' I said, stroking the soft square.

'Then you're mad,' said Matty. 'And you should see the design. *Frills!* And a petticoat. I think I've even got to wear matching pink knickers, imagine!'

'But it wouldn't look right if they didn't match. You're always dashing about and doing hand-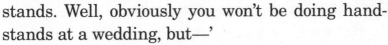stands. Well, obviously you won't be doing handstands at a wedding, but—'

'Don't count on it. Hey, wouldn't it look cool if I somersaulted up the aisle after Aunt Rachel? I bet everyone would have a right laugh.' Matty saw my face. 'I'm joking, silly.'

'You never know with you,' I said.

'Mum dragged me off to this lady's house to have a fitting for this awful dress. I didn't half look daft, standing there in my underwear. And one of the lady's daughters put her head round the door and saw me and poked out her tongue.'

'That was rude of her.'

'I cracked up laughing, actually. I'd have done the same. She's quite good fun. We talked a bit while our mums were having a cup of tea. Oh, and you'll never guess what, Tilly!'

'What?'

'We've nearly got the same name. She's called Martina, but everyone calls her Marty. Matty and Marty! Isn't that magic?'

'Not really,' I said. My voice sounded a bit croaky. I swallowed. 'It's just like you and me both being called Matilda.'

'Yeah, but Matty and Tilly still sound different. Matty and Marty sound like a double act or something, don't you see?'

'No,' I said, and I quickly changed the subject.

Chapter Three

Matty kept going on about this Marty girl. She had to go back for two more fittings for the bridesmaid's dress.

'I bet you think it's a right bore,' I said hopefully.

'Yes, it is, standing there on a table, with Marty's mum making me turn round and round ever so slowly while she pins up the petticoat hem and then the awful dress. I felt just like the little twirling ballerina inside my mum's music box. So then I stuck my arms in the air and did a little ballet dance, just a couple of steps, only I was too near the edge of the table and I fell off. Look at my bruise!'

Matty pulled up her dress there and then,

even though we were out in the playground. I saw the dark purple bruise on her skinny white thigh. So did a little gang of boys playing football. They all shouted and whistled. I'd have died of embarrassment but Matty just made a very rude gesture back at them. Miss Hope was on playground duty and glared, but Matty turned her back on her.

'I've got a big bruise on my bottom too, but I suppose I can't show you that here,' she said. 'Mum wasn't at all sympathetic. She said it was all my own fault for showing off. She was a bit embarrassed because the stupid frock tore just a little bit at the waist.'

'Oh no!'

'Marty's mum wasn't cross at all though. She said it was just the gathers part and she could easily fix it. She told Mum not to worry and said her Marty was always clowning about like that. She said we were so alike we could be twins!'

'You look like *twins*?' I asked, my heart thumping. 'You didn't say she had red hair.'

'She hasn't – she's got these mad blonde curls. We don't really *look* alike – it's more that we act alike.'

'Well. So do we,' I said. 'We act alike all the time. We play Warrior Princesses together and we do all the same sort of stuff.'

'Yes, I know, but we have different *personalities*, don't we?'

'What do you mean?' I said. My voice went croaky again. In fact I very nearly burst into tears.

'Well, I'm a tomboy and I like football and I'm messy and I hate frilly, girly things. You're a totally girly girl.'

'No I'm not! I'm a tomboy too,' I insisted. 'And I play football.'

Sometimes, if it was really warm when I went to tea with Matty, we didn't play in her bedroom. We went into her back garden and the three of us played a sort of piggy-in-the-middle football. I was nearly always piggy. Even little Lewis had much better ball skills than me. But I still *played*.

'You're rubbish at football,' said Matty.

I screwed my eyes up tight but I couldn't stop two fat tears rolling down my face.

'What's the matter?' said Matty, surprised. 'Why are you crying?'

'I'm not. I've just got something in my eyes.' I scrubbed at them with my fists.

'I haven't upset you, have I?'

'No,' I said. 'Of course not.'

'I think I have. I'm sorry,' said Matty, and she put her arm round me. 'Do you want to come to tea tonight?'

'Maybe not tonight,' I said.

I wanted to terribly, but Aunty Sue kept saying that I mustn't keep on going to Matty's house all the time. She said it was an imposition, though I wasn't sure what that meant. She suggested that I should ask Matty back to her place for tea.

I was horrified at the idea. I supposed Matty wouldn't mind a teacake and she'd probably like the pizza if Dad didn't make it back in time, but she'd hate it at Aunty Sue's. There wasn't anywhere we could play properly. We'd have to sit in the living room, which smelled of fusty old furniture. We'd have to sit on the sofa with her and watch all her quiz shows. We couldn't even play out in her garden because Uncle Eric didn't like anyone running about on his carefully mowed lawn, and anyway, he'd be there, fussing over his roses.

Dad had asked if I'd like Matty to come over one Saturday, when he didn't have to work. I wasn't sure about that either. Our new house was so quiet. It didn't seem as if a real family lived there any more. It was like a furniture showroom. And then of course Matty would start wondering about Mum.

She'd asked me lots of questions at first. Why did I go to Aunty Sue's house every day? That was easy to answer. I said my mum worked. She asked what job my mum did. I said she was an artist and had her own studio. Well, she had painted a lot of pictures once. Dad took them down from the walls of our old house and covered them in bubble wrap and stored them carefully in the furniture van but he didn't hang any of them on the walls of our new house. They were stacked at the back of our garage, still in their bubble wrap.

Matty was interested in my mum's mythical studio.

'Will you take me there? I'd love to see a real artist's studio,' she said eagerly.

'I wish I could, but my mum doesn't like to be disturbed,' I said uncomfortably, and then tried to change the subject.

After a while Matty stopped asking about Mum, which was a great relief. I wondered whether it might be possible for Dad and me to take Matty out somewhere one Saturday. Then we wouldn't have to be in our house. I thought of all the places dads took children for a day out. To the shops? No, that was more a mum thing. To the cinema? Lots of the children in Year Four had been to a big blockbuster film about dinosaurs and said it was great – but I didn't want to bring up the dinosaur subject all over again. Perhaps we could go to the zoo?

When we first moved here, Dad had taken me to the zoo every single weekend. The zoo had once been a huge treat, but the animals started to look sad and depressed. The elephant's wrinkled face looked mournful, the tiger padded up and down in agitation, the monkeys screeched anxiously. Even the comical waddle of the black-and-white penguins looked painful, as if their feet hurt. I didn't want to go to the zoo ever again.

So I didn't invite Matty that Saturday. I regretted it bitterly on Monday.

'Guess where I went on Saturday, Tilly,' said Matty when we met in the playground. 'It was wicked!'

'The zoo?' I asked.

'I wish! No, we went to have the last boring-boring-boring fitting for the hideous raspberry monstrosity, but then I got to play with Marty while our mums were chatting. Her bedroom is absolutely weird – all dinky and pinky and neat as a pin one end and totally messy with all sorts of mad toy animals the other end. Marty has to share with her older sister Melissa and she hates it. Anyway, we started playing this crazy game with a toy snake made out of tights. She's good at playing our sort of game, Tilly.'

I could scarcely breathe. Matty noticed my expression.

'Not as good as us though,' she said quickly. '*Anyway*, their dad had tickets to take them to the new dinosaur film, but Melissa wanted to go round the town with her friends, so they asked me instead. Oh, Tilly, it was fantastic. Super scary but in a good way. The best film ever. It's given me all sorts of ideas for Warrior Princesses. Princess

Powerful is going to win every single battle, just you wait and see!'

I tried to smile but my lips were too wobbly.

'What's up *now*?' asked Matty.

'I wanted to go to that dinosaur film with you,' I said.

'Well, you should have said.'

'I did say. Just now.'

'Yes, but it's too late now, silly.'

'I'm not silly.'

'Yes, you are. You keep getting fussed about stuff. It does my head in sometimes, though Mum says I've got to be tactful.'

'What? What do you mean? Why do you have to be tactful?' I asked.

'Well, you know . . .' Matty was fidgeting now, looking worried herself.

'No, I don't know. I don't know what you're on about. You're doing *my* head in,' I said.

'My mum says I've got to be careful not to upset you because of *your* mum,' said Matty in a rush.

'What about my mum?' I could feel little beads of sweat starting out under my fringe.

'Well . . .' Matty twisted her hands together and scraped her canvas boot tip along the tarmac of the playground. 'Because she's dead,' she mumbled.

'No she's not!'

'Oh, Tilly, my mum explained. I couldn't understand why your mum's never around and you have to hang out with that Aunty Sue lady, and even though you said all that stuff about your mum being an artist, it sounded like you were making it up. And you seem so sad sometimes. And when your dad comes to pick you up, he's all quiet and sad too. So Mum said she thought your mum had died and it made you both too upset to talk about it. She said I had to be extra nice to you because of it.'

'Well, your mum is talking total rubbish, because my mum isn't, isn't, isn't dead. She just doesn't live with us any more. So now you know and you don't have to be extra nice to me and make out you want to be my friend. Tell everyone in the whole class. See if I care,' I said, and I pushed her away and went running straight into school.

We weren't supposed to go into the classroom until the bell went. I went charging into the girls' toilets and locked myself into a cubicle and cried and cried. Sometimes I heard other girls coming in, and I pressed my lips together and pinched my nose so they wouldn't hear me sobbing. Matty came in too and called my name but I didn't answer, and after a while she went away.

The bell had gone now but I still stayed locked inside. I didn't want to face anyone ever again. I was in a terrible state by now. I'd run out of toilet paper so I had dribbles all down my face and I was all hot and sweaty and my head ached and my heart pounded. All the old ache for Mum started roaring inside me.

'Matilda?'

Oh no, it was Miss Hope's voice.

'Matilda!' I heard her walking along the cubicles, checking each one.

I tried to tuck my legs right up so she wouldn't see my feet. But she came to a halt outside my cubicle and tapped on the door.

'Tilly?' she said softly. 'Don't be silly, I know you're in there.'

'I'm not silly!' I shouted, though I'd never ever raised my voice to a teacher before.

I thought Miss Hope would be really mad at me, but she wasn't at all.

'Sorry. Of course you're not silly. *I'm* silly to say

so. And I *feel* silly talking to a door. Couldn't you unlock it so we can talk face to face?'

'No!'

'Then I'm going to have to go down on my knees and peer under the door just to make sure you're all right, and that will be embarrassing for both of us.'

I reluctantly unlocked the door.

'Oh dear, you poor little thing,' said Miss Hope. 'Let's get you mopped up.'

She had a couple of big soft tissues in her jacket pocket. She wiped me with them, and then ran some cold water in a basin and told me to bathe my face. I got my fringe wet by mistake, so Miss Hope stood me beside the hand dryers and smoothed my hair with her fingers so that it didn't dry sticking up. It was such a careful motherly thing to do that I started crying again.

'Oh goodness, no more tears. How about you and me popping into the staff room for five minutes? It should be empty by now. We'll have a cup of tea and a chat,' Miss Hope suggested.

I wondered about our Maths lesson, but Miss Hope said she'd left Mrs Avery, the classroom assistant, in charge. It was the first time I'd ever been into the staff room. I'd expected it to be like a hotel lounge with matching seats, but it was much shabbier, with odd chairs and battered sofas and low tables scattered with educational magazines and a big Krispy Kreme box.

'It was Mrs Jeffries's birthday yesterday,' said Miss Hope, nodding at the box. 'Shall we see if there's any left?'

There were two doughnuts with rainbow sprinkles.

'Well, look at that. Just waiting for us! They might be a little stale now, but a doughnut is a doughnut, don't you agree?' said Miss Hope. She patted her tummy. 'Though maybe I shouldn't. Perhaps you'd better eat them both quick. You're such a skinny little thing you could eat a whole boxful.'

She chattered away, making us both a mug of tea. My mug said DON'T WORRY, BE HAPPY. Her mug said WONDERFUL TEACHER!

'Did one of our class give you that mug, Miss Hope?' I asked, munching. The doughnut *was* a little stale, but still marvellous.

'I think it was from last year's Year Four. Or maybe the year before that. Are you going to have the last doughnut?'

'No, you have it.'

'That's what I'd hoped you say! Now, why all the tears this morning?'

I stared into my mug of tea, pretending not to have heard her.

'Did you and Matty have an argument?'

I sniffed and nodded.

'That's a shame. You two usually get on so well together,' she said.

'She's my best friend,' I said. I gulped. 'Well, she *was.*'

'I expect she still is,' said Miss Hope. 'So, what was this argument about?'

I pretended to be deaf again.

'I asked Matty, and she didn't want to tell me either, but eventually she said it was something about your mum,' said Miss Hope gently.

I shut my eyes tight, pretending that I couldn't see her either.

'Careful, you don't want to spill hot tea all down you,' said Miss Hope. 'Now, Tilly, I don't want to pry, but I gather from something your dad said that it's just you two at home?'

I nodded. 'Matty thought my mum was dead but she's not. She just doesn't live with us any more. But Dad and I don't talk about it. Please don't say anything to him, Miss Hope, or he'll get upset,' I begged.

'Well, I won't say anything today,' she said, which wasn't very reassuring. 'So how long have you and Dad been coping by yourselves?'

'Ages. Since I was in Year Two. We used to live in Albarn, but then we moved last year. Dad said it was a fresh start.'

'Do you still get to see your mum?' Miss Hope asked.

I shook my head. 'No. She came to see me lots at first, she really did, but now she lives abroad somewhere and it's too far away.'

'Oh dear, that's a shame. You must miss her a lot, Tilly.'

'I do. And so does Dad.'

'Yes, of course. So your aunty helps look after you too?'

'She's not a real aunty. Dad pays her to collect

me from school. He thought I'd like that better than going to after-school club.'

'And do you have a granny who lives nearby?'

'No. It's just Dad and me.'

'Well, you make a great team, you and your dad. But tell you what – if there's ever any girly thing you need to get sorted, you can always come and have a little word with me. OK?'

I nodded.

'There now. I suppose we'd both better get back to class now. Lick round your mouth – you've got rainbow sprinkles all over.'

'Miss Hope, what am I going to do if Matty isn't my friend any more?' I asked.

'I think she definitely wants to stay best friends with you,' she said.

'But she's got this other friend now, Marty. They went to the cinema together on Saturday. Marty's mum is making Matty a bridesmaid's dress.'

'Goodness, is Matty going to be a bridesmaid? I wonder if she'll wear her sparkly green trainers with her dress!' said Miss Hope, chuckling. 'Don't worry, Tilly. Matty's the sort of girl who likes to make lots of friends, but I'm sure you'll always be her best friend.'

I wasn't sure Miss Hope was right, even though she was a teacher. But when I went back to class and sat next to Matty, she looked at me anxiously.

'Are you OK? I truly didn't mean to upset you, Tilly. And I promise I won't breathe a word about you-know-who to anyone. You're still my best friend, aren't you?'

'I'm your best friend for ever, promise, promise, promise,' I said.

Chapter Four

'I've got the bridesmaid's dress,' said Matty in the playground. 'And it's truly hideous. I look a right idiot in it.'

'I bet you don't,' I said.

'Yes, I do. And I absolutely hate the shoes. They're deep pink and very pointy, with funny heels. I can't walk properly in them.'

'They've got *heels*?' I asked, awed.

'Not *high* heels. Little stubby silly things that make you turn your ankle. Oh, and the knickers! They've got frills! They look ridiculous. It will be total torture wearing them,' Matty wailed.

'You are funny. Most girls would give anything

to be a bridesmaid and wear a beautiful dress,' I said, sighing.

'Then you swop places with me at the wretched wedding,' said Matty.

'I wish I could.'

'No, really. You'd do it much better than me. I'm bound to trip or tread on Aunt Rachel's gown or something. I just know I'll get bored and mess about and get into trouble.'

'Then don't!'

'Yes, but I have this sort of itch to do it, and then I simply can't resist,' said Matty. 'I like it when people laugh at me. I even like it when they don't laugh and get cross instead.'

'You're a nutcase,' I said fondly. 'I wish I could come to your Aunt Rachel's wedding. I'd love to see you as a bridesmaid.'

'Then come! Oh yes, please come! It's at St Saviour's. It's in North London somewhere. You're not doing anything next Saturday, are you? Then come with us. You can squeeze up with Lewis and me in the back of the car. It'll be great to have you there. I'll tell Mum it's the only way I'll manage to behave. She likes you. She says you're a good influence on me,' said Matty.

She tucked her dress in her knickers and started

doing cartwheels. It was hard work keeping up with her.

'Did she really say that?' I asked, trying to talk to Matty's head as it revolved.

'She said it to my dad. I overheard. Oh, Tilly, it'll be so cool to have you there, especially afterwards at the reception. That's like a great big party in a hotel. You get lots to eat and it won't matter too much if I spill stuff down the dress because I'll have done my bit in the church. Then there's lots of dancing. You're quite good at dancing. Lewis is absolute rubbish – he just jumps up and down.'

'Are you *sure* your mum won't mind?'

'Of course she won't mind!' Matty assured me.

She ran to ask her the minute we finished school that afternoon. I followed her, though I could see Aunty Sue beckoning to me.

But Matty's mum was shaking her head. 'I'm sorry, girls. I'd love you to come too, Tilly, but you have to be properly invited to a wedding. Rachel will have booked a specific number of people at the reception, all of us sitting in special places,' she said.

'Tilly and I can share a chair. She's so skinny

she won't take up any extra room,' said Matty. 'She's desperate to come, Mum. She wants to see me in my stupid bridesmaid's dress.'

'It's not stupid, it's beautiful! Well, tell you what, Tilly. You come to have tea with us tomorrow and we'll dress Matty up in her posh frock and she can give us a little twirl. Would you like to do that? Shall I ask your Aunty Sue?'

'She's *not* my aunty,' I insisted, but we had to ask her. She looked a bit put out, but when Dad came to collect me I asked and he said yes, hurray, hurray!

So the next afternoon I didn't go to Aunty Sue's home and drink my milk and eat my teacake and watch *Pointless*. I went to Matty's, and we had little yoghurts and a banana each, and then Matty had to have a strip-down wash so she wouldn't get her bridesmaid's frock sticky or stained, and *then* she put it on.

I stared at her. She was still Matty above the neck, her red hair needing a good brush, and she wore grubby socks and trainers instead of the new pink shoes – but her raspberry-pink dress made her look like an angelic stranger. The soft, subtle colour was beautiful, even with her bright hair, and the silk hung perfectly, rustling slightly as she moved. The dress had been so cleverly cut and styled. Matty was scrawny, with sharp elbows and scabby knees, but the puffed sleeves made her arms look slender and graceful and the ruffles on her dress hid her knees altogether.

'Doesn't she look a picture,' said Angie proudly.

I nodded. 'She looks amazing,' I said.

'Amazingly hideous,' said Matty, pulling a gargoyle face. 'Ugh, I can't stand the way this dress feels, all slippery against my skin. I'm taking it off right this minute!' She started tugging at it impatiently.

'I like the way it feels,' said Lewis, picking up the hem of the skirt and rubbing it against his nose like a comfort blanket.

'Don't use it like a hankie!' said Angie. 'Matty, stop pulling, you'll tear those stitches all over again. What a pair you are. What am I going to do with them, Tilly?'

'Tickle them silly,' I said without thinking. It was what Mum used to say to me when I was little, and I was making a fuss or couldn't go to sleep.

'I'm going to tickle you silly,' she'd say, and she'd

lightly tickle my neck until I hunched up my shoulders and squirmed away, giggling helplessly, all worries forgotten.

I tried to tickle my own neck after she'd gone but it didn't work.

My face must have gone all sad now because Angie put her arm round me.

'Would you like to try on Matty's bridesmaid's dress to see what it looks like on you, Tilly?' she asked. She eased Matty out of her outfit, pulled my school dress off, and then slipped the wonderful pink silk over my head. I felt its softness whispering over my shoulders. She zipped me up carefully and then turned me round to look in the mirror.

I looked different too. The pink looked wonderful, making my mousy hair seem almost blonde. I was usually ghostly pale, but excitement made little pink patches on my cheeks. I was still too skinny but the dress draped me softly. I usually walked with my head bent, but now I stood up straight to show off the dress.

'Wow,' said Matty. 'That dress looks heaps better on you, Tilly.'

'No it doesn't,' I said quickly.

'Yes it does!' said Matty's mum. 'You

look as if you were born to wear that dress. I do hope you get to be a bridesmaid yourself soon, Tilly.'

I just shrugged. '*Me?*' I said, as if I'd never thought of such a thing before.

Then I had to take the bridesmaid's dress off again, and Angie put it in its plastic bag and took it away to hang in her own bedroom. Matty and Lewis and I had a good long game of Warrior Princesses before supper. Matty was inspired by the new film, and Princess Powerful urged her dinosaurs on to new and ever more violent action. Soon Princess Go-to-Sleep and Princess Pony were rendered powerless, all their own subjects savaged to death.

'It's not much fun if Princess Powerful *always* wins,' said Lewis.

'It is so. It's glorious fun,' said Matty, making Princess Powerful strut commandingly across the carpet, her dinosaurs bounding along behind her. She'd drawn red felt pen round their mouths and over their scaly chests to indicate their recent gorging.

'Bluey looks as if she's got lipstick on,' I said.

'Yes, she does rather, doesn't she?' said Matty. 'Perhaps she's in love with Scaly and is trying to impress him.'

She made Bluey and Scaly kiss, with funny slurpy sounds that sent Lewis into a fit of giggles.

'Yes, they're definitely in love,' I said. 'Hey, maybe they want to get married?'

'Dinosaurs don't get married,' Lewis spluttered.

'Dinosaurs can do anything we want,' said Matty. 'Great idea, Tilly. OK, let's get cracking. I'll make all the food for the wedding feast.'

'And I'll make Bluey her bridal gown,' I said.

'What will I do?' asked Lewis.

'You can get those old building bricks and build a church,' I suggested.

So Lewis built a church, using books too, as his bricklaying skills were basic and his first church came tumbling down before we'd got the dinosaurs arranged. Matty took a nearly new packet of plasticine and used the red strip to make a big meat cake, and fashioned a green strip into a leaf tart for the herbivores. I raided their dressing-up box and designed a beautiful wedding frock with a long train out of a cream chiffon scarf. I searched for a raspberry-pink scarf to use for bridesmaids' dresses for any likely little girl dinosaur, but I couldn't find anything pink at all.

I lined all the littlest dinosaurs up in a row and made them cry, 'We want raspberry-pink bridesmaids' dresses! Oh boo hoo, we can't be naked at Bluey's wedding!'

'I think they want a bridesmaid's *battle*dress,' said Matty. 'They're rufty-tufty tomboy girls.' She dug out an old pair of green and brown camouflage trousers from the back of her wardrobe. 'Cut these up!'

'I can't cut up your trousers!'

'They're too little for me now. They come halfway up my leg,' said Matty. 'And Lewis can't wear them because he's such a podge.'

'I don't *want* to wear them – they're stupid,' said Lewis.

The dinosaur girls didn't think their new dresses were stupid at all. I cut them each a dress, attaching it with little gold safety pins. Then I made a camouflage coat for Scaly, and a silver helmet out of a thimble.

Princess Powerful was the vicar, officiating at the front of the church. Princess Go-to-Sleep and Princess Pony assembled the cuddly toys and the ponies in neat rows. Princess Powerful wasn't very sure of the right words for the wedding service. Princess Pony prompted her, but when they got to the part where the assembly was asked if anyone objected to the wedding, Spiky-Thumb Dinosaur screamed that *he* wanted to marry Bluey.

Then Scaly objected to his cheek, and there was a terrible fight between the two males. They knocked everyone flying, even the poor bride. I was annoyed with Spiky-Thumb because I wanted to do the wedding properly. I kept trying to make the dinosaurs stop fighting, but Princess Powerful urged them on, and made all the bridesmaids join in.

'Good Lord, what's going on? It's like World War Three in here!' Angie was standing in the bedroom doorway, shaking her head at us.

'It's a dinosaur wedding, Mum, and Scaly and Spiky-Thumb are killing each other!' said Lewis.

Angie roared with laughter. 'You girls! What will you think up next? Look, declare a truce with the dinosaurs for half an hour while you come and eat supper. I'm just about to dish up macaroni cheese.'

'Oh yum!' said Matty, and she jumped up,

scattering the bride and groom and all their ferocious guests. It was so strange one minute the dinosaurs seemed so huge and angry: they roared around the room, their heads scraping the ceiling, their tails lashing against the walls, then the next minute they were just little plastic dinosaurs lying on their backs with their feet in the air.

It was also strange that everyone made such a fuss if I drew a few dinosaurs, whereas Angie found it funny when Matty made Scaly and Spiky-Thumb attack each other savagely. I knew why, of course. I was the girl who'd gone a bit weird ever since her mum had left her.

Matty was a bouncy girl with a lovely family so nobody thought she was weird, no matter what she did. I was a droopy girl with only half a family so Dad and Aunty Sue and Miss Hope were worried that I was disturbed when I was just playing normally. It wasn't fair.

It also wasn't fair that Matty was going to be a bridesmaid on Saturday, wearing the most beautiful dress in the world – and I wasn't.

'Matty's soooo lucky,' I said to Dad as he was driving me home.

'Yes, she is,' said Dad.

'I wish *I* was going to be a bridesmaid.'

69

'I know, love.'

'I've never ever been to a wedding.'

'Come to think of it, neither have I,' said Dad.

I didn't say anything else until we got home. It wasn't bedtime yet. Dad suggested we might watch a DVD together, but there wasn't anything I fancied. Dad brought out the battered cardboard box of Ludo that he'd had when he was a boy. We played one game, but it wasn't really exciting when it was just the two of us. So then we just sat on the sofa together, staring into space.

'Dad?' I said.

'Yes?'

'Dad, why didn't you and Mum get married?'

'Well . . . not all mums and dads marry, you know.'

'Yes, but didn't Mum *want* a lovely wedding?' I couldn't help thinking that if Mum and Dad had been properly married, she mightn't have gone away. If they'd been married, it would have taken a while before they could get divorced. Mum would still belong to us until then.

'Mum didn't fancy a wedding at all,' said Dad. 'She laughed at the idea. She said she couldn't stand the idea of prancing about in a white dress. She was always so funny and lively and unconventional. She always wanted to do things differently. You know what she was like, Tilly.'

'Yes,' I said uncertainly.

'You do remember her, don't you?' asked Dad, looking startled.

'Yes, of course I do. But I don't know how to think about her. Sometimes I just love her and want her so much. And sometimes I hate her for going away and not coming back,' I said in a very small voice.

'I feel exactly the same way,' said Dad, and he reached out and pulled me close for a cuddle. 'Tell you what,' he added, talking into my hair. 'We'll have a very special day out on Saturday. Where would you like to go?'

'Not the zoo,' I said.

'Not the zoo,' said Dad. 'Perhaps we could go shopping at the Flowerfields Centre?'

I knew Dad hated going shopping, especially at the Flowerfields Centre. I rather wanted to go, but I shook my head.

'Then how about an amusement park?' Dad suggested. 'You know, one with those roller-coaster rides.'

I thought about it. I knew Matty would be wildly envious if I told her I'd been to one. She was forever begging her mum and dad to take her, but they wouldn't because they thought Lewis was too little.

I'd never admit it to Matty in a million years but I felt I was maybe too little too. I hated the thought of being up so high and then swooping down, screaming my head off. I imagined my head literally unscrewing and spinning through the air like a ball.

'I think I might feel a bit sick on a roller-coaster ride,' I said.

'Well, that's a relief. I didn't really fancy it either,' said Dad. 'We'll cross an amusement park off our list. So, how about a *park* park? A big ornamental park with a lake and statues and little bridges?'

It sounded a bit boring, but I said yes. And it was actually quite interesting. There was an amazing crystal grotto like a very big dark cave with thousands of crystals glittering all around us. I held Dad's hand and imagined little goblins scuttling about our feet. I tried to get Dad to join in making up a little tribe of goblins, but he wasn't very good at it. He just started listing Dopey and Sneezy and all those other dwarfs in *Snow White*.

Then we climbed up to a Turkish tent at the top of a little hill and sat in it surveying the grounds below. Dad told me that servants used to come with refreshments for eighteenth-century people visiting the garden.

'What sort of refreshments?' I asked, wishing they still came now.

'Well, it's a Turkish tent, so perhaps they served Turkish coffee and Turkish delight,' said Dad, trying hard, because he knew he'd failed at the goblin game.

'Right, you pour the coffee and I'll open the box of Turkish delight,' I said, pretending.

'Oh look, I just happen to have some Turkish delight in my pocket,' said Dad.

It wasn't actual Turkish delight, it was a handful of Quality Street in shiny paper, which was actually even better. Dad let me have the caramel and nut wrapped in purple. He had a thin yellow toffee stick. Then I twisted the coloured wrappers round my finger and turned them into tiny glasses, and we toasted each other and drank pretend wine.

The best place of all in the park was a little

castle up another hill. It looked just like a picture in a fairy-tale book.

'Can we go inside?' I begged.

'I think it's just a folly, a pretend castle,' said Dad, but he was wrong.

There was a door, and you could go up a winding staircase right to the top and peer out of the turrets. All the rooms were disappointingly empty.

'Well, they're just waiting for us to move in and furnish it,' said Dad. Then he saw the excitement on my face. 'I'm pretending!' he added quickly.

It was still fun deciding on beautiful crimson carpets as soft as fur so we could pad about barefoot, and huge velvet sofas and Chinese cabinets for all our things, and two four-poster beds, a big one for Dad and a little one for me. It was strange how we could furnish the castle so splendidly when we didn't have a clue how to make our new house a comfortable home.

We stayed in the castle a long time, pretending we were the king and the princess of all the land, the meadows, the woods, all the way to the hazy blue hills on the horizon.

'Happy?' said Dad.

'Yes, happy-happy-happy,' I said.

We came down from the castle and walked all the way back through the park, our feet aching now. We spotted a walled kitchen garden near the entrance.

'Excellent,' I said. 'Let's see what we're growing, and then I'll decide what to cook for us for our supper, O King.'

'Promise it's not turnips, Princess,' said Dad, playing along with me.

But we were distracted from our vegetable survey by music and laughter coming from behind the wall. We went to have a look. There was a long white marquee all lit up with sparkling lights, with people in lovely clothes gathered inside.

'It's a party just for us!' I said. And then I realized. I saw a lady in a long white frock and a man in a black suit cutting a huge tiered cake. It wasn't a party. It was a wedding.

It wasn't Matty's Aunt Rachel's wedding. These

bridesmaids wore primrose yellow. They'd have looked much prettier in raspberry pink. One of them looked round and stared at us.

'Come on, we can't gatecrash a wedding,' said Dad.

We went back to the car park and drove home. We didn't pretend. We weren't in the mood any more.

Chapter Five

There were lots of official photographs taken at Matty's Aunt Rachel's wedding but I didn't get to see them until later. I just saw the photos on Matty's mobile phone. She smuggled it into school and showed me in the girls' toilets at break time.

They were mostly selfies: Matty and her aunt, in her white bridal gown holding her bouquet of deep pink roses; Matty and her two cousins, all in raspberry pink; Matty and Lewis and a boy cousin, all of them sticking out their

tongues; Matty still sticking out her tongue and crossing her eyes too; Matty licking her lips holding a huge ice-cream sundae. Someone else had taken photos of Matty on the dance floor, with a big stain all down the front of her bridesmaid's dress.

'Oh no, you've spilled something on it!' I gasped.

'What? Only a little bit. Well, I didn't get any on the skirt.'

'But what's the matter with the skirt? It's all hanging down at the back!'

'It's just the way I'm dancing. Oh no, wait a minute. I was mucking about under the table—'

'In your *dress*?'

'Shut up! You sound just like my nan. She was nag, nag, nag at me all day long, and she kept grabbing hold of me, licking a corner of her lacy hankie and then scrubbing at my face. Yuck! *Anyway*, when I got up from under the table, I caught the stupid heel of my pink shoes in the hem of my skirt, so perhaps that's why it's hanging down,' said Matty.

'Oh, Matty, you're hopeless,' I said.

'Yeah, that's what Nan and everyone kept saying. But Uncle Ethan was laughing at me – he's the one Aunt Rachel married. He's much, much nicer than Aunt Rachel. He gave all us bridesmaids presents. He gave my cousins Lucy and Rebecca dinky little silver bracelets, but do you know what he got me? A silver Swiss Army knife, those ones with all the little gadgets. It's seriously cool. I wanted to bring it to school but Mum said I might do someone serious damage and wouldn't let me. Wait till you next come to tea, Tilly. You'll be very impressed.'

'So long as you don't do *me* serious damage,' I said.

'Don't be daft – you're my best ever friend. And I've got a special present for you, only I mustn't say what it is. Mum says it'll spoil the surprise.'

'Go on, tell me!' I said, all agog.

'Nope. My lips are zipped,' said Matty, miming it. 'But you'll like it, honestly.'

I couldn't think what it could be. Perhaps it was a present from the wedding. Amanda had been a bridesmaid at a wedding and she'd brought a little white net bag tied with a white ribbon into school. She said it was a wedding favour. There were pink and white sugared almonds in the bag and she shared them with Cathy and me. I wasn't actually that keen on sugared almonds but I felt honoured all the same.

Perhaps Matty was going to give me another

wedding favour? But she seemed extra excited about this present. Maybe it was more than a few sugared almonds? Maybe Matty's Uncle Ethan had given her a dinky silver bracelet as well as a Swiss Army knife? I would love a silver bracelet! I became extra excited too.

I hoped Matty would invite me to tea that very day, but she didn't. She didn't invite me the next day either, though I'd told Aunty Sue I was sure she would.

'I wish you wouldn't keep messing me about, Tilly,' she said. 'Your dad says you can go to Matty's house any time you want, but it's not very considerate to me. I get your tea and some-times your supper in specially, and then at a drop of a hat you say you're not coming so it's all wasted!'

I didn't see how my tea and supper could be wasted. Teacakes kept for weeks in the cupboard and frozen pizza kept for months in the freezer. Aunty Sue liked to moan just for the sake of it. I wished I didn't have to go to her house. The days I didn't go to Matty's I'd be absolutely fine at home. I could make myself a sandwich and read a book and watch a DVD and draw and colour perfectly well all by myself.

I tried to remember what it was like when Mum was still with us and she came to fetch me from school. We had whippy ice creams on the way home, sometimes with two kinds of sauce *and* a chocolate flake. We played very loud music and danced. We even danced up and down on  the beds. We pretended that we lived in Greenland and the duvet was our igloo and Stripy teddy was a polar bear. Mum gave us each a big bar of chocolate and we pretended it was whale meat and blubber. We laughed and laughed, saying the word *blubber* over and over again.

We were always laughing in those days. We played dressing up, getting all Mum's clothes out of her wardrobe. She made me up to look like a fashion model and bought me a long blonde wig so I looked like a fairy princess. We painted together in Mum's room – she painted on canvas and she let me paint straight on to the wall.

When Mum left and Dad decided we had to move away and make a fresh start, he had to paint those walls over and over in white paint to cover up all my silly scribbles.

It wasn't always like that though, painting and laughing and playing games. But I didn't want to think about those times. It was generally safer not to think about Mum at all.

I had a whole long list of good things to think about. There was Dad for a start. My new blue bedroom. All my favourite books. My big set of Caran d'Ache crayons. Fish and chips for supper most Saturdays. And top, top, top of the list, my best friend Matty.

I kept wondering what this mysterious present was going to be.

'I *think* you can come to tea on Wednesday,' said Matty. 'But we won't know for sure till Mum comes to collect us. I have to check it's back.'

'What's back?'

'Ah, that would be telling!' said Matty, maddeningly.

I ran out into the playground with her on Wednesday afternoon. Angie was smiling and she did a thumbs-up sign to her.

'Hurray, it *is* back!' said Matty. 'OK, you have to come to tea right now!'

'Just let me tell Aunty Sue,' I said.

Aunty Sue wasn't at all pleased. 'I've told you a hundred times, Tilly, you have to give me some warning. If I'd known you didn't need me, I'd have gone into town or popped to the garden centre or had a cup of tea with one of my friends. But I've made the effort to come and meet you instead, so you must come home with me. You can go to tea with Matty tomorrow.'

'Can't you still do all those things now?' I asked.

'No I can't. It's too late in the day. And your daddy wants me to take you home and give you your tea. So stop arguing, dear,' said Aunty Sue. She said the word 'dear' as if it meant 'annoying little girl'.

'But Dad *likes* me to go to tea with Matty. And he pays you just the same each week, whether you have to look after me or not,' I said.

'Don't you dare talk to me like that!' said Aunty Sue, little pink patches standing out on her face. 'I shall have to have a word with your father. I'm not having a nine-year-old lay down the law to me.'

'What's the matter?' said Matty, running up to us. 'Oh please, dear Aunty Sue, you absolutely have to let Tilly come to tea with me tonight because we've got her a ginormous surprise and if I have to wait till tomorrow I shall simply burst. You do understand, don't you, Aunty Sue?'

'I understand that you're an affected little madam and you're a bad influence on Tilly,' said Aunty Sue. She said it under her breath. Perhaps she didn't mean us to hear, but we did.

We stared at her, shocked. Angie sensed something was wrong and came over to us, Lewis skipping along beside her.

'Hello! We're hoping Tilly can come to tea tonight, if it's all right with you?' she said politely.

'No, it's not all right,' said Aunty Sue. 'I've had enough. I'm going to phone your father, Tilly, and tell him he'll have to find someone else to look after you. Goodbye.' She turned on her heel and marched off by herself.

'Oh goodness,' said Angie. 'I didn't mean to upset her.'

'*I* upset her,' said Matty. 'She said I was affected and a bad influence.'

'But you're not! Not a bit. She's horrid to say that,' I said fiercely. 'She was really upset with *me*, because I'd much, *much* sooner go to tea with you than with her.'

'Still, I think your dad might be upset with all of us, because Sue has gone off in a huff and maybe won't look after you any more, Tilly,' said Angie.

'Tilly doesn't need Aunty Sue. She's got us. She can come to tea with us every day, can't she, Mum?'

'Of course she can,' said Angie. 'Would you like that, Tilly?'

'I would absolutely love it!' I said, though I was a tiny bit worried that Dad would fuss.

But then I forgot to be worried, because as soon as we got to Matty's home she said, 'Let's give Tilly her present now, Mum, please!'

Angie smiled and went to fetch something in a big protective bag. There was a glimmer of pink inside the thick plastic.

'Can you guess what it is, Tilly?' Matty said excitedly.

My heart was thumping hard in my chest. Angie unzipped the plastic, and there was the raspberry-pink bridesmaid's dress, soft and silky and unsullied.

'I've just collected it from the dry cleaner's,' said

Angie. 'They've got that horrible stain off *and* turned up the torn hem. It's as good as new now. We all wanted you to have it, Tilly, because you looked so beautiful in it.'

'You can play dressing up as a princess,' said Matty. 'And if anyone you know is getting married, you can offer to be their bridesmaid with a ready-made dress.'

'But it's *your* dress, Matty. What if *you* need to be a bridesmaid again?' I asked.

'Never ever again!' she said. 'And luckily no one in my family will ever ask me now.'

'You'd better phone your dad, Tilly, and tell him where you are,' said Angie.

My heart started thumping all over again. I hated worrying Dad. Angie dialled his number and then gave the phone to me.

'Pickard Brown Chartered Accountants, Michael speaking, how can I help you?' said Dad in his work voice.

'It's me, Dad,' I said, in a very small voice. 'It's about Aunty Sue.'

'I know. She's already been on the phone to me. I gather you were cheeky to her,' said Dad.

'I didn't mean to be. And then *she* was cheeky to Matty and me.'

'Well, don't let's go into it now. I'll come and pick you up from Matty's house when I get home from work – and then I'll try to find someone else to fetch you from school in the future,' said Dad wearily.

'But it's all right, Dad. It's all sorted. Matty's mum says I can always go to their house.'

'No you can't – it wouldn't be fair on them,' said Dad.

Matty took the phone away from me. She'd been listening to every word.

'It would be extremely fair, Mr Andrews, because we love having Tilly to tea,' she said. 'It's nowhere near as much fun when it's just Lewis. Please say she can come every day,' she begged.

'Well, I'll have a chat to your mother about it. Please thank her for having Tilly to tea tonight,' said Dad.

'Tilly's dad says thanks, Mum,' Matty called, hanging up. 'Come on, Tilly, let's go and play.'

'And me,' said Lewis.

Matty sighed. 'Do you *have* to come too, Lewis? Tilly and I never get to play on our own.'

'Me want to play too!' said Lewis in a baby voice, hanging his head.

'He's just acting like a baby to make Mum take his side,' Matty whispered to me.

Lewis stayed acting like a baby when Angie told us to let him play too. He pretended not to know how to play Warrior Princesses.

'No, me a baby!' he said.

He just sat on the floor squealing, waving his plump little fists at the dinosaurs and knocking them over like ninepins. Matty got seriously annoyed with him, but we couldn't help giggling too. Lewis was quite good at being a baby, making funny cooing sounds and then pretending he had a damp nappy. We ended up playing that he really was a baby. I made all my ponies trot round and round him, and then they galloped up and down his plump legs as if they were a race track while he laughed and laughed.

I wished I had a funny little brother. I wished I had Matty for my sister. I wished I had a mum and dad like Matty's, safe and warm and happy and always there.

I felt guilty when Dad came to collect me. He looked so pale and anxious, and his eyes kept blinking because they got tired looking at rows of figures on his computer all day long. He never said anything about his work, but I knew he didn't like this new job anywhere near as much as his old one. He'd worked in the accounts department of a big publishing firm. That's where he'd met Mum. She worked in the art department. Dad once said that he never ever in a million years thought someone like Mum would go out with him.

'Everyone was sweet on your mum,' he said.

It was the first time I'd heard that expression. I imagined Mum like a magic princess in a fairy tale, and everyone who looked at her turned sweet as sugar candy, melting like chocolate, sticky as toffee.

Dad was the strange little frog who came scuttling along, and Mum carelessly blew him a kiss, and then he turned into a handsome prince and carried her off so they could live happily ever after. Only they didn't.

'Dad!' I said, and rushed to give him a hug.

'Now then, Tilly,' he said. 'I don't like to hear that you've been rude. What are we going to do about poor Aunty Sue? She's very upset.'

'That Aunty Sue is horrible,' said Matty. 'She was rude to Tilly. And she was actually even ruder to me. But you don't have to worry, Mr Andrews, Tilly can come to tea with us every day now and it will be magic.'

'That's very sweet of you, Matty, but we can't possibly impose on your mum like that. Tilly's round here nearly all the time already,' said Dad.

'We love having her. Please let her come here,' said Angie.

'Then you must let me pay you properly for your trouble.'

'Of course you can't! Tilly's practically family.'

'Well, it's very kind of you. Are you really sure? You must let me know if it gets too much for you,' said Dad. 'Come along, Tilly, then.'

'You don't have to rush off straight away, do you? Let me make you a cup of coffee first,' said Angie.

'I think a beer would be a better idea,' said Tom, Matty's dad.

I could tell Dad just wanted to get home, but he smiled bravely and had half a glass of beer and some crisps, and then a cup of coffee with a home-made chocolate-chip cookie. He tried hard to make conversation all the time. I squeezed up on the sofa beside him and snuggled against him.

He kept thanking Matty's parents.

'It's no trouble at all,' Angie said for the fifth time. 'We love having Tilly. She's a very special little girl. You're doing a great job, bringing her up on your own.'

Dad and I stiffened. If we didn't say a word about Mum not being with us, we madly hoped that no one would notice.

'Thank you,' he mumbled eventually. 'Well, we really must be going now.'

'Don't forget your present, Tilly!' said Matty.

Dad had to be grateful all over again for the bridesmaid's dress. I sat in the back of the car with it spread carefully over the seat in its plastic wrapper.

'It is all right if I go to Matty's house, isn't it, Dad?' I asked.

'Yes, they're a very kind family. I can see you have much more fun there than with poor Sue,' he said.

'They're very, *very* kind to give me Matty's bridesmaid's dress. Just wait till you see it on me, Dad. I look almost pretty!' I said.

'You *are* pretty,' said Dad. *He* was being kind now. I knew I wasn't the slightest bit pretty. I didn't take after Mum in any way whatsoever. But when we were home and I put the dress on again, I truly did feel beautiful.

'Look, Dad!' I called, from the top of the stairs.

Dad came and looked. He put his hand up to shield his eyes, pretending to be dazzled. 'You look like a real princess. You'd outshine any bride,' he said.

'Dad, do you think I could be a real bridesmaid? Do you know anyone who's going to get married soon? Oh, Dad, I'd give anything to wear my dress to a real wedding,' I said.

Chapter Six

I got up ten minutes early every day and put on the bridesmaid's dress. I practised walking slowly and solemnly as if I were walking up the aisle, and I held my head high and clasped my hands as if I were holding a posy. I even practised bending down quickly and gracefully, twitching the imaginary bride's train into place. I stood patiently, still as a church pillar, pretending the ceremony was happening, and then I marched triumphantly round my bed and back again, humming my version of churchy organ music.

When Dad called that breakfast was nearly ready, I pulled off my bridesmaid's dress, smoothed it down gently, rubbing my cheek on the soft silk before slipping it back inside its protective plastic. I put on my ugly check dress for school and sloped off downstairs, back to being ordinary me again.

Whenever I was bored or stuck at school I tried to make a list in the back of my jotter of all the people I could think of who might need a bridesmaid in the next year. I was small but I was still growing. If the bridesmaid's dress fitted me perfectly now, it might be getting a bit too short and tight in nine months' time, let alone a year.

My list was small too.

No 1: Dad.

I had to put him first, even though I knew it wasn't very likely. Dad still loved Mum. I think he secretly hoped she might still come back, even though he told me firmly that it was never going to happen. He was particularly angry when she forgot my birthday. No present, no card, no phone call. We'd given up trying to phone her. She seemed to keep changing phones, and shortly after we set up Skype so that I could still chat to her, she changed her email address.

Dad pretended she'd sent him money for my birthday present and bought me sequinned trainers just like Matty's, but red, and a red-and-blue jacket like hers, and a big box of paints. He wrote on each parcel:

Sorry this is a bit late!
Hope you had a very happy
birthday, Tilly. Lots of love
from Mum

I half believed she might have put some money in his bank account, like he said. But then a whole month late a big parcel arrived that really was from Mum. It was an odd white dress covered with pink and red and yellow and green embroidery and a little wooden house full of strange little wooden people, most of them on their knees. The ones who were standing wore long white dresses and had brass plates stuck on their heads.

There was a postcard in the parcel. It had a picture of a lady with very thick eyebrows and lots of jewellery on the front. On the back it said:

Hi from Mexico! Think I missed
your birthday, sweetheart.
Love and kisses,
Mum

I tried on the very bright dress but it came down almost to the floor, like the dresses of the brass-plate wooden people. Dad said they were meant to be saints. This dress had very wide arms that flapped like wings. It didn't fit me anywhere and the material was stiff and scratchy.

'It's very . . . colourful,' said Dad.

'Yes, isn't it,' I said doubtfully.

'Perhaps you could wear it to a party?'

'Everyone would laugh at me.'

'Matty wouldn't,' said Dad.

'Matty would laugh harder than anyone,' I said. 'Matty wouldn't be seen dead in a dress like this.'

'You could take the dress to school for show-and-tell,' Dad suggested. 'You could read up about Mexico, and take the house too. I bet Miss Hope would be very impressed.'

'Dad! We don't do that kind of thing in the Juniors,' I said.

I put the Mexican dress in my wardrobe. It's stayed there ever since, right at the back. I tried keeping the house of wooden people on my windowsill, but they all had fierce eyebrows like the lady on the postcard. It was easy to imagine they were staring at me. I couldn't forget about them, even in the dark. In the end I put them in the wardrobe too.

'Do you think Mum's on holiday in Mexico?' I asked Dad.

'Maybe. Or maybe she's actually living there. Who knows?' he said.

'I think she's on holiday,' I said. 'I expect she'll come to see me when she gets back home, wherever her home is now. Maybe she'll decide she wants to live with us again.'

Dad didn't say anything for a little while. Then he took a deep breath. 'I think we have to get used to the idea that Mum isn't ever coming back,' he said.

I couldn't get used to the idea, but I didn't argue. I wasn't sure whether Dad really meant it or not. If he *did*, then maybe he was ready to meet someone new. I played with the idea of a stepmother in my head. All stepmothers in fairy tales were wicked. Snow White's stepmother wanted her chopped into pieces by a huntsman and, failing that, made a couple of serious attempts at poisoning her. Cinderella's stepmother didn't go that far, but she kept her as a servant and wouldn't let her go to the ball.

Real stepmothers didn't seem quite as extreme. One girl in our class, Lydia-Jane, said her stepmother was always nagging her, and she couldn't stick her – but Lydia-Jane was a mean, lazy girl who didn't seem to like anyone. Amanda had a stepmother, and saw her every other weekend when she went to stay with her dad. She said her stepmother let her try on her make-up and have two puddings when they had their Sunday lunch at the pub. That sounded good. Amanda said her stepmother was young and pretty, with long hair. I wasn't so keen on having a young, pretty stepmother. Mum was the youngest, prettiest mother ever – and look what happened.

I thought Dad should go for someone kind and friendly who would like looking after us. I couldn't quite picture her in my mind. She'd have to like pretty clothes, to appreciate my raspberry silk bridesmaid's dress. Perhaps she might be a little like Mary Berry, only younger? It would certainly be a bonus if she made us wonderful cakes.

The Great British Bake Off was on television that evening. I always liked to watch it, fantasizing about the sort of cakes I might make. Dad wasn't so keen and generally looked at stuff on his iPad when it was on.

'Could you watch with me, Dad?' I asked. 'Please?'

He pulled a funny face but put his iPad down and watched obediently.

'I love this programme. And I love Mary Berry,' I said.

'Is this a big hint?' Dad asked.

'Oh, Dad! How did you guess?' I said excitedly.

'I know my girl,' he said, patting my knee. 'But I'm not sure it's going to work. I don't know the first thing about making cakes. I suppose I could find a recipe for a sponge cake somewhere – that must be quite simple. I could let you do the icing and decorating part. Would you like to do that, sweetheart?'

'Oh yes! But that wasn't actually what I meant, Dad. I wanted us to watch Mary Berry. She's lovely, isn't she?'

'Well, yes, I suppose so.'

'How would you feel about marrying Mary Berry, Dad?'

'*What?*' Dad snorted with laughter. 'Oh, Tilly, what on earth are you going to come out with next?'

It was ages and ages since I'd heard him laugh like that, so I didn't mind that he was actually laughing at me.

'I don't know what's so funny,' I said, though I'd started to giggle myself, because Dad's laughter was so infectious.

'Well, of all the women in the world to suggest! To start with, Mary Berry's married already. And then she's very famous and probably very rich, so she certainly wouldn't be interested in someone dull and ordinary like me. And for all she's quite glamorous she also happens to be old enough to be my mother, maybe even my grandmother,' Dad spluttered.

'I didn't mean marry *actual* Mary Berry. I meant someone a bit like her. Someone . . . mumsie.'

Dad stopped laughing. 'Mumsie?' he said.

'I don't mean like Mum. I mean someone who *acts* like a mum.'

'Ah. Well. I get you now,' said Dad. 'And I suppose you're all set to wear your bridesmaid's dress at my wedding?'

'Yes! Wouldn't it be lovely! Oh, Dad, please!'

'Tilly, I don't know any ladies like that.'

'What about at your work?'

'The women in my office are either respectable married ladies of a certain age or young girls with lots of make-up and very high heels who go clubbing all the time.'

'Don't you see any likely interesting ladies on your way to work?'

'I can't just go up to a total stranger and say, "Hello, likely interesting lady, would you like to go out with me?" I'd get myself arrested.'

'Then you could try a dating website. I could help you write your profile! *Nice kind man, middle size and middle weight, quite good-looking in a dad sort of way, clever at maths, very reliable, one small well-behaved daughter.* There! Brilliant! Let's put it on a website right now.'

'Absolutely not.'

'Don't be shy, Dad.'

'Stop it now, Tilly.'

'You can't actually stop me. I could wait till you're out in the kitchen or asleep or something and set it all up on the website and pay with your credit card,' I said. I was just joking, but Dad took me seriously.

'Tilly.' He pulled me on to his lap and tilted my chin so I had to look him in the eye. 'Tilly, I understand, I really do, but I need you to put this daft idea right out of your mind. I don't want to meet any lady. I don't want to get married. And I don't ever want you going on any website using our details, do you hear me? It's very dangerous. Anyone could answer. They could pretend anything they wanted. There are some very sick, twisted people in the world. Now promise me you won't touch my iPad and go on the internet, not unless I'm with you and you're looking something up for school. Promise me!'

'I promise, Dad,' I said.

I crossed Dad off my list. I couldn't think of anyone else. I asked Matty to help me when we were at school. We thought hard. She kept asking me about aunties and cousins and friends of the family, but Dad and I didn't seem to have any.

'What about . . . your mum?' said Matty, lowering her voice. 'Didn't she have any friends?'

'She's got lots, but we don't see them any more,' I said.

'Oh,' said Matty. She fidgeted, doodling on my list. I'd already sketched a border of miniature bridesmaid's dresses all round the edge. Matty's doodles were wild spirals and dots and dashes and they made the page look very messy. I didn't say anything but I minded.

'Tilly?' Matty said, her head still bent, doodling away. 'Tilly, I know I'm not supposed to ask, but *why* did your mum leave?'

'I don't know,' I said.

'But you must know,' she persisted.

I stared at my miniature bridesmaid's dresses until they blurred into one pink ribbon.

'She just . . . went.'

'You mean you woke up one morning and she'd packed her case and disappeared?'

'No. Well, almost. She'd been acting a bit weird for weeks. Months, maybe. I can't remember properly,' I said.

I could remember everything, but I didn't like to. There were lots of times when Mum wasn't happy and funny and lovely. Times when she stayed in bed and pulled the covers over her head when I tried to talk to her. Times when she shouted at Dad. Times when she slammed out of the house and went off for hours.

Sometimes I thought it was because of me. I couldn't learn the dance she was teaching me or kept on about something silly at school or tried to tell jokes that weren't funny enough.

Dad told me again and again that it wasn't because of me.

'I think it's me,' he said miserably. 'I can't ever think of the right thing to say. I can't ever think of any romantic surprises. I never do anything exciting and spontaneous. We were fine for a while, because she liked being looked after, but now she's bored with me.'

Mum and Dad had a terrible row one night. I tried not to listen but I couldn't help it. I don't think they went to bed at all – they just stayed up shouting. Well, Mum shouted. Dad hardly said anything.

They were sitting at the kitchen table when I got up the next morning. Dad was in his pyjamas, his face white, his eyes red. Mum was dressed in her prettiest top and her tightest jeans. She had a suitcase by her side. I stared at the suitcase and started trembling.

'I'm going away for a little holiday, Tilly,' she said.

'Oh don't, please don't!' I cried. I ran to her and climbed onto her lap. 'Can't we come with you, Mum?'

'No, Tills, I need to be by myself for a bit. I've got a lot of thinking to do. You stay with Dad and be a good girl,' said Mum.

'But when will you be coming back?'

'I don't know.'

Dad made a little choking sound. He went out to the downstairs toilet. I pulled Mum's head closer and whispered in her ear.

'Can't *I* come with you, Mum?'

I hated remembering that. It was horrible of me to try to walk out on Dad too. But I just wanted to be with Mum so much. It didn't matter anyway. Mum wasn't having it.

'No, I have to be by myself. Don't start crying, Tills. You're better off without me. You both are. Now come on, slide off my lap. I've got to go now. This is awful for all of us,' she said.

She kissed me goodbye. She waited until Dad came out of the toilet and kissed him too. Then she walked out of the front door with that one suitcase. She didn't come back that night. Or the next or the next or the next. She didn't come back for months.

Dad and I were so happy when she suddenly

turned up on the doorstep. We thought she'd come back for good. She hugged us and kissed us and said how much she'd missed us. We didn't notice at first that she didn't have a suitcase with her. She hadn't come back – she was just visiting to make sure we were all right.

She wasn't stupid: she could see we weren't all right at all; we were all wrong without her. But she still went again. She came back three more times, just for a day. She never even stayed the night. All the times in between we waited for her. Whenever we heard a car drawing up nearby, or footsteps, or the squeak of our front gate, we jumped up, ready.

That was why we moved away. Dad said we had to start a new life. We couldn't stay waiting for ever. I was terrified Mum wouldn't be able to find us the next time she came back.

'Maybe she won't come back at all,' said Dad. 'Anyway, I've left our forwarding address with the new people in our house, the neighbours, Sylvie, all her friends. Mum will find us if she wants to.'

Mum obviously didn't want to.

I didn't tell Matty any of this. It was too sad.

She was staring at me, waiting for an explanation. I just shrugged my shoulders helplessly.

'Oh well,' she said. She chewed her pen. It was actually my pen, and she was making little nibbly marks.

'Don't muck it up,' I said.

But then she jerked and bit off the entire top.

'Matty! My pen!'

'What? Sorry! I didn't mean to,' she said, spitting the top out. 'I've just had the most wonderful idea!'

'What?'

'You can advertise. Offer your services! Rent-a-bridesmaid!'

Chapter Seven

'Rent-a-bridesmaid,' I said slowly.

'You could make yourself a little profile on the internet,' said Matty.

'No. I can't. Dad made me promise that I would never do anything like that on the internet. He says it's dangerous.'

'Yes, but hundreds of thousands of people do it. And he needn't know.'

'But I'll know. And I'll feel terrible if I break my promise.'

'Oh, Tilly, you're such a hopeless goody-goody wuss. Tell you what, *I'll* do it for you – on *my* iPad, so your dad couldn't possibly find out. There!

Problem sorted!' said Matty triumphantly.

'I'll still know though. I'll still be breaking my promise. No, I can't do anything on the internet,' I said.

'Well, how are you going to advertise then?'

'I know exactly,' I said. 'I'll put an advert in Sid's window.'

When we went up to Matty's bedroom to play, the Warrior Princesses stayed sleeping in their cardboard-box palace. The dinosaurs and cuddly toys and ponies lay on their backs, immobile. Lewis lay on his back too, arms and legs out like a starfish on the rug. He sang all the songs he knew, pop songs and theme tunes to television shows and advertising jingles and Christmas carols. He sang very loudly, and when he didn't know the right words, which was often, he made up rubbish. It was very distracting, but at least it stopped him interfering with our important task.

Matty and I were compiling our advert for Sid's window. I tore out a page from my drawing book, made it into a neat square, and started working on another bridesmaid's dress border while Matty made a rough draft of the wording because I couldn't think what to say. I could make up a profile for Dad in a heartbeat but I was stuck when it came to describing myself in a positive manner.

'It's easy-peasy,' said Matty, scribbling away, and then read out:

'Very pretty, sensible nine-year-old has barely worn gorgeous pink designer bridesmaid's dress with matching accessories. Will attend any wedding ceremony and add that perfect stylish touch to your wedding photos. Very small rental fee for one day.'

'Matty! I'm not in the least pretty!'

'Well, you do look quite pretty in that yucky dress.'

'Sensible?'

'Well, you *are* sensible, except when you go all moody on me.'

'I haven't got matching accessories.'

'Of course you have. You can wear my pink shoes. They did get a bit scraped at the toes when I danced, but you could colour them in with your felt tip. And you can wear those awful pink frilly knickers. Mum washed them and I'm never wearing them again, believe you me,' said Matty.

'I don't want to charge a fee either. I'll be someone's bridesmaid for nothing,' I said.

'You've got to be professional. They won't take you seriously if you say you'll do it for free,' she said. 'Go on, write out the advert. Your handwriting's neater than mine.'

'I'm not putting I'm pretty. It's not true and it sounds like showing off.'

'No it doesn't. And if you *don't* put that, they'll think you're hideous and no one will want you to be their bridesmaid,' said Matty.

'You can't say stuff like that – it's mean. You can't help the way you look. Everyone should have a chance to be a bridesmaid.'

Matty sighed. 'I'm simply being practical. OK, if you're someone's little sister or niece and you happen to be ugly, then they maybe won't mind too much. You're probably stuck with them anyway because of family pressure. I'm positive my Aunt Rachel didn't want to have me as her bridesmaid

111

because I look stupid in frills and she knew I'd muck about, but Grandma insisted. You're not a family bridesmaid, though. You're a professional selling your services, so you need to reassure people you'll do a good job and look the part. Now write the wretched thing and let's play. I'm getting bored with the whole subject.'

'Me too, and I don't even know what you two are whispering about,' Lewis sang.

I still wasn't sure, but I wrote Matty's words in my best fancy handwriting and then put the card carefully in my school bag. I didn't know how I was going to get to Sid's to put it in his window, but I decided to think about that problem later. The Warrior Princesses awoke and leaped from their palace, preparing to do battle. We managed a great game before our lasagne and salad supper.

'Mm, something still smells good,' said Dad when he came to collect me.

'We've still got heaps left. You're very welcome to a plateful,' said Angie.

'Oh no! No, I wasn't hinting! I was just commenting, that's all. No, I've got my own supper at home, honestly,' said Dad, blushing painfully. 'You're being wonderful looking after Tilly like this. You can't look after me too!'

'You look as if you might need a bit of looking after,' said Angie. 'Come on, sit down and have some supper.'

But Dad wouldn't – he was far too embarrassed.

'Oh dear, I don't know how to make it up to Matty's mother. She absolutely refuses to take any payment for having you,' he said in the car going home.

I suddenly had a crafty idea.

'Let's give her a little present then, Dad. Sid's shop is always open early. Let me run in on our way to school in the morning and I'll choose her a big box of chocolates. I'll use my own pocket money.'

'That's a brilliant idea,' said Dad.

I felt a bit guilty then. Very guilty, in fact. But it didn't stop me running into Sid's shop the next morning with my purse and my advert in my school bag. Luckily Dad couldn't find anywhere to park outside, so he said he'd drive round the block while I bought the chocolates.

I did buy chocolates, the biggest purple box in the shop.

'Is it your mum's birthday?' Sid asked.

I wriggled. 'No, they're for my friend's mum,' I said. 'And can I put an advert in your window, please?'

'Is this for another lady to look after you? What happened to the last one? Did you play her up?' he asked, looking amused.

'No, this is for me,' I said, handing it over.

Sid peered at it, sucking his teeth.

'I don't quite get it. You want to be someone's bridesmaid?' he said. 'It doesn't usually work like that, does it? Aren't you supposed to be asked by the bride and groom?'

'Yes, well, this is the modern way,' I told him.

'Does your dad know about this?'

'Yes, of course.' It was a downright lie and I felt dreadful, but I was scared Sid wouldn't accept the advert if I said no.

He still didn't seem too keen on the idea. 'I've never heard of this bridesmaid malarkey before. People advertise themselves as cleaners or child-minders or odd-job men or as a man with a van – little kids don't advertise themselves as bridesmaids.'

'Perhaps I'm starting a whole new fashion,' I said.

'Hmm. I'm going to ask a lot of questions if

anyone seems interested in this advert of yours. And if you get any replies, you'd better let your dad vet them carefully. *If* you get replies,' he said. 'People don't want a stranger for a bridesmaid. And they'd want to choose their own bridesmaid's dress, surely?'

I glared at Sid. 'I will get replies, just you wait and see,' I said. I paid for the chocolates and the advert and marched towards the shop door. I held my head up high and didn't look where I was going, so I tripped right over a crate of milk waiting to be shelved.

'Whoops! You'd better not do that walking up the aisle in your famous bridesmaid's frock,' said Sid, cackling with laughter.

I swept out, still trying to look dignified. Dad drove past and I jumped in the car.

'Oh yes, good choice,' he said, nodding at the chocolates. 'Matty's mum will like them.'

She did really like them, and seemed especially touched when I told her I'd bought them with my own pocket money.

'That's so sweet of you, Tilly. But you mustn't ever do it again. We *love* having you round here.'

She opened the box of chocolates right away and let us choose one.

'Yes, we especially love having you here,' said Lewis, his cheek bulging with the chocolate Turkish delight. 'Mum doesn't usually let us have chocolates.'

Matty chose the caramel. I had the nutty one, my favourite. Angie had the strawberry cream and smacked her lips.

'Don't listen to Mum,' said Matty when we were up in her bedroom. 'Please buy her a box of chocs every week.'

'Every *day*,' said Lewis.

'I might have to!' I said, suddenly realizing something. I needed an excuse to go back to Sid's shop every day for my replies.

I didn't have enough pocket money to buy a big box of chocolates every day – or even every week. But I thought up a cunning plan I could just about afford.

'Could we stop off at the newsagent's again this morning?' I asked Dad the next day when we were in the car going to school. 'Matty's mum loved her chocolates so much that I thought I'd buy her just a little bar every day as a tiny treat. Don't you think that's another brilliant idea, Dad?'

'Not really. I think that's going a bit over the top,' he said.

'But it'll still come out of my pocket money. It won't cost you a penny,' I insisted.

'It's not the money, you silly sausage. It's sweet of you, but I'm sure Matty's mum wouldn't want you to spend all your savings on chocolate, especially not for her. The one box was a nice gesture, but you don't need to go over the top,' said Dad, and he accelerated past Sid's shop.

I stared back in anguish. I imagined Sid with a huge pile of cards and letters for me, all asking me to be a bridesmaid. How long would he keep them? How would I ever get Dad to stop off at the shop? Could I secretly slip out of the house and fetch them all by myself? Could I ask Matty's mother to trail all the way to Sid's after school, when it was at the opposite end of town to her house?

I was so taken up with worrying over the problem that I barely paid any attention in our first lesson, Literacy. I doodled bridesmaid's dresses compulsively all over several pages of my jotter while Miss Hope droned on about the media and different types of reportage.

'Tilly!' she said suddenly, right in my ear.

I'd been so anxiously absorbed that I hadn't realized she'd crept up on me. I jumped violently and everyone laughed, even Matty.

Miss Hope shook her head at me. 'Oh dear, what are you drawing now?' she said, and picked up my jotter. She peered at all the dresses, each identical, and looked puzzled.

'They're not dinosaurs, Miss Hope,' I said quickly.

'So I see,' she said. 'No, they're very carefully designed dresses. You've drawn them very well, Tilly, but I'd prefer you to concentrate on the lesson, if you don't mind.'

'Yes, Miss Hope,' I said miserably.

Miss Hope went back to the front of the class and carried on. She said she wanted us all to divide into pairs and start a special project, our own newspaper. We had to report on a week of news, but we had to write our features according to what kind of newspaper it was. It could be serious reporting, or very sensational. We could concentrate on important issues or family matters or sport or fashion.

'I expect you'll want to do a page of dress designs, Tilly,' said Miss Hope.

'Yuck, I hope not,' said Matty. 'Let's do a newspaper totally devoted to sport. What sort of sports get reported on, Miss Hope? Can we write about skateboarding?'

'Well, why don't we all bring a newspaper into school tomorrow and see for ourselves?' she said.

Bring a newspaper.

Hurray!

'Miss Hope says we've got to bring an old newspaper to school tomorrow,' I told Dad.

'But we haven't got any newspapers. I read the news online,' he said.

'So can I buy one from Sid on the way to school?' I asked.

'Well, it's a bit daft, buying one specially,' said Dad, but he gave in.

The next morning I went charging into the newsagent's on the way to school. I picked up the first newspaper I saw, found the right money, handed it over to Sid, and grinned at him expectantly.

'Yes?' he said. 'Do you want chocolate or crisps?'

'I want my replies, please! I'm Matilda, the girl who put the advert in your window,' I said.

'Replies?' said Sid. 'You didn't get any replies. I said so, didn't I?' He shook his head – but he had a gleam in his eye.

'You're teasing me!' I said. 'I did get replies, didn't I?'

'Well, yes, to my total surprise, you did.' Sid rummaged in a drawer and brought out one Basildon Bond envelope. 'Here we are. Your reply.'

'Where are all the others?' I asked merrily.

'What do you mean, others? There aren't any others. I'm amazed you got the one. Take it then. And you'd better hop it now – your dad's hooting his horn at you.'

'I was sure I'd get heaps of replies,' I said.

'Well, you never know. You might get more. You've paid for a week, so your card stays in the window a few more days. You can always pay for another week after that if you've got money to burn,' said Sid.

I stuffed the one envelope in my school bag and trailed out of the shop clutching my newspaper.

'In you get, quick,' said Dad. 'What's up?'

'Nothing,' I said.

I thought I'd get a whole sackful of replies. I'd imagined myself attending weddings all summer, wearing my beautiful raspberry-pink bridesmaid's dress Saturday after Saturday until the end of September. I'd planned to go through all the replies with Matty so she could help me choose the most promising invitations. But at least I had *one* reply. I could get to be a bridesmaid once.

All through breakfast club, I kept putting my hand inside my school bag and stroking the smooth envelope. But I couldn't even take one peek at it before Matty arrived. The moment she got to school, I streaked across the playground towards her – she was hopping up and down, waiting.

'Did you get to go to the newsagent's? Did you get many replies? Where are they, stuffed in your school bag?' she gabbled.

'I've got one,' I said, fishing for it.

'One?' said Matty, wrinkling her nose.

'I expect I'll get lots more,' I said quickly. 'Let's look at this one!'

I slit the envelope open carefully and drew out the letter. The writing was very clear and neat, sloping gently to the right, with lovely loops. I looked at the signature first.

Iris May Bloomfield. I said the name aloud delightedly. It was such a wonderful flowery name. I pictured Iris May Bloomfield, certain she'd be very pretty, probably with long fair curly hair.

She'd have deep blue eyes – that's why she was called Iris. She'd have a lovely figure, perfect for a long creamy-white dress, and she'd carry a bouquet of pink roses on her wedding day to match the subtle colour of my dress.

Dear Matilda, said the letter.

I'm going to be married at St John's Church this coming Saturday 29 May at 12 noon. My fiancé and I think it would be delightful to have a bridesmaid in such a pretty frock. Would you and your mother like to come round to my house, 37 Ringstead Gardens, one day after school so we can discuss it?

Yours sincerely,
Iris May Bloomfield

Chapter Eight

'**D**-a-d?' I said, going home in the car from Matty's that evening.

'What is it?' said Dad. 'I can always tell you've been up to something when you use that tone of voice!'

'Dad, I've been asked to be a bridesmaid! Truly! Isn't it wonderful!' I said.

'Oh, darling, that *is* wonderful. I'm so happy for you. So who's getting married? Someone at school? It's not one of the teachers, is it? Miss Hope?' he asked.

'Oh, Dad, don't be daft! No, it's Iris May Bloomfield, isn't that a lovely name! She wants us to come round to her house one afternoon. Well, she asked if I'd come with my mum, but I'm sure she won't mind if it's you, Dad.'

'But who is this Iris May Bloomfield? You've never even mentioned her before,' he said.

'Well, I don't exactly know her yet,' I said, fidgeting a little. 'That's why she's asked us round to her house.'

'So if you don't know her, how on earth has she asked you to be her bridesmaid?'

'W-e-l-l . . .'

'Come on, Tilly, spit it out,' said Dad.

'I actually advertised,' I mumbled.

Dad very nearly drove straight into the car in front. He went down a side road and pulled up altogether, then switched off the car engine. He turned and looked at me.

'You *advertised*?' he said.

'Please don't be cross, Dad,' I said.

'Didn't we have a serious discussion about the dangers of advertising on the internet?' Dad demanded.

'Yes, but this wasn't on the internet. I swear it wasn't. I wrote out my advert on a piece of paper and paid to put it in Sid's window,' I said.

'Oh, Tilly!' said Dad. He suddenly started

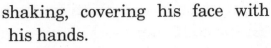 shaking, covering his face with his hands.

'Dad? Oh, don't cry! I'm sorry, I'm terribly sorry, I didn't mean to upset you,' I said, unbuckling my seat belt and trying to wrap my arms round his neck.

'I'm not crying – I'm laughing,' Dad snorted. 'Though I'm cross too. You *mustn't* advertise yourself like this, even if it's just in Sid's window! Let me see this reply.'

I fished in my school bag and handed it over. Dad read it carefully.

'Well, she certainly sounds very nice – but it's still very bizarre. I think we'd better drive straight round to Ringstead Gardens and explain to this lady that you took it into your own head to do this,' said Dad.

'But will you still let me be her bridesmaid?'

'I don't know.'

'Oh please, please, it's my only chance of wearing my bridesmaid's dress and it means *so* much to me!'

'I know it does, sweetheart. Well, let's wait and see what Miss Bloomfield is like,' said Dad, starting up the car again.

'We can't go *straight* there. We have to go home first so I can put on the bridesmaid's dress. And I've got ink all over my fingers and my socks are grubby and I'm sure my hair's a mess,' I said, panicking. 'She'll never ever say I can be her bridesmaid unless I make myself look a little bit pretty.'

'You do look pretty, sweetheart. She won't be expecting you to be all dressed up. And I've told you I'm not at all sure I *want* you to be her bridesmaid. Let's just wait and see. Now, Ringstead Gardens . . . I think it's off to the left somewhere.'

Dad drove up and down several streets before we found Ringstead Gardens. I'd imagined it as actual gardens, with little houses covered in honeysuckle and roses and my Iris May blooming inside the prettiest. The real Ringstead Gardens were modern houses with very boring strips of grass, scarcely a flower in sight.

'Oh,' I said. 'I didn't think it would look like this.'

'Let's have another look at that letter. I don't think it *can* be Ringstead Gardens. I think this is special housing for the elderly. No one here's going to be needing a bridesmaid!' said Dad. 'Perhaps it's Ringstead Crescent or Lane?'

But there was no mistaking the clear copper-plate writing on the letter.

'Well, we'll knock on the door and see for ourselves,' said Dad, pulling up outside number 37.

It looked a little more interesting than all the other homes. The white lacy curtains at the window were tied with pink satin ribbons, and several twirling china ballerinas danced along one windowsill. A large white cat lay in the other window, idly washing its front paws.

'Oh, look at the cat, Dad! I wish we could have a cat,' I said.

'Well, maybe one day. When we get settled,' said Dad, though we'd been in our new house quite a while now.

He knocked on the green front door. There was a little wait. He knocked again. 'I don't think she can be home yet,' he said.

But then the door opened and a very small lady stood there, smiling at us. A very small, very *old* lady, with pink cheeks and white curly hair and a pink jumper and white slacks, as pretty as a packet of marshmallows.

'Hello!' she said, sounding pleased to see us.

'I'm so sorry, I think we've come to the wrong place,' said Dad. 'We're looking for a Miss Bloomfield.'

'That's me,' she said. She looked at me. 'And I think you might well be Matilda!'

'I am,' I said. 'I look a bit of a mess because I've been at school, and then I was round my friend's house. I don't usually look as scruffy as this. And when I put my bridesmaid's dress on, I look totally different, I promise – and I'll have pink shoes to match. I'll even have a pink petticoat and knickers but they won't show.'

'I'm sure you'll look beautiful, dear. Do come in, both of you. Let's have a cup of tea,' said Miss Bloomfield.

Dad looked a little anxious, but I marched in boldly, determined not to lose my chance of being a bridesmaid. She led us into the living room. It was small but very cosy, with crotcheted blankets on the backs of the sofa and chairs. There was a large cat basket with a plump cushion, but the cat clearly preferred the windowsill. It surveyed us lazily, and didn't seem to mind when I went to stroke it.

There were several photographs of the cat in silver frames, and one big photograph of an elderly weather-beaten man with a big grin, looking like a sailor in a storybook. He must be Miss Bloomfield's fiancé!

She made us a proper pot of tea, with milk in a willow-pattern jug and sugar in lumps in a matching bowl. There was a plate of little fairy cakes too, white icing with pink sprinkles and pink icing with white. She and I both picked pink ones. They were absolutely delicious. The icing tasted of sweet raspberries.

She smiled again. 'Pink's my favourite colour,' she said.

'Then you'll love my bridesmaid's dress,' I said. 'What colour will you be wearing, Miss Bloomfield? Will it be white?'

'Well, yes, I am,' she said.

Dad and I nodded politely. I tried to picture her in a long white bride's dress with a veil. It was quite a struggle. A long dress would trail on the ground and trip her up; a veil would be even more cumbersome.

Miss Bloomfield laughed. 'I'm not wearing a conventional bride's dress, dears. Come with me, Matilda, and I'll show you my wedding dress.'

She took me into her bedroom, a lovely little pink-and-white room, with a white toy cat on her pink pillow. There was an outfit hanging outside her wardrobe: a white dress with pink stripes, with a matching pink jacket.

'Oh, it's lovely!' I said.

'It doesn't look too girlish, does it?' she asked, a little anxiously.

'No, it's lovely. Very pretty. And my bridesmaid's dress will go with it perfectly,' I told her.

'That's what I thought! We'll set each other off a treat,' she said. 'You won't mind being at an old folk's wedding, will you? It's going to be very quiet – Mr Flower and I are only having a few guests. We'll be having a little do down at the church hall after. Nothing fancy, just a few sandwiches and sausage rolls, that kind of thing. And I've made my own wedding cake. Want to see it?'

'Oh yes, please! I've never had wedding cake,' I said.

She took me into her kitchen. It was even smaller than the other rooms, so you could hardly turn round in it, but incredibly neat and tidy. Miss Bloomfield couldn't quite reach her top shelf of pots and pans and tins, but she had a handy silver ladder propped against the wall. She climbed it with surprising speed and seized a big cake tin patterned with flowers. She descended the ladder much more carefully, holding the tin protectively against her chest.

'Here, have a little peep,' she said, easing off the lid.

The big white cake took up almost the whole of the tin. There were icing rosettes piped all the way round and a little marzipan couple stood in the middle, holding hands. The woman had white hair and she was wearing a white dress with pink stripes.

'They're too big, those stripes, but I can't work miracles,' said Miss Bloomfield. 'And that's Mr Albert Richard Flower, my fiancé, bless him.'

The marzipan man was much rounder than Miss Bloomfield, and his face was very pink, without any hair at all. She'd made him a very smiley mouth.

'He looks very happy to be marrying you,' I said.

'I hope he is,' said Miss Bloomfield. 'He's been married before, and he has grown-up children. I hope they don't mind too much that he's marrying me. It's my first time to be a bride. I've had a few gentleman friends in my time, but I've never so much as been engaged before. Do you like my ring?'

She held out her hand to show me. It was like a little flower itself, a tiny amethyst with diamond chips as petals.

'It's lovely,' I said.

'Isn't it?' Miss Bloomfield agreed. 'I can't help holding out my hand and admiring it every now and then! I feel just like a silly young girl all over again.'

Dad came into the kitchen with our tea things neatly piled on the tray. 'Thank you so much, Miss Bloomfield. So, as you and Tilly are getting along like a house on fire, I presume you'd like her as your bridesmaid?'

'If you don't mind?'

'Well, I was a bit taken aback at first. I had no idea she'd taken it into her head to advertise herself! But I know she's set her heart on it,' said Dad.

'I've set my heart on it too!' said Miss Bloomfield. 'I'd been really wishing I could have a little bridesmaid. I don't have any great-nieces and neither does my fiancé. We don't know any little girls at all. I was really taken with the advert in

Sid's window. So, if we're all in agreement, we just need to discuss the rent,' she said, twinkling.

'The rent?' said Dad.

'For Matilda.'

'Tilly said she was for *rent?*' Dad repeated, astounded.

'She stresses that it's a very small rent,' said Miss Bloomfield. 'What sum did you have in mind, dear?' she asked, turning to me.

'I – I'm not sure,' I said. 'Actually, you don't really have to pay me anything.'

'Of course you're not going to be paid anything!' said Dad. 'Good heavens, Tilly, what's got into you? It's bad enough to advertise yourself – but to suggest someone pays for your services is totally beyond the pale. I'm so sorry, Miss Bloomfield.'

'No, I think Tilly – may I call you that, dear? – is simply being professional,' she said.

'That's what Matty said,' I told her.

'Ah, I thought Matty might be involved too,' said Dad.

'Matty's my very best friend,' I said proudly. 'Actually, it was her bridesmaid's dress first. But she gave it to me as a very special present, because I like it so.'

'I can't wait to see it,' said Miss Bloomfield. 'And

I definitely want to rent you dressed up in it. Name a sum! How about . . . ten pounds?'

Ten pounds! I'd seen a wonderful new tin of felt tips in the shops for exactly that sum. My own crayons were getting a bit worn now, even my best set, and my pink had run out altogether, because I'd drawn so many bridesmaid's dresses. Dad only gave me a pound a week pocket money, though he made sure he gave it to me every single Saturday. Mum used to give me as much as twenty pounds sometimes – but other times she forgot altogether. I really wanted Miss Bloomfield's ten pounds, but I didn't want to upset Dad. He was shaking his head determinedly.

Then I had a sudden idea.

'You can have me totally rent-free, Miss Bloomfield, but perhaps I can ask a special favour?' I said.

'Tilly!' said Dad.

'Could you teach me how to bake cakes?'

'Oh, I'd love to do that! I'll be going away for a few days to the Isle of Wight for my honeymoon, but as soon as I'm back we'll arrange our first cake-baking session. Mr Flower and I haven't quite decided where to live just yet, so at the moment we're going to try week and week about, first at my home and then at his. He lives at number twenty-seven so he's only a minute away! Now, about Saturday. Can you be here by eleven, do you think? Then we can sit down and have a cup of tea to steady ourselves. I expect I'll be feeling a bit wibbly-wobbly. It's not every day a woman gets married, especially at my age! Then we'll just wander down to the church. It didn't seem worth ordering a car when it's only five minutes' walk. Mr Flower is a little anxious that it might rain, but I can always take an umbrella.'

'If it rains, I'll drive you round to the church myself,' said Dad.

'Oh, that's so kind of you, Mr Andrews,' said Miss Bloomfield. 'You're invited to the little reception afterwards, of course. And perhaps your wife would like to join us? I'm sure she'd like to see Tilly as a bridesmaid!'

There was a little pause.

'Tilly's mother is abroad at the moment,' said Dad. 'So it will be just Tilly and me.'

'Of course, dear,' said Miss Bloomfield, tactfully not enquiring further.

'Miss Bloomfield? I couldn't possibly ask my best friend Matty to your wedding, could I? As it was her bridesmaid's dress in the first place. Please could she come too?'

'Of course she can come,' said Miss Bloomfield, beaming.

'I *do* like Miss Bloomfield,' I said to Dad in the car going home.

'Yes, so do I,' he said. 'I don't want you to ever try this trick again, Tilly. It is a miracle that it has turned out wonderfully. She's a lovely lady. And I shall feel very proud on Saturday seeing you in your pretty bridesmaid's dress.'

I waited till we were nearly home.

'D-a-d?'

'Now what?'

'*Is* Mum still abroad?'

'Well, she was. She sent us the postcard from Mexico, remember?'

Of course I remembered. It was in my private treasure box, along with one of Mum's earrings, her blue nail-varnish bottle and her old perfume. The varnish had dried rock hard. I'd secretly sprayed myself every night so I could imagine Mum leaning over me in bed, giving me a hug. The perfume bottle was empty now, but there was still the ghost of a smell whenever I pressed the nozzle.

'Do you think she might have sent lots more to our old house, Dad?'

'No, love. I made sure all cards and letters would be forwarded to our new address.'

'What about parcels? Perhaps Mum sent me another parcel? She did for my birthday,' I said, unwilling to give up.

'Tilly, I think we've got to accept that Mum's forgotten about us,' said Dad.

'That's stupid! She can't possibly have *forgotten* us,' I said. 'We remember every little thing about her.'

'Well, I don't mean she's literally forgotten us. She's just probably got other things to think about now,' said Dad.

'More important than us?' I said. 'I don't understand.'

Dad sighed. 'I don't understand either, Tilly. But there's no point dwelling on it. We'll just feel even more unhappy. But I promise I do know just how much you miss Mum.'

'I don't miss her *all* the time. Just sometimes. And I wish she could see me on Saturday. I know I'm not really pretty like Mum, but I do look quite good in my dress.'

'You're *much* prettier than Mum,' said Dad.

'You're just saying that. Dad, could I try leaving a message on Mum's phone and emailing her too, to tell her about Miss Bloomfield's wedding, just in case she wanted to come,' I said in a rush.

'Tilly, you know Mum's changed her phone number and her email address,' said Dad.

'Yes, but maybe she still checks her old ones, just to see there aren't any important messages,' I persisted.

'Well, you can have a go if you like. But I don't think you'll have much luck,' said Dad.

I tried when I got home. A little voice inside the phone told me that Mum's number was unavailable. And my email bounced back. So that night I tried to send a thought-message through the air.

I opened my window wide to make it easier. I stood there in my pyjamas, sending the same message again and again, until I started shivering.

Please come back on Saturday morning, Mum.
Come and see me be a bridesmaid
at St John's church at noon. You'll love
my dress – it's absolutely beautiful.
Please, please, please come!

Chapter Nine

Mum didn't come on Saturday.
Matty didn't either.

'*This* Saturday?' she said when I asked her at school.

'Yes, isn't it exciting? You will come, won't you? Don't pull faces at me, though – I have to stay very serious. Oh, Matty, I'm getting nervous now just thinking about it! Did you get very nervous when you were a bridesmaid for your Aunt Rachel?'

'No, I just felt a right fool. Especially when I had to follow the bride and they told me to keep my head up because no one wants a stooping bridesmaid, and yet I also had to keep my head down because they were all terrified I'd stomp on

Aunt Rachel's hem and tear it. Honestly! So I kept looking up and down until I felt my head was going to nod right off my neck.' Matty demonstrated her technique. I could see why her mum sighed whenever she talked about the wedding.

I rather wanted Matty's mum to see *me* as a bridesmaid.

'So you will come, won't you? St John's Church at noon. I so want you to see what I look like,' I said. 'If I look all scared and trembly, you can give me the thumbs up and your special smile, and then I'll feel better, won't I?'

'Mmm,' said Matty. 'Well, I'll see if I can come, but actually I think I might be going out on Saturday. If it's *this* Saturday. I mean, I absolutely know I can come the Saturday after.'

'Well, that's not much use. I can't get Miss Bloomfield to change her wedding day! Oh, Matty, *please* come. I want *someone* to see me in the bridesmaid's dress.'

'Your dad will be there, won't he?'

'Yes, I know, but he's just *Dad.* Weddings aren't really his thing.'

'They're not mine either! And it isn't as if this is a *proper* wedding anyway,' said Matty. 'You said this Miss Bloomfield is ancient and she'll just be inviting a few of her chums from some old folks' group.'

'Don't be mean! I didn't say that, not in those words. It doesn't matter that she's a bit old. You can get married at any age. And she seems so happy too. And *I'm* happy that I'm getting to be a bridesmaid at last. Don't spoil it,' I said, clenching my fists. 'What are you going to do that's so important that you can't come to the wedding?'

'Don't get so het up! I'm going to the zoo, if you must know. And don't get upset, but I'd much sooner see a lot of monkeys and tigers and elephants than some stupid old wedding,' said Matty. 'If you were absolutely honest, you'd far sooner see a whole lot of animals too.'

'No I wouldn't. I hate zoos! They're horrible places. I wouldn't be seen dead in a zoo,' I declared. I was being reasonably truthful, because zoos always made me think of those desperately sad Saturdays after Mum left when it was all Dad and I could think of to do together. But I didn't want to tell Matty that, so I started to pretend I objected

to zoos on principle. Which I actually did too.

'Think of all those poor wild animals cooped up in cages like they're in prison. They want to be running free in the jungle or the savannah or wherever they live,' I declared.

'Free to be shot at. Free to starve to death. Free to be eaten by some other bigger animal,' said Matty. 'Most of the animals in zoos are specially bred there anyway. And they're not in cages nowadays – they're in big enclosures.'

'Oh, shut up about your stupid zoo,' I said.

'Well, you shut up about your stupid wedding,' said Matty.

We barely talked to each other for the rest of the day. It was very awkward seeing as we sat right next to each other at school. Miss Hope paused midway through the afternoon, putting one hand on my shoulder, and one on Matty's.

'What's up with you two today? You're normally natter, natter, natter, but now you're as quiet as little mice. You'll be growing whiskers next and twitching your noses,' she said. 'Watch out. I might turn into a cat.' She pulled a magnificent cat face, baring her teeth and miaowing.

Matty and I couldn't help giggling. Then we were somehow friends again, just like that. She didn't say sorry. I didn't say sorry. But we kept making cat faces at each other and collapsing into giggles. Miss Hope had to tell us off eventually but she couldn't help smiling too.

We made cat faces all the way home, miaowing at the tops of our voices. Lewis joined in too, even louder.

'For goodness' sake, calm down, all you pussy-cats,' said Angie. 'Or I might have to throw a bucket of water over you.'

Matty and I pretended to throw water over each other and laughed even harder. It felt so good to laugh and be so silly. I hadn't laughed till my stomach ached for so long.

When we got to Matty's house, Angie said she had half a mind to give us cat food for our snack. She looked in her special treat tin instead and broke a chocolate wafer biscuit into four sticks.

'KitKat!' she said, giving Matty and Lewis and me one stick each with a glass of milk, and eating the last herself. Then we went upstairs to play, though we were still all in such a silly mood that we didn't manage the usual game of Warrior Princesses. Matty seized one of Lewis's soft toys. It was originally a podgy zebra, but Matty insisted it was a cat.

'Yep, it's a killer cat. Watch it grow! It's ginormous, the hugest cat in the whole universe and it's hungry, it's soooo hungry, it's going to eat up all your other animals, Lewis. It's going to eat *you*.' Matty made the zebra-cat leap at Lewis's neck, which made him squeal.

'Stop it! Stop it, you're making it too real,' Lewis shrieked, batting at Matty with both hands.

'It *is* real,' she said. 'All the cats in the world have mutated and are getting bigger and fiercer and hungrier.'

'Better watch out when you go to the zoo on Saturday then,' I said, a little tartly. 'All the lions and tigers will be bursting out of their cages to gobble you up, Matty!'

'I'm almost glad I'm not going!' said Lewis, diving for his bed and cowering under his duvet.

'You're not going?' I said. 'Why on earth not? Your mum and dad wouldn't leave you behind.'

'*We're* not going. It's just Matty, the lucky thing,' said Lewis, muffled.

I looked at Matty. She didn't quite look back at me.

'Who are you going with, Matty?' I asked.

There was a long pause. Matty picked up Princess Powerful.

'Come on, let's stop mucking about with silly baby toys and play Warrior Princesses,' she said, as if she hadn't heard my question.

'Who are you going to the zoo with, Matty?' I repeated, though I already knew.

She still wouldn't say it though. She just started fussing with Princess Powerful, making her do kick-boxing so that all my ponies fell down like skittles.

'She's going with that Marty,' said Lewis, sticking his head out of the duvet. 'And it's not fair that they didn't invite me.'

'Why didn't you tell me, Matty?' I asked very quietly.

'Because I knew you'd go all weird on me. Like you are now,' she said.

'I'm not being weird,' I said, though I knew my voice sounded strange. My heart was thumping. I seemed to be thumping all over. Even my eyelids pulsed. '*You're* the one who's being weird. Why do you want to keep secrets from me when we're supposed to be best friends?'

'It's not a secret. Look, it's no big deal. I'm going to the zoo with Marty and her family. She Skyped me.

145

They're all going this Saturday and Marty thought I might want to come too. Simple,' said Matty.

'So she's your best friend now?' I said. I didn't mean to say it. The words just blurted out of my mouth before I could stop them. It sounded so lame, so pathetic, so needy.

'She's not my *best* friend. *You* are. She's just a *friend* friend. I don't get you, Tilly. Why can't we both have heaps of other friends? It's more fun that way,' said Matty impatiently. She was making Princess Powerful do karate chops with her arms. It looked like she wanted to karate-chop me.

I didn't have heaps of friends. I didn't spend any time with Cathy and Amanda now. I didn't get in touch with any of the girls from my old school. I just wanted to have *one* best friend. And now it looked as if she might be getting fed up with me. I wasn't fun enough.

I hadn't been fun enough for Mum either.

I started to cry before I could stop myself. Matty sighed. She tried to put her arm round me. I wanted to hug her but I pushed her away instead.

'OK. Be like that. You really are a baby sometimes,' said Matty, and she stormed out of the bedroom.

I collapsed in a heap on the floor, howling.

146

'Don't cry!' said Lewis, wriggling out from under the duvet.

I jumped, because I'd forgotten he was there. He squatted down beside me.

'Don't get upset,' he said. 'Matty and I are always having arguments. But then we make it up. It will be all right.'

'Best friends aren't supposed to have arguments,' I wept. 'She'd much sooner have this Marty as her best friend.'

'Well, Marty is very funny,' said Lewis. Then he realized he'd been tactless. 'But you're nicer, Tilly, promise. Look, *I'll* be your best friend if you like.'

I felt worse than ever then. I gave him a proper hug, and then we tried to play our own Warrior Princesses game, but it wasn't the same without Matty. We kept listening for her footsteps but she didn't come back.

She was in the kitchen with her mum. I felt worried. She'd be telling her mum, and then her mum was probably being understanding but saying she had to try to be kind to me. I went hot and squirmy just imagining it.

I didn't know what I was going to do. I couldn't

keep going to Matty's house after school if we weren't best friends. I was pretty sure Aunty Sue wouldn't take me back – and I didn't want to see her ever again anyway. Dad wouldn't let me go home by myself. I was stuck. I was the weird girl that nobody wanted.

But it turned out I was getting in a state pointlessly. When Angie called Lewis and me down for supper, Matty grinned at both of us.

'Hey, *I've* made supper, all by myself – well, nearly. Look, prawn stirfry, yummy! I chopped all the veg and then I stirred and fried, didn't I, Mum?'

It was as if the quarrel had never happened, though we were both careful not to mention Saturday.

I'd been so looking forward to the wedding and wearing the bridesmaid's dress. I tried it on again that evening, instead of getting into my pyjamas at bedtime. I held the skirt out and forced a smile as I looked in my mirror. Did I look pretty in the dress? It was a bit too big for me, even when I tightened the sash at the back. And maybe I was too pale to wear raspberry pink. Perhaps I looked stupid.

Matty was right. It wasn't a proper wedding. It was just two lonely old people deciding to live together. It wasn't as if they were family, *my* old people. I hardly knew Miss Bloomfield. I'd never even met Mr Flower. I was just a rented bridesmaid.

Dad knocked on the bedroom door. 'Are you in bed yet, Tilly?'

I didn't answer. Dad waited, and then opened the door a crack.

'Tilly? Oh, you look a picture!' he said.

'No I don't,' I sniffed.

'Are you crying? Here, let's take your dress off – quick we don't want tearstains all down the front,' said Dad.

He helped me pull it over my head. 'That's right. Now, I'm going downstairs to make something. Hang up your dress, put on your pyjamas and hop into bed, lickety-split.'

I did as I was told and waited. Dad was a little while. Then I heard him coming up the stairs, his footsteps slow and careful. He had a mug in each hand when he came in.

'Tea?' I said, surprised.

'Much better than tea,' said Dad.

It was hot chocolate with whipped cream and

tiny little pink and white marshmallows floating on top!

'Oh, Dad! And you've even got marshmallows!'

'I saw them in Sainsbury's when I was shopping on the way home. They reminded me of Miss Bloomfield. I thought I'd have a go at making us a proper hot chocolate as a little treat,' said Dad. 'Take a sip. It's not too sickly, is it?'

I took a proper gulp. 'It's lovely, Dad,' I said, licking my lips.

'That's good.' Dad sat down on the side of the bed, careful not to jog me. He gently dabbed at my eyes with a tissue and then rubbed round my mouth too. 'You've got a lovely little cream moustache.'

'This *is* a special treat, Dad,' I said.

'Yes, well, we don't have enough treats nowadays, do we?' Dad sipped his own mug of chocolate. He looked down at my duvet, making his finger hop from flower to flower on the blue-sky background. 'We did the right thing moving here. We needed to make a new start. Only we've not really *started*, have we? We've been a bit stuck, two silly old saddos. But now we're going to have fun.'

'We're not very good at having fun, Dad,' I said. 'Not when it's just you and me.'

'Well, we're going to have to try harder,' he said.

'The wedding's going to be fun, isn't it? You'll love wearing your bridesmaid's dress.'

I nibbled a marshmallow. 'I'm a bit worried about it now,' I said. 'Maybe I just look stupid in it.'

'Nonsense! You look absolutely lovely. I'm going to be so proud of you my heart will burst,' said Dad. 'Just you wait and see.'

Chapter Ten

When I woke up on Saturday morning, I crept into Dad's room. He was fast asleep, curled up in a ball as if he were still a little boy. He'd kept the bed he used to share with Mum when we came to the new house. It looked too big for just one person. I climbed in beside him and cuddled up to his back.

'It's the wedding day!' I whispered.

He murmured my name in a pleased sort of way but he didn't wake up properly. I tried a few wriggles and nudges to see if that would help but he started gently snoring. I felt too fidgety and nervous and excited to stay cuddled up for long.

I eased myself out of bed again and went to put on the immersion heater so that I could have a really big hot bath this morning. I checked on my bridesmaid's dress again, as if it might have flounced off by itself during the night. It was hanging up outside my wardrobe, as fresh and silky and pink as ever. I rubbed the frilly hem against my cheek, loving its feel.

I held the dress up against me and practised walking very slowly and importantly around my bedroom, though it was a bit difficult in my flip-flop bedroom slippers.

'Will I make a good bridesmaid?' I asked Stripy and Blue Bunny.

I made them nod their heads enthusiastically. I tried playing a game with them, but it wouldn't become real – I just stayed me playing with two cuddly toys like a baby. I got my crayons and my drawing book and started to draw Stripy and Blue Bunny instead, making them pose for their portraits. They were a bit small on the page so I drew some other animals around them. Monkeys and elephants and tigers. Then I drew two girls looking at all the animals. One girl had bright red hair and badges all over her jacket and sparkly trainers. I drew the other girl in a mad clown outfit with a tiny bowler hat and enormous baggy trousers with braces. I gave her a big round red nose and a silly grin. Then I scribbled all over her. I scribbled all over the whole page and then tore it out, scrumpled it up and threw it in the wastepaper basket.

I peeped into Dad's bedroom, but he still wasn't awake. I wandered back into the kitchen and stole a shortbread biscuit. I wasn't really hungry, and after one bite just licked the sugar off. Then I washed my sticky hands and started another drawing. It was a proper picture this time. I started with St John's Church. It was difficult remembering exactly what it looked like, but I knew it had a little spire and stained-glass windows and a grassy garden with roses. I drew Miss Bloomfield standing beside the rose bed in her pink-and-white wedding frock. She was hand in hand with Mr Flower. I tried to remember what the old man looked like in the photograph at Miss Bloomfield's. I drew him wearing his best suit, with a rose in his buttonhole.

Then, last of all, I drew me in the raspberry-pink bridesmaid's dress. I made my hair a bit longer and thicker and blonder and coloured my eyes very blue and gave myself cupid lips, just to look prettier on the page. This wasn't cheating. It was something called Artistic Licence.

Then I had to spend ages colouring in all the boring bits like the sky and the grass. Sometimes I couldn't be bothered to do it neatly, but this time I did my best to make the sky an even blue with little fluffy clouds, and I coloured the green grass in little vertical dashes to look like individual blades of grass.

Dad came into the kitchen in his pyjamas just as I was finishing.

'Hello, Tilly! I'm so sorry I slept in, lovey,' he said, yawning. Then he saw what I was doing. 'My goodness, let's have a look at your picture. It's a little masterpiece! You must have been up half the night.'

'It's me at the wedding in my bridesmaid's dress,' I said.

'I can see that,' said Dad. 'You've done it all so carefully – and I love the way you've drawn Miss Bloomfield. Tell you what, why don't you give

155

her the picture as a little wedding present? I'm
sure she'd think it very special indeed.'

'Do you think so?'

'I know so! Now, let's put the immersion on, so
you can scrub yourself as pink as your pretty
dress,' said Dad.

'I've done it!'

'Clever girl. Then let's have breakfast now. We
don't want you spilling your cornflakes all down
your dress.'

Dad made the tea while I set out the cornflake
bowls and put two slices of bread in the toaster.

'We make a good team together, you and me,
don't we?' said Dad.

'Yes, we do,' I said.

We gave each other a high five and smiled. We
were a team with the most important member
missing, but we were still a team.

I found I didn't want to eat much breakfast,
even though Dad let me sprinkle my cornflakes
with rainbow sugar as a treat.

'Eat up, poppet,' he said.

'My tummy doesn't feel right,' I said, rubbing it.

'I expect you're just a bit nervous,' said Dad.
'I wonder if Miss Bloomfield's feeling a bit nervous
too.'

'I do like her. I wish I had her as a granny,' I said wistfully.

I didn't have any proper grannies. Dad's mum had died when I was still a baby. Mum's mum lived in Spain somewhere with a new husband, but she'd never seemed very interested in me. She'd never got on with Mum either.

'Maybe Miss Bloomfield wishes she had a little granddaughter just like you,' said Dad. 'Come on, try a bit of toast and honey if you really can't finish your cornflakes.'

I did my best, and then went to have my bath. I washed my hair too. I wished I could style it properly. I couldn't help remembering the way Mum sometimes played hairdressers with me and gave me elaborate topknots. I brushed my damp hair and fiddled around with it this way and that, but it didn't work. In the end I just let it hang down to my shoulders, and gave my fringe an extra brushing so it wouldn't go all kinky. At least it was soft and shiny.

Then I put on the raspberry-pink underwear and the raspberry-pink dress and the raspberry-pink shoes, and stood back and looked at myself in the mirror.

'Do I look OK, Dad?' I asked, running to show him.

157

'Oh, darling! You look as pretty as a picture!' he said.

'So do you, Dad. Well, as *handsome* as a picture,' I told him.

He was wearing his office suit because he didn't have any other, but he was wearing a new shirt – a *pink* new shirt, with a navy and pink tie.

'I didn't want to let the side down. I'm the father of the bridesmaid after all,' said Dad. He looked at his watch. 'Well, shall we set off? You can't really do anything wearing that beautiful dress. We don't want you getting it all creased. We're going to be very early, but Miss Bloomfield said she'd like a bit of moral support. Pop your jacket on, sweetheart.'

'*Dad!*'

'It's quite chilly outside. Though thank goodness it isn't raining.'

'There's absolutely no way you can wear a denim jacket over a bridesmaid's dress!'

'You can take it off when you get to the church.'

'No! You have to look right the moment you step outside the house. Do you think Miss

Bloomfield will be wearing her fleece over her bridal outfit? I think not!'

'Well, you're both going to get goose pimples,' said Dad, but he didn't argue further.

We drove over to her house. Dad had cleaned the car specially last night and fixed some white satin ribbon in a cross over the bonnet like a real wedding car. I was bothered about crushing my silky dress, so I sat very still in the back with the skirt spread all around me and then eased myself out of the car.

'There! You still look pretty as a picture,' said Dad. He had his hands over his eyes, pretending to be dazzled by my beauty.

We walked up the path to Miss Bloomfield's house. We knocked. We knocked again. We looked at each other. We knocked a third time.

'Perhaps she's a bit deaf,' said Dad.

'But she answered her door almost immediately before,' I said. I pushed open the stiff letterbox. I saw part of the hallway, but it was empty. 'Miss Bloomfield!' I called loudly. 'Miss Bloomfield, it's me, Tilly, and my dad.'

There was a muffled sound. I waited a few seconds – and then Miss Bloomfield came towards the door. She was wearing something large in faded blue. It looked like a dressing gown.

She opened the door, but only a chink. 'Hello, Tilly. Hello, Mr Andrews,' she said. Her voice was husky.

'Oh, Miss Bloomfield, aren't you very well?' I asked.

'That's right,' she said. 'I – I won't invite you in just in case you catch anything. I think I'd better go straight back to bed.'

'But you can't! It's your wedding day!' I said.

'I don't think there's going to be a wedding,' said Miss Bloomfield, and a tear trickled down her pale cheek. 'I'm so sorry.'

She tried to close the door, but Dad gently held on to it, stopping her.

'Let us come in and make you a cup of tea,' he said softly. 'You look as if you could do with one.'

He went inside, holding Miss Bloomfield's arm, helping her along to the kitchen. I followed them, my heart thumping. No wedding! So I couldn't show off my raspberry-pink bridesmaid's dress after all. Then I noticed the slump of Miss Bloomfield's small shoulders and I felt horribly guilty. It was far, far worse for poor Miss Bloomfield.

Dad sat her at her kitchen table. He put the kettle on and found the willow-pattern teapot and the matching cups and saucers. He looked at me and made a little waving motion, indicating that I should go over to Miss Bloomfield. I shuffled towards her shyly, not quite knowing what to do.

She gave a little snorty sniff and then murmured an embarrassed apology. My arm went out automatically and I patted her shaking shoulder. She felt very small and frail underneath the bulky blue quilting.

'There now,' said Dad, pouring boiling water into the teapot. He stirred the tea leaves around. When he poured the tea, it came out a very pale lemon colour.

'Oh dear. I don't think I gave it time to brew. Tilly and I make do with tea bags and mugs at home. It looks very weak.'

'So do I!' said Miss Bloomfield, trying to make a little joke. She fumbled in her dressing-gown pocket and then dabbed at her eyes with a crumpled lace hankie.

'So the wedding is definitely all off?' Dad asked gently.

'Maybe. No, definitely. I just don't know,' said Miss Bloomfield helplessly.

Dad looked at his watch. 'Well, we've got just under an hour for you to think about it,' he said.

'What's *happened*, Miss Bloomfield?' I asked, unable to bear not knowing any more. 'I thought you were so looking forward to marrying Mr Flower.'

'I was, I was,' said Miss Bloomfield, having to dab her eyes again.

'Did you have a terrible argument?' I asked.

Dad shook his head at me. 'Tilly, it's none of our business,' he said.

Miss Bloomfield was nodding. 'Just last night. I can't believe it. We've never had a cross word before. We've been such friends, Albert and me, always getting on fine and dandy. And we were getting on so well last night too. We had an early supper at his house, so I could then help him pack for our honeymoon. It was fish and chips, from the shop up the way. We generally have that when we eat at Albert's, though it's always a little greasy and tends to give me indigestion. So I said that I'd cook him a nice piece of steamed plaice with new potatoes in the future, and I'd make sure he had good home-cooking. He got a bit shirty and said he'd always thought of steamed fish as invalid food and there was nothing wrong with bought fish and chips – it was his favourite meal.'

'Oh, that's exactly the sort of argument Matty and I have. She's my best friend,' I said. 'But we always make up afterwards.'

'But this was just the start, you see. He said my cooking was all very well, very prettily done, but he actually preferred takeaways, especially Indian meals. Well, I took umbrage at that, because I can't bear curries. They play havoc with my tummy and make the house reek for days, and I said as much. Then I had a bit of a sulk myself because I pride myself on my cooking, but I tried to stay pleasant. I said I'd go into his bedroom to start on his packing and he said he'd do it himself. So we had the silliest argument about that.'

'Yep, *just* like Matty and me,' I said.

'It was a bit of a shock when I saw the state of his bedroom. So untidy! Newspapers and old socks and dirty coffee mugs every which way, and the bed not even made properly. And his so-called packing! He'd just flung his shirts in the bottom of his case where they'd get all creased and shoved his shoes on top, would you believe! So I tipped it all out and started folding the shirts properly, and he came in, and instead of being grateful said I was being childish. So I got a bit waspish then, and he said very unpleasantly that he was being hen-pecked before he was even married.'

'Oh dear,' said Dad.

'I was so upset I blurted out that maybe we should call the whole wedding off in that case, and I stormed out of the door. I thought he'd run after me. Or at least call round at my house ten minutes later. But he didn't. And I certainly wasn't going to go grovelling to him. I hardly slept all night, worrying. And then this morning I tried phoning but he didn't reply. So he obviously doesn't want to make up.' Miss Bloomfield burst into fresh tears. 'And now it seems so silly. I don't know how I could have spoiled all my chances over a plate of fish and chips! I'd eat nothing else for the rest of my days if only I could share my life with Albert.'

'I'm sure he's feeling just as wretched as you,' said Dad. 'Why don't you give him another ring? Or even get dressed and pop round?'

'I'm not going to go running after him!' Miss Bloomfield insisted, shaking her head so that her curls bobbed about. 'If he really wanted to marry me, he'd be round here knocking at my door, wouldn't he?'

And at that very moment there were three loud knocks on the door.

'Aha!' said Dad. 'Right on cue!'

'It won't be him. I'm sure it won't be him. It'll probably be the postman, or one of the neighbours, or – or—' Miss Bloomfield gabbled.

There were three more loud knocks.

'Why don't you go and see?' said Dad. 'Or he might give up and go away.'

Miss Bloomfield literally jumped up, for all she was an old lady. She ran into the hall, her old slippers falling off in the process. We followed her and Dad gripped my hand as she opened the door. I clutched him back.

Please let it be Mr Flower! I wished as hard as I could.

Chapter Eleven

It *was* Mr Flower, hardly visible behind an enormous bunch of purple irises and a giant pink balloon with the words *Forgive Me!* in silver lettering.

'Oh, Albert!' Miss Bloomfield gasped.

'Dearest Iris. Will you?' He bobbed the balloon. 'I am so, *so* sorry. I can't understand what got into me. I don't know how I could have been so silly. And, tell the truth, I'm heartily sick of take-away food and I can't wait to eat your delicious meals every day. Just call it pre-wedding nerves.'

'I was so silly too, storming out like a hysterical young girl. But I did so hope you'd come after me.'

'I thought I would only make it worse. I couldn't stand the thought of any further cross words. I was so upset with myself I hardly slept.'

'Me too, me too!'

'And so I thought I'd rush out to the shops first thing this morning to give you a surprise. I had to go to three florist shops to find the irises, but I'd set my heart on getting them.'

'So that's why you didn't answer your phone!'

'You phoned me?'

'To beg you to forgive me. And when you didn't answer, I thought the wedding was all off, so I didn't even bother to get dressed this morning. I didn't know how to get hold of little Tilly here, and I couldn't face telling all our friends that the wedding was off. I just went back to bed and pulled the covers over my head.'

'But . . . *is* the wedding off?' asked Mr Flower. 'Please say you'll still marry me, Iris.'

'If you'll still have me, Albert,' she said.

Dad looked at his watch. 'Then you'll have to get a move on! You're due at the church in ten minutes!'

Miss Bloomfield gave a little shriek. She looked down at her old dressing gown and then ran one hand through her tousled silver curls.

'Oh my Lord! What must I look like!' she said.

'You look truly beautiful,' said Mr Flower gallantly. 'I'm a very lucky man.'

'Why don't you stroll to the church, Mr Flower, while we let Miss Bloomfield get ready. You can explain if she's a little late. I'll drive her and Tilly to the church,' said Dad.

'You're a gentleman, sir,' said Mr Flower, and he gave Dad a funny little salute.

Then he scurried off, while Miss Bloomfield rushed to the bathroom. I tied the *Forgive Me!* balloon to a table leg and then went to find a jug big enough for the flowers.

'I'll fill it, Tilly. You don't want to risk splashing your pretty dress with water,' said Dad.

'Oh! My dress! They didn't even say they liked it!' I said, holding out the raspberry-pink skirts sadly.

'I think they only had eyes for each other,' said Dad. 'But I keep telling you that you look absolutely gorgeous. Good enough to eat. Ooh, yum yum, a wonderful girl-sized raspberry lolly. Let me eat you all up before you melt!' said Dad, smacking his lips.

I giggled. 'Oh, Dad, I do like it when you're funny!'

'Then I'll try to be funny more often,' he said. He looked at his watch again. 'How long do you think it will take Miss Bloomfield to get ready? Your mum used to take hours, remember?'

I nodded. 'And then sometimes when we *thought* she was ready she'd suddenly change her mind and re-do her hair and put different clothes on.'

'Well, let's hope Miss Bloomfield's not the same, or she really will miss her own wedding,' said Dad.

'No I won't!' she called. We heard her coming out of her bathroom and tearing into her bedroom. 'I'm not going to miss this wedding for all the tea in China.'

'Or all the coffee in Brazil,' said Dad.

'Or – or all the water in the tap,' I said.

'Two minutes and I'll be ready!' Miss Bloomfield shouted.

She was as good as her word. She was wearing her pink-and-white outfit with very pretty pink shoes with little heels, just like mine.

'We've got the same shoes, nearly!' I said delightedly.

'Mine pinch my poor old feet – but who

cares? Us girls have to suffer to be beautiful. And, Tilly dear, you really do look beautiful in that lovely frilly dress. My, my! I'm so lucky to have you as my bridesmaid.'

'You look beautiful too, Miss Bloomfield,' I said. She really did. Her eyes were bright, her cheeks were flushed pink, and she'd put a dab of lipstick on her smiley mouth. Her curls were fluffed out so that they looked like a silver halo round her head. She clutched her pink rosebud bouquet as if it were a pretty handbag containing her life savings.

'I'm so sorry to have kept you waiting, dears,' she said. 'Am I very late, Mr Andrews?'

'Better late than never,' said Dad, offering her his arm.

He escorted us both to the car. Old folk were leaning out of their windows, watching.

'Good luck, Iris! Have a happy day! My, you look a picture! He's a lucky man!' they called cheerily. Miss Bloomfield's cheeks went even pinker as she gave them a wave.

Then we drove to St John's Church and Dad helped us both out of the car. There was an elderly lady waiting in the porch in a navy lace dress that was a bit too short. She had matching dark-blue eye shadow and too much very red lipstick. She looked a bit like Princess Powerful when Matty had scribbled on her with felt pen.

'Oh my, there's Julie dolled up to the nines!' Miss Bloomfield murmured.

Julie was going through a little pantomime, tapping her wrist to indicate the time and waving her hand in the air to suggest Miss Bloomfield should hurry up.

'Wherever have you been, Iris?' she hissed as we got closer. 'It's ten past twelve! We've been hanging around for ages. How could you keep poor Albert waiting? He's still in great demand, you know. He might have chosen one of us instead!'

Miss Bloomfield gave her a sharp look which clearly meant *As if!*

'It's the bride's prerogative to be a little late for her wedding,' said Dad.

'And who are you?' asked Julie. 'And who's this lovely little bridesmaid?'

'They're family,' said Miss Bloomfield firmly. 'Could you hold my bouquet for me, Tilly?' Then she looked at Dad. 'I wonder, would you escort me down the aisle, dear?'

'I'd be delighted to,' he said.

They edged round Julie and I followed, giving my raspberry silk skirts a quick fluff. Organ music started up and we processed forward, little Miss Bloomfield hanging onto Dad's arm, me following two paces behind. I kept my head up, walking slowly, concentrating hard on not turning my ankles in Matty's pink heels. My hands were suddenly damp with nerves and I had to hang on tight to the rosebud bouquet.

The wedding guests were all in the first three rows, craning round to see Miss Bloomfield. They all smiled and nodded their heads appreciatively because she looked so pretty in her pink and white. Then they looked at me – and smiled even more! They muttered to each other.

'What a little darling!'

'Did you ever see such a poppet?'

'Such a beautiful dress – and she sets it off a treat!'

I felt my heart thumping hard with joy beneath my raspberry-pink silk bodice. They thought I looked lovely. *Me!*

Mr Flower stood at the front of the church, gazing at Miss Bloomfield as if she were an angel stepped down from the stained-glass windows. He took her hand and she looked up at him radiantly.

I sat down in the front pew beside Dad. He gave me a wink and a little thumbs-up. Julie came tiptoeing elaborately up the aisle and sat beside us. She bent forward to whisper to me, her violet perfume making my nose tickle.

'What a pretty frock, dear,' she said. 'I'm Mrs Robinson. My husband passed away three years ago. I'm Iris's dearest friend. I offered to be her matron of honour but she said she wanted to keep things very simple. She didn't breathe a word about a little bridesmaid. So, are you Iris's great-niece?'

Dad leaned forward, his finger to his lips, because the vicar had started his Dearly Beloved speech. Julie subsided huffily. I wriggled forward on my seat, listening to the words. I imagined

Mum standing beside Dad at the altar, with me as their bridesmaid. I could see Dad there, I could see me – but Mum was very hazy. I couldn't picture her in a smart pink-and-white outfit. I knew she'd never wear a proper long white bride's dress. Mum wore short dresses or tight jeans, the last things to wear at a wedding. And it wasn't just Mum's clothes. I couldn't get her face to assume the right expression. I'd never seen her looking up at Dad as if he were the most wonderful man in the whole world.

I watched as Miss Bloomfield and Mr Flower said their vows, promising to love each other until death did them part. Then Mr Flower put a thin gold band on Miss Bloomfield's tiny finger, and gave her a kiss, while everyone in the congregation sighed happily. Well, Julie sniffed.

Then Dad and I followed Miss Bloomfield – no, Mr and Mrs Flower! – into the vestry where they signed the register, and then we came out to a fresh burst of organ music. Mr and Mrs Flower walked back down the aisle together, her arm tucked in his, and I followed again, smiling back at everyone. There were more lovely comments, louder this time, and I was so delighted it was hard to carry on walking slowly and regally. I wanted to skip, to run, to dance, to twirl round and round until my raspberry-pink skirts whirled like a spinning top.

Then we were outside in the church garden. There wasn't an official photographer, but everyone whipped out their mobile phones and took photos of Mr and Mrs Flower. They asked me to be in the photos too, and Mrs Flower made Dad come and pose as well. 'Seeing as you're family!' she said, with a little wink.

Julie tried to get into a lot of the photos – 'because I'm the matron of honour', she kept saying, though she was nothing of the sort.

Then we crossed the road to the White Lion pub and went to their back room, where they'd laid out plates of sandwiches and sausage rolls and little pizza triangles.

'Oh Lord, I forgot the cake!' said Mrs Flower.

'Give me your keys and I'll go back for it,' said Dad.

Mr Flower protested, saying he'd nip back himself, but Dad insisted.

'He's a lovely man, your dad,' said Mrs Flower.

'Well, he takes after his "aunty",' said Mr Flower, and they both chuckled. 'Happy, Iris?' he added.

'Very,' she said.

'No regrets?'

'None at all.'

'Let's hope we've had our first and last little tiff,' said Mr Flower.

Mrs Flower nodded, and blew him a kiss.

'Oh my, look at the lovebirds,' said Julie. She cooed over my dress some more, stroking the silk and holding up the skirts to admire the petticoat. I twitched away from her, scared she was going to lift the skirts higher to see my matching knickers.

Mr Flower was busy buying everyone drinks. He put aside a pint of beer for Dad and bought me a fizzy lemonade.

'Here you are, dearie. You're the prettiest little bridesmaid I've ever seen. You've really made our day. Well done, sweetheart,' he said. 'Now, come and sit with Iris and me and let's tuck into all that food.'

'Grab us a couple of those serviettes, please, Albert. Tilly and I don't want to spoil our dresses,' said Mrs Flower.

I ate very carefully even so, leaning right over my plate and holding my lemonade glass with both hands. Dad sat with us too when he came back with the cake. It seemed too splendid to cut.

'You must save the little marzipan figures at least!' I said, so Mrs Flower wrapped them up in another paper napkin and tucked them into her handbag. I imagined the little marzipan Flowers smiling at each other secretly in the dark depths of her bag while the real Flowers smiled at the table. I saw they were eating one-handed, so they could still hold each other's hand under the cloth.

The cake looked even more delicious inside, a fluffy sponge with three layers of cream and jam. Mrs Flower cut it up carefully, arranged the slices on a big serving plate, and then asked me to take it round to everyone.

'We'll keep you a big slice with lots of icing and a marzipan flower,' she said, putting it on a little plate for me.

I carried the big plate of cake around, offering it to everyone.

'Aren't you a helpful little girl?'

'Such a little sweetheart.'

'Lovely manners – and so helpful!'

It was fantastic being treated as if I were

wonderful when all I was doing was passing round a plate of cake. I liked being with all these old people. And they all liked me. It was so easy to make friends.

Then the landlady of the pub brought out trays of sparkling wine. 'Let's have a toast to the bride and groom, ladies and gents!' she shouted.

Everyone raised their wine glasses and I held up my lemonade and we all repeated 'The bride and groom!' and drank to them.

'Speech, speech, speech!' Julie cried.

'No, no, Julie, we don't want any speeches whatsoever,' said Mrs Flower in a sudden fluster. 'You know I go all to pieces if I have to do any public speaking.'

'Then you mustn't make a speech, my dear, because I want you to stay deliciously all in one piece,' said Mr Flower gallantly. 'There's only going to be one speech, and I'm the one going to make it. Don't worry, folks. It's going to be very short and sweet.'

He stood up and cleared his throat. 'I'd like to tell you all something. This is the happiest day of my life!'

Everyone went *Aaaah!* Mrs Flower gave him a little nudge, blushing.

'I'm so lucky. I was happy enough pottering away like an old codger, but when Iris came into my life I could scarcely believe my luck. And I still can't! Doesn't she look a picture in her lovely bridal outfit! And I'll tell you who else looks a picture too – our little bridesmaid, Tilly. Stand up, Tilly dear, and give us all a little twirl.'

It was my turn to blush as I gave the briefest flick of a twirl.

'Your being here is like the icing on the cake for Iris and me. So we'd like to give you a little present.' Mr Flower fumbled in his pocket and brought out a small box. He held it out to me, smiling. 'Here's to Tilly, the prettiest, pinkest bridesmaid ever!'

Everyone toasted *me* this time, as I opened the box. There was a necklace inside, a little chain with a delicate silver charm in the shape of a flower.

'It's a flower, see, to remind you of us Flowers,' said Mr Flower.

Mrs Flower did up the clasp for me and I thanked them both fervently and held the little charm tight in my hand, stroking it for luck. I was struck dumb with happiness.

Dad was usually very quiet in company too, but

he chatted away to Mr and Mrs Flower, asking them all about their honeymoon plans, and talking about his own holidays in the Isle of Wight when he was a little boy.

'Is the Isle of Wight a really nice place?' I whispered.

'Yes, it's got lovely beaches, and I liked going round Osborne House where Queen Victoria lived,' said Dad. 'I remember there was a wonderful playhouse for the royal children in the gardens. You'd like that.'

'Could we go there one day? Maybe for a holiday?' I asked.

We hadn't had a proper holiday since Mum went. Well, we'd tried going to EuroDisney a few months after she left, just for three days. It didn't really work. It was too loud and bright and cheerful, and everyone was in families. Dad and I felt quieter and sadder and lonelier than ever.

We could still feel quiet and sad and lonely sometimes – but it would be peaceful paddling in the sea and making a sandcastle and seeing the special Osborne playhouse.

'Yes, we'll go there. In the summer holidays. Deal!' said Dad, and he held out his hand. I gave him a high five.

'Oh goodness, I wish people wouldn't do that silly high-five thing,' said Julie. 'It's so American. Why can't you shake hands properly? I always tried hard to teach my children manners.'

I was very, very glad I wasn't Julie's child.

'Don't you agree with me, Iris?' said Julie.

'It's a bit late in the day for me to start having children,' said Mrs Flower. 'But Albert and I are discussing getting a little dog when we get back from our honeymoon. And we'll do our best to train him to do little tricks, but we won't really care if he shakes his paw or does a high five, just so long as he's happy.'

Julie sniffed. Mrs Flower laughed and said something quietly to Mr Flower that set him chuckling. Julie sniffed again.

'I hope she's not making a fool of herself,' she said. 'They're all lovey-dovey now, but I'm not sure it's going to work out, you know. They're two such different temperaments. Albert's so relaxed and easy-going, but Iris can be very pernickety at times, very set in her ways. I can't see them always agreeing.'

'I think they'll get on perfectly. Never a cross word,' said Dad firmly.

Someone put some money in the old jukebox in

the corner and some ancient pop song started playing: 'Save the Last Waltz for Me'.

'Come on, Iris! Come on, Albert. You haven't given us a first waltz yet!' someone shouted.

Mr Flower stood up, gave his new wife a little bow and held out his hand. 'Would you do me the honour of a waltz, Mrs Flower?'

'I'd be delighted, Mr Flower,' she said.

I thought they'd just shuffle around for a few bars of music and then sit down again, but they seemed to be serious ballroom dancers. Mr Flower stood upright, his arms outstretched. Mrs Flower reached up to him, clasping him with one hand, the other resting very lightly on his arm. They stood poised and then plunged into the dance, swooping and twirling round the tables and chairs in the crowded room, their faces rapt.

Everyone clapped and cheered them, and their cheeks grew pinker and they smiled a little, but they didn't miss a beat. They were so impressive that someone set the record spinning again the moment it had finished.

Mr Flower motioned with his hand for everyone else to join them. Couples got up and did their best, enjoying themselves even though they weren't serious dancers like the Flowers. There were more single ladies than men. They were all looking hopefully at the two widowers drinking beer together in the corner. Julie was particularly blatant, tossing her hair and laughing loudly at nothing in particular. The old men put their pint glasses down reluctantly and turned to the ladies nearest them. The remaining women started dancing together instead, taking it in turns to steer each other round.

Julie looked scornful. She downed a very large gin and tonic and kept staring at Dad. He fidgeted uncomfortably, then bent his head close to mine.

'You don't think she's waiting for me to ask her to dance, do you?' he whispered.

I nodded.

'Oh help!' said Dad. He took a deep breath. 'Julie, I do hope you don't mind not dancing. I'm afraid I haven't a clue how to do this ballroom lark,' he said in a rush.

'Oh no, thanks very much,' said Julie. 'I'm very happy to sit this one out. Don't feel sorry on my account. It's a bit pathetic anyway, making out this old pub is blooming Blackpool Tower ballroom.'

'Well, everyone seems to be having fun even so,' said Dad. 'Especially Iris and Albert, and that's all that matters.'

'Oh, the little lovebirds,' said Julie. 'Well, I hope it lasts. Mr Albert Flower can be very fickle, you know. He was sweet on me for a while. Very keen, he was. But he's not really my type, so when I made it plain I wasn't interested, he was suddenly all over poor Iris like a rash. And she was so desperate after all these years of spinsterhood that she wouldn't listen when I warned her. She's always been naïve. Well, downright stupid at times.'

Dad and I flinched.

'Oh, come on,' said Dad nervously. 'Don't take that tone, not at their wedding. It's such a special day.'

'I see you're one of life's romantics,' said Julie scornfully. 'Was your wedding day so special then?'

There was a little pause. I took a large gulp of my fizzy lemonade.

'Oh, I see!' said Julie. 'So, are you divorced then?'

'Tilly's mum and I are . . . separated,' said Dad.

'Ooh, sorry! I've clearly touched a nerve there,'

said Julie. She leaned across Dad to me. 'So are you one of those suitcase children, living part of the time with Mummy and part of the time with Daddy here? Poor little thing!'

I looked at Dad. He was staring at his empty plate, looking so sad. I felt the lemonade fizzing inside me.

'I live all the time with my dad and it's lovely,' I said. 'Now I wish you'd shut up and stop being so nasty.'

'You rude little madam! You could do with a good smack-bottom,' said Julie. She rose to her feet and marched off to the ladies'.

Dad shook his head at me. 'You *were* rude, Tilly. Very rude,' he said sternly. Then he smiled. 'But I don't blame you one little bit. Nosy old bag!'

The waltz record finished and this time some-one put on an old Abba song.

'Even I can bop about to this,' said Dad. 'Come on, Tilly, let's dance.'

We danced in and out of the tables. I'm not that great at it, and Dad does really cringe Dad-dancing, but it didn't matter at all. Mr and Mrs Flower did an amazing jive together as if they were still teenagers, but nearly all the other guests just jiggled about, waving their hands in the air. Then we all swopped partners and I danced with lovely Mr Flower and one of the other old men and two different ladies, and Dad danced with all the others. I even saw him offer to dance with Julie again, just to try to make friends, but she shook her head haughtily.

Then Mr Flower consulted his pocket watch and said they'd better be off soon to catch their train to Portsmouth for the ferry to the Isle of Wight. There was a lot of kissing and hugging and more congratulations. Julie went surprisingly tearful and hugged both Flowers as if they were going to Australia instead of a little excursion to the Isle of Wight.

Dad drove the four of us to collect their suitcases and then to the railway station. We stood on the platform with them and then waved them off, wishing them well again and again.

'Promise you'll keep in touch, dears?' said Mr Flower.

'You must come to tea the minute we come back. And we must arrange a baking day, Tilly!' Mrs Flower called.

We really did seem to have become family now.

'Oh, I absolutely loved being a bridesmaid,' I said on the way home. 'I wish I could be one all over again!'

We were passing Sid's as I spoke. And I had a sudden thought.

'Dad, Dad, could you pull up? I need to pop into Sid's for a minute. There might just be another reply to my advert!'

'I very much doubt it, sweetheart. And I think renting yourself out once is more than enough,' said Dad.

But guess what!

Chapter Twelve

'Another request, Dad. Someone *else* wants to rent me!' I said triumphantly, waving the letter like a flag.

I read it quickly as Dad drove away. 'Oh, Dad, I absolutely *have* to do this wedding!'

Dad sighed heavily. 'No! I'm not letting you carry on like this, Tilly. I'm not having my daughter renting herself out!'

'But look what a lovely day we've had with Mr and Mrs Flower.'

'That was different. It was just a very small informal wedding for two dear old people,' said Dad.

'Dear old people who have become like family to us now.'

'Yes, they have. But it's highly unlikely that this lady will be like dear Iris,' said Dad. He gave a quick glance at the letter as he drove. 'What's her name? Something Smith?'

'It's a man, Dad. Simon Smith.'

'He's the one fixing up bridesmaids?' said Dad. 'Are you going to be a secret for his bride?'

'He hasn't got a bride. He's got another bridegroom,' I said.

'Oh Lord.'

'He's marrying Matthew Castle. It's not in St John's or any other church. He says they're not religious so they're going to a registry office for their wedding. Oh, Dad, please can I be their special bridesmaid?'

'Absolutely not,' said Dad.

He wavered a little when we got home and I made him read Simon's letter for himself.

Dear Tilly,

I love your advert! You're very good at drawing. Your dress looks truly beautiful. No wonder you're determined to wear it at a wedding.

My partner Matthew Castle and I are getting married

in a couple of weeks. We've been together nearly twenty years!
We're not religious so we're having a simple registry office
ceremony in the Guildhall, with fifty of our family and friends
attending. However, we've had a peep at the venue and it does
look a little too much like an office. We're going to bring
flowers and we'll be wearing our Sunday best, so to speak
— but we thought a special little bridesmaid would be the
finishing touch.

It would be perfect if you could come. You will
need to discuss it carefully with your parents, of course.
They might not be happy about the idea. But if they agree,
perhaps your mum or dad might like to ring me on my mobile
— 07779 54321 — and then we can meet one evening and
discuss arrangements.

With best wishes,
Simon Smith

'There, Dad! Doesn't he sound nice?' I said.

'Yes, I suppose so. Very nice. But I still don't like
the idea of your being a bridesmaid for strangers.'

'Yes, Simon says you might not be happy about
the idea,' I said, tapping the letter.

'Hmm, well, that's annoying too, because I don't
want him to think I'm prejudiced.'

'Couldn't we just phone him and meet up and see what he's like?' I wheedled. 'Please, Dad. Today's been the best fun I've had in ages and ages.'

'I know. And I've enjoyed it too. Well, let me think about it. Let's have a cup of tea and that extra slice of cake Iris gave us to take home. I'm peckish all over again.'

Dad made the tea in our special initial mugs. He had M for Michael and I had T for Tilly. There was an L for Laura, Mum's name, which we couldn't bear to throw out, but we kept it right at the back of the china cupboard. I divided the cake carefully and put the halves on two different plates. We sat down on the sofa together and I reached for my mug. Dad had filled it very full, almost to the top.

'Careful!' he said. 'Better go and take off your bridesmaid's dress first. You don't want tea stains all down it if you're going to be wearing it to another wedding.'

'So I can go to it!' I gasped.

'I said *if*, Tilly.'

I didn't push him further. I knew he was going

191

to give in. I changed into my pyjamas and hung my bridesmaid's dress up carefully, fluffing out the skirts. I examined it all over for stains or little rips and was very relieved to find it was still pristine.

I drank my tea and ate my cake and then lolled around on the sofa with Dad watching television. His mobile pinged with a message. Dad won't let me have my own mobile yet, which is incredibly mean and old-fashioned of him, but there's nothing I can do about it. I have to wait until I'm ten.

Matty has her own mobile, needless to say.

'Here. Message for you, Tilly,' said Dad, handing me his phone.

Was ur dress success with wrinklies???
Zoo was Ace. Monkeys RUDE.
Their red bums!!! LOL. Matty.

She'd added three smiley faces for good measure.

☺☺☺

I fidgeted, not sure how to reply. Maybe I didn't even want to. I hated it when Matty called dear Mr and Mrs Flower and all their friends wrinklies.

Well, Julie really *was* wrinkly – so much so that her thick powder got caked in her creases, but that wasn't really her fault. Mrs Flower had a dear little face with hardly any wrinkles at all.

I was even more upset that she'd said the zoo was ace, using capitals for emphasis. I pictured her having a brilliant time with that awful Marty, both of them shrieking idiotically at the monkeys.

I'd always loved the monkeys best when Dad and I used to go on our Sunday trips to the zoo. I laughed at them when they scampered about or made faces or snatched food from each other – but I felt like crying when the mother monkeys cuddled their babies, running their fingers tenderly through their fur. There was nothing remotely funny about their neat little bottoms tucked under their tails.

Matty clearly meant the baboons, which actually did have pretty startling behinds. Fancy not knowing the difference.

Ur stupid. U mean baboons, not monkeys,

I started texting.

Dad was looking over my shoulder. 'Hey, don't send that,' he said. 'It doesn't sound very friendly.'

'Well, I'm not sure I *want* to be friendly. I'm a bit sick of her. I'm not sure I even want her for my best friend any more,' I said. 'She can be so stupid at times.'

'Downright stupid,' said Dad. He said it in a squeaky old-lady voice. He sounded just like Julie.

That shut me up. I deleted my message and got my drawing book and crayons. I wondered about doing a zoo picture, but I'd already done that. I drew Mr and Mrs Flower on their honeymoon instead. I didn't know what the Isle of Wight looked like, but it seemed safe enough to draw them on a sandy beach. I gave Mrs Flower a pretty sundress with a floral print. Mr Flower wore a big bright shirt and shorts down to his knees. They were both in deckchairs eating ice creams.

The beach all around them looked a bit empty, so I drew Dad and me too, building a sandcastle together. I filled in the rest of the sand with palm trees, though I wondered if they were a little tropical for the Isle of Wight. I wanted the trees there so I could draw lots of different monkey families on their holidays. I drew a row of tiny deckchairs along the branches so the mum and dad monkeys could bask in the sunshine, while the baby monkeys slid down a slide into a paddling pool on the sand, and then scampered all the way to the top again to repeat the experience.

They looked so funny that I couldn't help chuckling, even though I'd invented the joke myself. Dad peered over my shoulder and he laughed out loud, telling me I was a brilliant artist. He'd said that several times to me in the past, but then he'd always added, 'You obviously take after Mum,' which always upset us both. But this time he didn't say it, just went on remarking on the monkey antics and shaking his head at my invention.

I think he was exaggerating simply to make me feel good – but it certainly worked. I returned Matty's text just before I went to bed.

Dress mega success. Luv monkeys too.
Tilly x

Dad brought me breakfast in bed on Sunday morning (a bowl of apricot yoghurt with a real apricot cut up on top, and then toast and honey) and then we lazed around in our pyjamas in the living room. Dad browsed the Sunday papers on his iPad and I did another drawing. It had a monkey theme again, because I wanted Dad to like it.

I drew a monkey wedding, with a little monkey bride in a white dress, a matching white ribbon tied on the end of her tail, and a miniature bunch of bananas for a bouquet. The groom balanced a top hat on his head, and wore a tail coat and striped trousers, but I left his funny monkey feet bare. They had a bridesmaid, of course – in fact they had a whole troupe of bridesmaids processing two by two. The older taller ones were walking upright, holding out their silk skirts carefully, but the little ones at the back were gambolling about on all fours, their dresses tucked into their frilly knickers.

I called Dad to have a look, and he laughed and told me I was brilliant again. I coloured it all in, while Dad listened to that funny old *Archers* programme on the radio. Two of the Archer men were deep in discussion about a new type of combine harvester. I decided to start a *third* monkey picture, with a countryside setting this time, though I wasn't at all sure how to draw a combine harvester or even a tractor, but Dad said I'd better go and have a bath and get dressed instead.

'Can't I stay in my PJs all day?'

'Well, you can, but you'll look a little odd going out to lunch in them,' said Dad.

'We're going out to lunch? Yay! Can we go to Wagamama?'

'No, we're going to have a Sunday roast today – well, I think we are.'

'In a pub? Can I have a fizzy lemonade again?'

'We've been invited to lunch at someone's home.'

'Really?' I was puzzled. We never went out to lunch with anyone. 'Did Matty's mum ask us?'

'No, though she's always said we'd be very welcome.'

'So who *is* it? Dad, stop messing about and *tell* me!'

'We're going to lunch with your friend Simon,' said Dad.

I stared at him, wrinkling my nose. My friend Simon? The only Simon I could think of was a horrible boy in my class who always picked his nose and made me feel sick.

'Not Simon in Miss Hope's class?' I asked incredulously.

'No, *your* Simon. The potential bridegroom,' said Dad.

'But we don't know him. We haven't phoned him yet, though I do hope you do soon.'

'I phoned last night, after you were asleep.'

'Oh, Dad, I wanted to listen too!'

'Yes, well, *I* wanted to check everything out first.'

'And did he sound nice?'

Dad smiled. 'He sounds incredibly nice. We had a really long chat. And then Simon invited us for lunch. So chop chop, Tilly. You can have first bath.'

I skipped upstairs and rushed to get ready.

'Should I wear my bridesmaid's dress, Dad, so they can see what it looks like?' I asked.

'No, you need to keep it spotless. But we'll take it with us in the car so they can have a look at it,' Dad called from the bathroom.

'Yes, but they'll be taking a look at me too, and I don't look anywhere near as pretty when I'm not in the dress,' I said.

'You'd look pretty in a plastic bag,' said Dad.

'But you would say that, wouldn't you. You're my dad.'

'Well, dads are allowed to be prejudiced,' said Dad. 'But you look lovely, honestly.'

I wasn't at all convinced. I looked very pale and ordinary when I wasn't in raspberry silk. My hair wouldn't fluff out properly and my T-shirt and jeans looked too ordinary. I put my best dress on instead, navy with bluebirds flying all over it. I hoped it looked OK with my denim jacket. My socks were clean but they weren't bright white any more. I worried that Simon and Matthew might think me a bit scruffy. I hoped they'd be so distracted by my sparkly trainers that they wouldn't notice my socks.

Dad made an effort with his clothes too. He wore his jeans, but they were his best pair, and he put on a proper white shirt.

'Should I wear a tie or not?' he asked. 'A tie looks smarter, but I don't want to look as if I'm trying too hard.'

I gave Dad a sideways look. He never usually fussed about clothes.

'Guys like Simon and Matthew are generally very well turned out,' he said sheepishly.

Dad was generally right about things, but he was wrong about Simon and Matthew. They definitely weren't very fashionable. Simon was quite plump, with very short hair because he was going quite bald at the front. He wore an old sweatshirt with a star and baggy jeans and old canvas shoes.

'Hi – you must be Michael – and this is Tilly! Hey, Tilly! You look just the way I imagined. And is this the famous dress?' Simon said, peering at the cellophane bag. 'It's a fantastic colour. And you'll look fantastic in it.'

I liked him straight away. So did Dad. Simon led us into his sitting room. It had Sunday papers all over the big sofa and lots of books everywhere and, best of all, a big white Staffie with a sparkly pink collar lying on her own little sofa. She raised her head and barked at us, but in a very friendly manner.

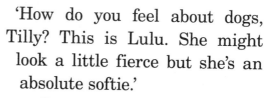

'How do you feel about dogs, Tilly? This is Lulu. She might look a little fierce but she's an absolute softie.'

'I think she's lovely,' I said enthusiastically. 'Would she mind if I patted her?'

'She'd like it very much,' said Simon.

'Careful though, Tilly,' said Dad anxiously, clearly fussed about Lulu's large jaw stuffed with big teeth.

'I promise she loves children,' said Simon. 'I often take her to school.'

I stared at him. I had a comical vision of him in a sweatshirt with a badge and little shorts and rolled-down socks.

'I'm a teacher,' he said. 'Well, I'm actually head of Larch Road Infants, but I still like to do as much teaching as I can.'

'I loved it in the Infants,' I said, stroking Lulu carefully. She seemed to enjoy it, because she gave a little sigh and lolled against me.

I remembered finger painting and the water trough and the playhouse where we played Mums and Dads. And I had a mum as well as a dad then, and she came to collect me every afternoon and I skipped home hanging on to her hand tightly, as if even then I was scared she'd run away from me.

There was a lovely smell of cooking wafting through the house and the sound of whistling.

'Is your partner a teacher too?' Dad asked.

'No, he sells second-hand and antiquarian

books, mostly on the internet now, but he still has a little shop in Market Lane,' said Simon.

'Castle Books!' Dad and I cried in unison.

It was our absolute favourite shop! We'd stumbled across it by chance when Dad went to the market to buy fruit and vegetables. We'd wandered off down the alleyway hauling carrier bags of oranges and apples and potatoes, past poky little shops selling second-hand clothes, dish-mops and dusters, and old vinyl records, and right at the end was Castle Books. It was as small and shabby as the other shops, but the wall above the shop window was painted with castle turrets and pretend crumbling brickwork so that the shop looked like a real castle.

When we went inside, we saw the books had long since erupted from the shelves and had spread like lava over most of the floor. We had to step very carefully, but the larger piles of old art books made very useful seats if we wanted to browse. There was a special children's section filled with old Ladybird books and tattered Enid Blytons and half a shelf of Noel Streatfeild paperbacks that I was steadily buying with my pocket money.

We'd got to know the bookshop owner, a smiley,

scruffy man with curly hair and a curly beard, and generally a curly smile on his face. And now that exact same man came into the living room, a stripy apron over his T-shirt and jeans.

'Hello, I'm Matthew Castle,' he said politely – and then he did a double-take. *'Hello!* You're *you*! Si, these are my special customers! What a coincidence.' He grinned at me. 'So *you're* our little rent-a-bridesmaid!' he said.

'Yes, please,' I said.

I rolled back the cellophane and showed them my bridesmaid's dress. 'Do you like it? I've got a matching petticoat and pink shoes. They actually rub my feet a bit but I could try wearing socks – I need some new ones anyway. And I could put a pink ribbon in my hair if you like. It might make me look a bit prettier,' I gabbled.

'You'll look adorable!' said Matthew.

'You'll be our finishing touch – beautiful proof that this is a special wedding, not a visit to an insurance office,' said Simon.

'If you wanted a bridesmaid, why didn't you

ask one of the children at your school?' Dad asked.

'I didn't even think of it until I saw Tilly's enchanting advert in the newsagent's shop. But then how could I possibly choose between all my assorted Infants? If I singled out some similarly pretty little child, I'd be accused of gross favouritism and the other mothers would hate me. Ah, what about Tilly's mother? I take it she's in favour of Tilly being our bridesmaid?' Simon asked. He saw Dad and me exchange glances. 'Sorry. I think I've put my foot in it,' he said quickly.

'Are you a single parent, Mr Andrews?' Matthew asked.

'Call me Michael, please. Well, yes, I suppose I am now. I'm bringing up Tilly. I know it's a bit unusual, but—'

'Not unusual at all. I've got two single dads at my school, and they're both doing a splendid job, like you, Michael,' said Simon.

'I don't know about splendid,' said Dad. 'In fact I've been a bit rubbish at it one way and another.'

'Tilly, do you like cooking?' said Matthew.

I nodded. 'I can cook heaps of things,' I boasted.

'Well, that's great, because I could do with a bit of help in the kitchen. Come on, lovely.'

So we left Dad and Simon having a bit of a heart

to heart while we went to cook. I peered at all the pots on top of the stove and got a bit worried.

'I don't think I can do that sort of cooking,' I admitted. 'I know how to boil eggs and I can do baked beans on toast, but I've never done a proper meal.'

'That's my job. You're going to be the pudding girl,' said Matthew. He took a large blue glass bowl out of the fridge. 'Trifle! I've done the boring bit – the sponge and the jelly and the custard. I want help with the topping. Do you think you could whip up some cream for me and then do the decorating?'

I *loved* decorating the trifle. Matthew showed me how to whip the cream with a funny whisk, smoothing it all over the top of the custard, and then I set about making it pretty. Matthew gave me glacé cherries, almonds, little green sticks of angelica, small pink icing roses, tiny silver balls and rainbow hundreds and thousands.

'Which should I use?' I asked.

'Whatever you like. All of them!' said Matthew.

I edged the trifle with a circle of alternate cherries and almonds, and then I started filling in the rest. Matthew showed me how to put more cream in a little bag and then squeeze it out of the nozzle so that it made a little creamy whirl. I topped each with a pink rose, snipping tiny pieces of angelica to look like stalks. I circled the middle rosy whirl with little silver balls and then sprinkled the hundreds and thousands all around.

'Oh my, it's a work of art!' said Matthew. 'Pop it back in the fridge while I get the chicken out of the oven. Can you get the table properly laid, sweetheart? Cutlery in the top drawer, napkins in the drawer underneath – and let's arrange those pretty flowers and put them on the table too.'

We'd bought them a slim bunch of carnations, very ordinary ones from a garage because we couldn't find a proper flower shop open. I looked for a vase, but Matthew brought out a set of eight little blue glasses.

'Fill each one half full of water and then pop one carnation in each,' he suggested.

It made the flowers look very special when I arranged them in a row along the wooden table.

'There are two flowers left over,' I said.

'Well, we won't waste them,' said Matthew. He

stuck a carnation each side of my hair, like slides. 'Very pretty. I think you'd better reproduce the look on our wedding day.'

When we called Dad and Simon into the kitchen for lunch, Dad looked strange, and his eyes were a bit red, almost as if he'd been crying. I looked at him anxiously, hoping he'd be able to enjoy his lunch. It was a wonderful lunch too: the chicken with special bread sauce, crisp roast potatoes, cauliflower, runner beans and peas. Matthew carved and dished out the meat, and then pulled the wishbone with me. I ended up with the bigger end, so I got the wish.

I closed my eyes tight, wondering what to wish for. I could wish that everyone would admire my trifle. That Dad would stay happy. That Matty would be my best friend for ever. That I would look lovely for Simon and Matthew's wedding. That the Flowers were blooming on their honeymoon. So many different wishes! But in the end I wished the same old wish, though I knew it would be wasted.

I wish Mum would come back!

Some of the other wishes came true anyway. Dad cheered up, especially after he'd had a glass of wine with his lunch. All three men clapped when I fetched the trifle from the fridge, and told me it was absolutely delicious when they ate it, as if I'd made it all by myself.

When Dad and I were back home, he seemed to go a bit quiet and sad again.

'Are you all right, Dad?' I asked, hovering beside him. 'You do like Matthew and Simon, don't you? You don't mind if I'm their bridesmaid?'

'I'm thrilled you're going to be their bridesmaid. They're lovely guys. I had a really good talk with Simon and he was so understanding.'

'Did you talk about . . . Mum?'

'I was mostly talking about you, Tilly. I've been so worried because I know how sad you've been, and I've been a bit of a wet week as a dad.'

'No, you've been a lovely dad,' I said.

'I wish,' said Dad. 'But anyway, Simon said you're happy and well-adjusted and seemed to think I'd done a reasonable job with you – and he's a head teacher, so he really does know about children.'

'And I know all about dads, and you're the best,' I said, and gave him a big hug.

Chapter Thirteen

I had heaps and heaps to tell Matty at school the next day. I told her about the Flower wedding before school. I told her more at playtime. I told her during lunch and when we were playing ball in the playground afterwards. She listened carefully and made all the right noises and even said she was sure I had looked lovely in the bridesmaid's dress, but somehow she didn't really seem *interested*. She even yawned when I was telling her all about the Flowers.

'Matty! Don't act like you're bored!' I protested, bouncing the ball at her.

'Well, you have gone on and on about it, Tilly.

Still, I'm truly glad you had a chance to be a bridesmaid and wear that stupid dress,' said Matty, bouncing the ball even harder.

'It's a *beautiful* dress. The most beautiful bridesmaid's dress ever. And I'm going to be wearing it again, not this Saturday but next,' I said happily, throwing the ball high in the air.

'Really? You got another reply?'

'Yes, and Dad and I went to Sunday lunch with them, and they're soooo nice, and they're thrilled that I'm going to be their bridesmaid,' I said triumphantly, giving her an easy catch.

'Is this another old couple then?' Matty asked, bouncing the ball herself and then kicking it again and again, doing Keepie Uppie.

'No! Well. Sort of middle-aged. Simon's a teacher, though obviously not at our school, and Matthew has that lovely bookshop by the market,' I said.

'Two men?' said Matty. 'Rats, you made me miss the ball! Why do they want a bridesmaid?'

'Well, because they want their wedding to look weddingy.'

'Yes, but the whole point of being a bridesmaid is that you're a maid of the bride, and you're supposed to sort out her dress and veil and all that stuff. You can't do that if there are two grooms,' said Matty, bouncing the ball hard at me.

'Don't be mean,' I said. The ball stung my hand slightly. Perhaps that's why I had to blink my eyes hard.

'I'm *not* being mean. I'm just pointing out a fact, that's all. I'd have thought you'd have wanted to be a bridesmaid at a proper fancy do like my Aunt Rachel's, seeing as you're so fixated on weddings. Though goodness knows why. The food was OK at Aunt Rachel's, but apart from that I was bored out of my skull and I felt a right twit in all those frills. Why can't they have bridesmaid's *trousers*? If I ever get married, I'll definitely wear trousers instead of a bride's dress.'

'Well, you'll look stupid then,' I snapped.

'No I won't. I'll have white trousers, with a white jacket, and white boots,' said Matty. 'I'll look seriously cool.'

'You'll look seriously dirty, because you won't be able to keep anything clean even for five minutes,' I said. I threw the ball at her. Hard.

She threw it back even harder. I ducked, but it caught me on the forehead.

'Ouch!' I bent over, clutching my forehead.

'Tilly? Oh, Tilly, are you OK?' Matty asked.

'No!'

If I'm absolutely truthful, it didn't hurt *that* much, but it meant I could have a little cry. Matty saw the tears and started panicking.

'Oh no, I hit that bit above your eye. I think that's your *temple*, and my dad knew someone once playing cricket and they got hit on their temple and they died! They dropped down dead there and then!' she wailed.

It was obvious to both of us that I *hadn't* been instantly struck dead but I started panicking too. Matty clutched my hand and we ran up to the teacher on playground duty – our own Miss Hope.

'Miss Hope, Miss Hope, I think Tilly's dying and it's all my fault!' Matty shouted. 'I hit her on the temple!'

'She didn't mean to, she truly didn't,' I said, because she was still my best friend even though we were quarrelling, and I didn't want her to be arrested for attempted murder.

'Hey, hey, calm down, girls,' said Miss Hope. She smoothed back my hair and looked at my forehead carefully. 'I think you'll live, Tilly. You might get a little bruise, but that's all. It's just a minor bump.'

I couldn't help feeling disappointed. I rather wanted my head to swell alarmingly and my whole forehead to turn black and blue. Still, I was relieved for Matty's sake.

She flung her arms round me and gave me a hug. 'I'm so sorry, Tilly!' she said.

I hugged her back. 'I'm sorry as well. I think I might have been trying to hit you with the ball too, but my aim isn't as good as yours,' I admitted, feeling ashamed.

'You two!' said Miss Hope. 'You're best friends and yet you keep quarrelling as if you were worst enemies. What was it all about this time?'

'Being a bridesmaid,' I said.

'I see,' said Miss Hope, though it was clear she didn't.

I started explaining, and it took so long that Miss Hope sat down on the step by the canteen and we sat on either side of her. She seemed very worried about my rent-a-bridesmaid advertisement, but was reassured when I told her all about the lovely Flower wedding and how special it had been.

'Yes, I think it sounds a very special wedding,' said Miss Hope. 'And romantic too. It just shows that you, you can fall in love at any age.'

'I don't think I'm going to fall in love,' said Matty. 'I think weddings are rubbish. Especially all the fancy clothes. I'm wearing trousers if I ever get married. You are allowed to wear trousers at your own wedding, aren't you, Miss Hope?'

'You can wear anything you want,' she said.

'What would you wear at your wedding, if you were ever thinking of getting married?' Matty asked.

'Matty!' I hissed, because it wasn't the sort of thing you should ask your teacher.

Miss Hope was used to Matty, and just laughed again. 'I'm *not* actually thinking of getting married, but if I were, then I know I wouldn't want to wear a white meringue dress. I'd look silly in it anyway, and I'd have to go on a serious diet. Talking of which . . .' She felt in her pocket and brought out a bar of dairy milk chocolate with caramel. 'This is my secret treat when I'm on playground duty. It's my chocolate comfort diet. Want to share with me?'

She broke it into thirds and we all munched happily.

'You still haven't said, Miss Hope,' Matty persisted. 'Might you want to wear trousers too?'

'Not trousers. I haven't got the figure for them either. Oh, I don't know what I'd choose. I'm going to a wedding soon and I still haven't decided what to wear just as a guest. I'm hopeless at buying clothes. I suppose I'd like something elegant and slim-looking, but not so tight that it showed all my lumps and bumps.' She sketched a shape in the air.

'I think that would look lovely, Miss Hope,' I said politely. 'And would you have a bridesmaid?'

'Well, I don't have any little nieces, so in the extremely unlikely event that I get married in the near future, I'll bear you in mind, Tilly. And you too, Matty, if you ever get your bridesmaid's trousers,' said Miss Hope. 'Now, what did *you* do this weekend, while Tilly was having such an exciting time in her bridesmaid's dress?'

'I went to the zoo and it was absolutely ace. Especially the monkeys! They were so gross! And then Marty and I had such fun imitating them, and this old granny lady said we were very rude little girls.' Matty started giggling, and then clapped her hand over her mouth, looking guilty.

'Yes, you should certainly be ashamed of your-self,' said Miss Hope, trying to look stern.

But I knew why Matty had suddenly stopped talking. *Marty-and-I-had-such-fun.* Each word was like a little punch to my stomach. But I hated to see Matty looking so upset now. I really didn't want to be a Julie-type friend.

I made a big effort. 'Did you and Marty like the lemurs?'

'Oh, we absolutely loved the lemurs!' Matty said. She chatted about them till the bell went for afternoon school. She talked even more about them when we were going back to her place. And she talked about the lions and the tigers. And the elephants. And the penguins. And the petting zoo with the rabbits and the guinea pigs. And she went on and on about the goats, because they tried to eat Marty's cardigan.

I wouldn't have minded if they'd eaten Marty herself as well as her wretched cardigan, but I smiled valiantly. Matty looked incredibly relieved. It was Lewis who eventually said, 'Just shut up about your trip to the boring old zoo and let's play Warrior Princesses.'

So we did. I decided that one of Princess Power's dinosaurs had a silly, self-satisfied face – very much how I imagined Marty. I played with total determination, encouraging my troupe of ponies to gallop in a herd. They all reared up when Princess Pony whistled and knocked DinoMarty flying. Then they galloped over her for good measure. It was very enjoyable and Matty didn't suspect a thing.

Matty ran ahead for supper while Lewis and I were still washing our hands.

'Honestly, Matty does go on and on sometimes,' said Lewis.

'Yes, she does,' I said.

'About that zoo.'

'Yep.'

'And Marty.'

'Mmm,' I said, swishing soap round and round in my hands.

'She's OK, I suppose,' said Lewis. 'She's funny.'

I said nothing at all. My hands were becoming incredibly clean.

'But she's not as much fun as you, Tilly,' Lewis persisted.

'Oh,' I said. 'Well. Thank you. But I'm not sure Matty thinks that.'

'Oh, she does. She said so,' said Lewis.

'Really?' I said breathlessly.

'Yes, I asked her on Saturday night after we

went to bed, when she was going on and on about all the funny things Marty had done at the zoo. I said, "Matty, is Marty your new best friend now?" And do you know what she said?'

'What?' I said, struggling to sound casual. I scooped up some soap suds and blew at them, as if I didn't have a care in the world.

'She said, "Don't be daft, Lewis. Marty's a very good friend and I like her a lot, but you know perfectly well that Tilly is my best ever friend and she always will be."'

'She really truly said that?' I asked, abandoning all attempt to pretend I didn't care.

'Yes, she did. And I don't blame her. You're *much* more fun than that Marty.'

I gave Lewis a big soapy hug. I decided I liked him very, very nearly as much as Matty herself.

Matty and I got on wonderfully all week – at school and at her home. Then, on Friday after school, Angie came into the bedroom and started searching in all the cupboards and drawers.

'What are you looking for, Mum?' Matty asked.

'Those armband things you used to have – you

know, the inflatable ones you wear to help you swim. I thought Lewis might like them tomorrow,' she said.

So there was going to be another outing on Saturday, and this time Lewis was invited too. I squashed one of my ponies between my knees and started combing his mane very fiercely with a little plastic brush.

'I don't need them, Mum. I'm sure I can swim heaps better now. I won't need armbands – I'll just whizz up and down the pool,' said Lewis.

'Yeah, as if,' said Matty. 'You can barely swim two strokes and then you have to put your foot on the bottom of the pool. You can't swim at all.'

'Don't be mean, Matty,' said Angie, scrabbling through odd shoes and strapless school bags and headless dolls at the bottom of the wardrobe. 'Honestly, you two! Why do you have to get everything in such a mess and muddle?' She didn't sound particularly cross, though, and when she backed out of the wardrobe, she stepped carefully over our three princesses and their assorted armies.

'I can so swim,' Lewis muttered. 'I just put my foot on the bottom of the pool to check it's there.'

'Can you swim, Tilly?' Matty asked. 'I can swim a whole length without stopping – *and* back again.'

I didn't say anything. I just bent my head and held the pony tight. Matty misunderstood. She shuffled towards me on her knees and put her arm round me.

'It doesn't really matter if you can't swim, Tilly. It's easy-peasy really. And *you* can wear the arm-bands, seeing as Lewis says he can swim OK.'

'Perhaps we can wear one each,' said Lewis. 'You can come tomorrow, can't you, Tilly?'

'You're going swimming with Marty?' I said.

'I'm not sure. I think Dad and I are going shopping.' I didn't want to go swimming with Marty. I didn't want to do *anything* with Marty.

'We're not going with Marty,' said Matty. 'This is just us – well, Mum and Dad and Lewis and me. We're going swimming in the Lido now it's warm enough. We're going to have a picnic too. Do come! Couldn't you go shopping with your dad on Sunday instead?'

'Maybe I could,' I said, my heart thumping. 'If – if that's OK?'

'Of course it's OK,' said Angie. 'And why not invite your dad too? Does he like swimming?'

I tried to think. We'd never been to a swimming baths together, though I'd gone to the pool once a week at my old school. When we were on holiday,

Mum and I sometimes went swimming, but Dad generally minded our stuff on the beach. Perhaps he couldn't swim?

'I'm not sure,' I said. 'I don't think he does.'

'Well, ask him anyway. Never mind if he doesn't want to come. We're probably setting off about half past two, when our lunch has gone down,' said Angie. 'Ah! Look what I've found!'

The armbands were tucked up tightly in an old pair of Spider-Man pyjamas. They both had hankies tied round them. Angie held them up, looking quizzical.

'Oh yes, I remember. I was pretending they were my twin babies ages ago. The hankies are their nappies,' said Lewis.

'Those nappies must be pretty wet by now,' said Matty, laughing. 'Oh, Lewis, you are soooo crazy. Isn't he, Tilly?'

'No, I think he's fun,' I said. 'I wish I had a brother like Lewis.'

I wished I were part of a family of four. I loved Dad very much, but it was sometimes lonely being just a family of two.

When Dad came to collect me, Angie asked if he'd like to go swimming at the Lido.

'I'm not really a swimming kind of person, but

thanks very much for asking,' Dad said predictably. 'Still, I'm sure Tilly would love to go.'

I was quiet in the car going home. When Dad was preparing his supper (a Scotch egg and a tomato and oven chips – he didn't generally bother to do real cooking), he asked me if I was all right.

'You do want to go swimming with Matty, don't you?'

'Yes.'

'But?'

'But I wish you'd come too, Dad.'

'Oh, Tilly. I'm rubbish at swimming. Not like your mum. She swam like a little fish. Remember our seaside holidays?'

'Yes.'

'Darling, I'm so sorry Mum's not around to go swimming with you,' said Dad, putting his arm round me.

'*You're* around. I want you to come,' I persisted.

'But you love being with Matty and her family. You don't need me to come too, you funny old thing.' He bent down and rubbed his cheek on the top of my head.

'I *do* need you. I want us to be a family too,' I said. 'I don't mind if you can't swim. I tell you what,

you could borrow Matty's arm-
bands instead of Lewis.'

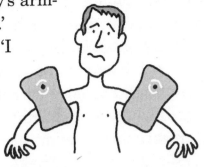

Dad laughed then. 'I
don't think so! I can
swim a bit. Just not
very well. I never
learned properly as a
child. Look, I'll come
along too, and watch you having fun in the pool.
I'll even put on a pair of swimming trunks if that
will make you happy. I just won't go swimming
myself, OK?'

'OK,' I said. 'You promise?'

'Yes, I promise,' said Dad.

We settled down on the sofa to watch television
together, and when Dad's oven chips were ready,
he shared them with me.

In the morning he phoned Matty's mum and
said he'd changed his mind and would like to come
too. Then he shut himself in his bedroom
to try on his swimming trunks.

'They're a bit big for me now,' he called. 'Just as
well I'm not intending to swim. Imagine the
embarrassment if they fell off as I dived in! You'd
better check your costume too, Tilly. Heavens,
you've had it for a couple of years. It's probably way

too small for you now. We'll have to nip out to the shops and buy you another.'

But my swimming costume still fitted me perfectly. I hadn't grown very much at all since Mum went. I remembered the last time I'd worn it. It still smelled very faintly of suntan lotion. Dad always rubbed it on my back and shoulders for me. Mum never bothered with suntan lotion and went golden brown every summer. I remembered her running into the sea in her red bikini, her hair blowing in the wind. I chased after her, calling, 'Mum! Mum! Wait for me!' I thought she'd forget all about me and swim out towards the horizon, and then there would be no one to catch me and pick me up if a wave knocked me over. She'd waded out through the shallows, and then I saw her dive right under the water. I couldn't see her for ages and I started to panic, dashing into the sea after her – and then, all of a sudden, she burst out of the waves right in front of me, laughing and hugging me tight.

I loved that moment. I replayed it in my head time after time. I even dreamed it – but it got all mixed up and horrible in my dreams. Mum simply swam away from me, far out to sea, and I shouted myself hoarse, but she went further and further until I couldn't see her head bobbing along any more – there was just wave after wave of empty water.

I felt panicky now just remembering, but I stared at myself in my bedroom mirror and looked straight into my eyes.

'*Stop it, stop it, stop it,*' I hissed. 'Stop thinking about Mum. Don't let her spoil everything. You're going swimming with Matty and her family, and Dad's coming too, and *next* Saturday you're going to be a bridesmaid all over again, so you've got to feel happy.'

I unhooked my bridesmaid's dress from where it was hanging and held it up under my chin. I looked at my raspberry-pink reflection and managed to calm myself down.

'Tilly? What's the verdict on your swimming costume?' Dad called.

'It's fine, Dad,' I called back. 'Absolutely fine.'

And I was absolutely fine after that too. Dad and I did do a little shopping, but just at the Saturday farmer's market down the road. We wanted to contribute to the Lido picnic. We chose a big bottle of apple juice and a beautiful home-made coffee-and-walnut cake.

'I'll be able to make us cakes soon, Dad, when Mrs Flower has given me baking lessons,' I said.

She'd sent us a postcard from the Isle of Wight telling us that she was having a grand time with Mr Flower and they both hoped we'd go round to tea as soon as they got back.

I wanted to carry the cake to the Lido, but it slid about in its box and it made my arms ache trying to hold it steady. Dad carried it instead, with the apple juice in his backpack, along with our swimming costumes and towels. We were meeting Matty and her family inside the Lido, but I hadn't realized how crowded it would be. Dad and I peered at the wooden decking around the pool and the grass further back and the turquoise water itself, but we couldn't see them anywhere.

'Oh well, we'd better go and change into our swimming costumes now we're here,' said Dad.

The men's and ladies' changing rooms were entirely separate, of course.

'Will you be all right by yourself, Tilly?' Dad asked anxiously.

'Of course, Dad. I'm not a baby,' I said, sauntering into the ladies' – but I was actually a bit worried, not sure where to take my clothes off and how to work the little keys in the locker. All the other girls my age were with their mums. But it was simple enough to watch what other people did, and when

I'd locked my clothes away, I pinned my key to my costume so that I wouldn't lose it.

When I came out of the changing room, I couldn't see Dad for a moment, and that did make me catch my breath. I stood clenching my fists, staring at all the hundreds of strangers all around me. I walked over to the men's changing room, but Dad wasn't there either.

'Are you all right, lovey?' said a man coming out, his little boy riding on his shoulders.

'I think I've lost my dad,' I said in a very tiny voice.

'Isn't that your family over there? Look, they're all waving at you,' said the man.

I turned round. There was Dad, looking thin

and white in his swimming trunks, his towel slung round his shoulders, standing with Matty and Lewis and Angie and Matty's dad, Tom – and, yes, they were all waving at me.

'Hi, Tilly!' Matty called, running over to me. 'Wait till we get changed! Don't go swimming without us!'

Dad and I found an empty spot on the decking and spread our towels out, saving the rest of the space for Matty's family. When they joined us, we all sat and chatted for a little bit, but then Matty got fidgety.

'Come *on*. We're at a swimming pool. We've got to *swim*!'

'That pool's a bit too big,' said Lewis. 'I want to go in the little pool.'

'That's just for babies,' said Matty scornfully.

'Why don't you two dads go in the big pool with Matty and Tilly, and I'll go in the little pool with Lewis,' said Angie.

'No, I'm not really that keen on swimming,' said Dad. 'I'll sit and watch the picnic. We don't want anyone sneaking a slice of our cake, do we, Tilly?'

So Dad stayed on the decking. Angie and Lewis went off hand in hand to the little pool.

Matty started pulling me towards the deep end.

'What about starting at the shallow end?' I suggested.

'It's too crowded down there. It's much more fun up at the deep end,' said Matty.

'Is that OK, Tilly? How far can you swim?' said Tom.

'I can swim a length. Maybe two or three lengths, though I get out of breath,' I said, truthfully enough – but I didn't add that I hated going out of my depth. I was in Lewis's camp – I liked to put my toe down on the bottom every now and then, just to prove it was there.

Still, I wasn't going to have Matty calling *me* a baby, so I clambered down the steps of the deep end and pushed off bravely. We swam backwards and forwards, careful to keep out of the way of some big boys who were mucking about, with Tom treading water beside us, checking we were all right. At first I held my breath and went a bit trembly, but after a while I got used to it. In fact it was almost fun. I stuck my hand out of the water and waved at Dad, and he waved back and gave me a thumbs-up sign to show that he was proud of me.

'I'm getting a bit cold. Do you mind if I have a quick swim to warm up?' Tom asked. 'I can see you two are like little fish and won't come to any harm.'

He sped away, doing a quick crawl.

'My dad swims ever so fast, doesn't he?' said Matty.

'Mmm,' I said, wondering if she were casting aspersions on *my* dad.

'Let's have a race,' Matty suggested. 'One, two, three, *go!*'

She was half a width away before I could turn myself round and swim after her. I knew I was actually just as good a swimmer as Matty, if not better. I sped up determinedly, head down, arms pushing down, legs kicking hard. And then suddenly I was hit hard, knocked right down under the water.

I thought someone was attacking me. I'd forgotten the big boys on the edge. One had forgotten to look below and had dived straight on top of me. I thought someone was deliberately trying to push me under the water to drown me. I opened my mouth to scream and water rushed in, choking me. I tried to kick to get my head above water but I floundered helplessly. I really was drowning!

But then arms were around me, tugging me upwards, and suddenly I was free of the water, gasping in clear air. And so was Dad, his hair flattened in a fringe, water streaming off him.

'Oh, Dad!'

'Oh, Tilly!'

We neither of us had any breath left till we got to the side. We clung there, both of us panting.

'You saved me, Dad!' I said at last. 'And you can't even swim.'

'I can swim enough to save my girl,' he said.

Then Matty came swimming up to us, and Tom, desperately apologetic. We all got out and Angie and Lewis joined us, and after we'd all towelled ourselves nearly dry, we started on the picnic.

Angie had made egg-salad brown baguettes, with carrot sticks and grapes to nibble. Our coffee-and-walnut cake wasn't anywhere near as healthy – but it tasted marvellous. We'd forgotten to bring a knife so we had to tear chunks of cake off with our hands, which was great fun.

Angie had brought paper cups so we could drink our apple juice more decorously. We all drank a toast to Dad for being such a hero, which made him blush. I licked the cream off my lips and leaned against my dad, smiling up at him.

He was the best dad in the whole world.

Chapter Fourteen

I ate so many suppers the next week, it was a wonder I actually fitted into my bridesmaid's dress on Saturday. Simon and Matthew asked Dad and me round to supper on Wednesday so we could discuss all the details for the Big Day. I'd already had fishcakes and peas at Angie's, but I managed a big plate of bacon and potato pancakes and apple sauce and sour cream with Simon and Matthew.

Then, on Friday after school, I had tomato soup and chicken salad at Angie's. Afterwards Dad picked me up early and we went round to the Flowers'. Dear Mrs Flower had made fancy sandwiches and home-made sausage rolls and three kinds of cake – a Victoria sponge with buttercream, a chocolate cake with icing and a jam Swiss roll.

'Help yourself, Tilly dear,' said Mrs Flower. 'Take a selection of sandwiches.'

'And don't miss out on the sausage rolls,' said Mr Flower. 'I've already sampled two and they're tip-top.'

'And you must try a slice of each cake and tell me which you like best, and then we'll have a go at baking it when we have our first cookery session,' said Mrs Flower.

'They're all very yummy,' said Mr Flower. 'My wife's a marvellous cook.'

He said 'my wife' very proudly and Mrs Flower blushed.

I very much wanted to sample a slice of each cake, but after I'd eaten a couple of sandwiches and the sausage roll I was starting to feel uncomfortably full. I reached for a slice of cake after all, but Dad was keeping an eye on me.

'I'm not sure that's a good idea, Tilly. You don't want to make yourself sick, pet. It's a big day tomorrow!'

'Why's that then, Tilly?' said Mrs Flower.

'I'm going to be a bridesmaid again,' I said.

'Oh my, you *are* a one! Look, dearie, I'll cut you

a big slice of each cake and wrap them up in tinfoil and we'll pop them in one of my cake tins. They'll stay nice and fresh for several days, so you tuck in over the weekend.'

'And meanwhile I'll tuck in here, if I may,' said Dad. 'Tilly's already had some supper at her friend's house but I haven't eaten anything since lunch, and that was only a bag of crisps.'

'You need looking after, matey,' said Mr Flower, offering him cake. 'Follow my example and find yourself a nice new wife. Not that there's anyone to compare with my Iris. I've got the pick of the bunch, I have,' he said. 'Pick of the *bunch*, see,' he repeated, so we wouldn't miss the pun.

'All right, Albert, that's enough!' said Mrs Flower, though she giggled.

'So, did you have a good time on the Isle of Wight?' Dad asked, taking a huge bite of cake.

'Marvellous!' they said in unison.

They told us all about their itinerary, day by day – the visits to neighbouring towns, the boat trip, the tour round Osborne.

'And we went down to the beach most days,' said Mr Flower.

'Nothing beats sitting in a deckchair in the sunshine,' said Mrs Flower.

Mr Flower was very brown but Mrs Flower was still pink and white because she'd worn a sunhat, though she said her legs were brown because she'd taken her tights off every day to go paddling.

When we'd finished eating, Dad sat in a chair and I sat on the pouffe beside him, while Mr and Mrs Flower sat on the sofa together, holding hands and looking very sweet. They'd brought us back a special present from the Isle of Wight – a little glass ornament in the shape of a lighthouse. It was filled with different coloured layers of special Isle of Wight sand. They'd bought one for themselves too. It was sitting on Mrs Flower's mantelpiece, but they were going to take it with them and display it on Mr Flower's windowsill next week when they were staying in his house.

Dad had taken quite a few photos of their wedding day and showed them on his mobile phone, asking them to choose which ones they liked best so he could have them developed as proper glossy photos. He'd taken snaps of all the guests too.

'Oh my, look at this one of your pal Julie!' said Mr Flower. 'She's watching us have a dance, and her mouth is all puckered like a cat's—'

'Albert!' Mrs Flower interrupted. She shook her head at the photo. 'Poor Julie,' she said gently.

'Oh, look at this photo! That's a beauty!' said Mr Flower.

It was one of me standing in front of them, holding out my dress, while Mr and Mrs Flower smiled at each other over my head.

'Yes, that's my favourite photo too,' I said.

'You were the star of our wedding,' said Mrs Flower.

'So who's tying the knot tomorrow?' asked Mr Flower.

'It's two lovely gentlemen called Simon and Matthew,' I said.

'Oh my, that's very modern,' said Mrs Flower.

'Well, I'm sure you'll make their wedding day too,' said Mr Flower. 'You must come round and tell us all about it.'

'Yes, you will come round again soon, won't you?' asked Mrs Flower. 'We consider you both family now.'

'That makes us very happy,' said Dad. 'I wish we could stay longer today but I think I'd better take Tilly home. She needs to have an early night.'

'Oh yes, we can't have a bridesmaid with dark circles under her eyes,' said Mrs Flower.

I gave them both a kiss goodbye and thanked

them for our present. Then we went home. I actually nodded off to sleep in the car, but when I was home in bed I found I was wide awake again.

There was a full moon and my curtains weren't drawn properly so I kept propping myself up on one elbow and peering up at the bridesmaid's dress. It was grey instead of raspberry pink in this eerie light, but it still looked beautiful. I crawled down to the bottom of the bed so I could reach out and touch the hem. It was still silky soft. I stroked it carefully, and then held it to my cheek, loving the feel of it.

I hoped I was going to be a good bridesmaid for Simon and Matthew. I couldn't help feeling nervous, even though I'd been a bridesmaid before. I wasn't quite sure what the ceremony at the registry office would be like. Simon and Matthew didn't seem to know either. Perhaps there wouldn't even be a ceremony. Maybe we'd just stand in a queue and then someone behind a counter would stamp a form to say they were married! If it was going to be just like visiting a post office, I'd have to be extra decorative and bridesmaidy to make up for the lack of ceremony. I'd have to psych myself up to walk around swishing my silk skirts and pointing my toes in my tight pink shoes, and maybe even attempt a little dance. My tummy turned over at the thought, but I liked Simon and Matthew so much that I wanted to make their wedding really special.

Much to my relief, I didn't have to do anything extra at the registry office. Someone had hung a frieze of silver wedding bells around the walls, and there were two big vases of roses and lilies. There were lots of people in colourful clothes sitting on rows of chairs and standing down the sides and at the back, all smiling happily at Simon and Matthew.

Simon and Matthew were looking unexpectedly smart in grey suits. Simon had a blue shirt with a white collar and Matthew had a lilac shirt with little white flowers. They'd both had haircuts. Matthew had even trimmed his beard.

They both told me I looked lovely, and then I walked hand in hand with them to stand in front of the registrar. I'd expected an official-looking man, very brisk and businesslike, but it turned out to be a blonde lady in a frilly white blouse and a pale blue suit and white high heels, as if she were a wedding guest too.

She welcomed everyone in a friendly manner and said that it was a very happy day. Then she started the actual ceremony. She had a book in her hand, but she barely glanced at it, saying all the words looking straight at Simon and Matthew. When she declared they were married, everyone in the room started clapping and cheering and she didn't seem to mind at all. Simon and Matthew hugged each other, and then they hugged me too.

'Happy wedding day!' I said to both of them.

When we came out of the registry office, all the guests threw confetti and rosebuds over Simon and Matthew – and me too! I especially liked having rosebuds in my hair. Lots of people were taking photos on their smartphones – and there was one woman in jeans and a denim jacket who took more photos with a very elaborate, expensive-looking camera. She made Simon and Matthew stop and pose properly.

'I'd love a picture of you with the little brides-maid too,' she said. 'I hear she's a rent-a-bridesmaid. Brilliant idea!'

'Ask your dad, Tilly. This is our friend Jane who works for the local paper,' said Matthew.

'You mean Tilly's photo might be in the paper too?' said Dad. 'I'm not really sure about that.'

'Oh, Dad, I'm ever so sure! Oh please let my photo be in the paper. It would be so lovely if everyone could see it!' I exclaimed.

I imagined Matty's surprise. Cathy and Amanda and the whole class would be impressed. Simon might even stop picking his nose! The Flowers would be thrilled for me. Sid would laugh and show everyone the local newspaper. It would maybe spread far and wide. Perhaps some of the big daily papers would print my photo too. And maybe Mum would casually open a news-paper in some coffee shop and see me. Then she might feel proud of me and come rushing home to see me and . . .

'All right then, Tilly, no need to

look so wistful. You can have your photo taken,' said Dad.

So Jane took *lots* of photos of Simon and Matthew and me, and then we went down the road to La Terrazza, their favourite Italian restaurant, with all the guests following behind. It was like a carnival. I held Dad's hand and skipped along. The restaurant had arranged a long table at one end, and then lots of circular tables filling the room. The wedding guests sat here and there, calling to each other, pointing out spare seats.

Dad and I hovered, not quite knowing where to sit down.

'Come and sit with us!' Simon called.

'I want Tilly next to me!' Matthew shouted.

So Dad and I got to sit at the top table, with Simon and Matthew, Simon's mum and sister, and Matthew's mum and dad and very old granny in a wheelchair. We all had pink champagne! Well, I had one tiny sip, and then my own special glass of pink lemonade with a fancy straw and a little cocktail stick of fruit.

We all toasted Simon and Matthew and wished them every happiness – and then Simon and Matthew stood up and toasted *me*!

'Here's to Tilly, the prettiest little bridesmaid in the world,' said Matthew.

'To Tilly, who's made our wedding so special,' said Simon.

All the guests stood up and raised their glasses and shouted out, *'To Tilly!'* One of the ladies at the table nearest us had an especially big smile on her face. She was very curvy and looked amazing in a tight red dress with a white patent belt. Her long blonde hair waved to her shoulders. It was tucked behind one ear, showing her little silver-moon earring.

That earring was very familiar. So was her face. I suddenly pictured her with her hair pinned up and wearing a pinafore dress.

'It's Miss Hope!' I gasped. 'Dad, Dad, look, it's Miss Hope, my teacher!'

'Good heavens! Are you sure?' he said. 'Miss Hope always seems so serious and schoolmarmy, but she looks amazing now. If it really *is* her.'

We still weren't absolutely sure, and we couldn't go up to her and find out because the wedding meal was being served: melon and Parma ham, then spaghetti carbonara, then chicken with green beans and sauté potatoes, and *then* delicious creamy tiramisu, with coffee and little amaretti biscuits. I could hardly move after eating all that, and I breathed shallowly so I wouldn't strain the seams of my bridesmaid's dress too much.

Every now and then Dad and I peered over at Miss Hope – or indeed Miss Hope's twin. She was chatting with this person and that, gesturing and laughing.

'She absolutely *can't* be Miss Hope,' said Dad.

But she absolutely *was*. She came over to the top table when we were at the coffee stage, her hips swaying, wearing extraordinary high heels.

'Hello, Mr Andrews. Hello, Tilly. My goodness, don't you look beautiful! And you haven't spilled the tiniest drop on your lovely dress. Unlike your slurpy old teacher – look!' She pointed to an unfortunate stain on her front. 'I was so eager to eat my tiramisu that I took an enormous spoonful and half of it went down my dress. I'm going to the ladies' to see if I can mop it off.'

'I can't believe you're here too, Miss Hope,' I said.

243

'Simon and I are old chums. We met when we did our teacher training and we've kept in touch ever since,' she said.

'Well, we only met him a couple of weeks ago,' said Dad. 'Tilly here put an advert in the newsagent's—'

'Renting herself out as a bridesmaid – I know!' said Miss Hope, laughing. 'But I had no idea she was hired for this wedding too!'

'Hey, Sarah, how do you know each other?' Simon called.

'Tilly's one of my pupils!' she said.

'Well, lucky Tilly!' said Simon.

'No, lucky me. Tilly's one of my favourites,' said Miss Hope.

'I thought teachers weren't supposed to have favourites,' said Dad.

'We're not. You're not meant to have heard that!' she told him.

One of the Italian waiters put some music on – 'Somewhere Over the Rainbow' – and Simon and Matthew got up to do a slow dance in the middle of the floor while everyone clapped. Miss Hope sat in their place and started talking to Dad. Simon's mum was talking to me, admiring my dress, so I couldn't hear what they were saying properly. I think it was about me, and I heard Dad ask something about my drawing. Miss Hope sounded very reassuring when she answered.

Then Simon came back and asked *me* to dance. I felt a bit shy because I had no idea how to do that kind of slow dance, but luckily it was a bouncy tune so we could just jiggle about as we liked. Then Matthew asked me to dance, and by this time there were lots of couples on the small patch of floor.

I looked round – and saw Dad and Miss Hope dancing! At first I thought they looked the most unlikely couple in the world, Miss Hope so blonde and curvy in her red dress and high heels, and Dad so slight and pale and grey in his best suit – but after a while I got used to the way they looked. They seemed more used to each other too, shouting over the music and laughing. Dad's usually rather a hopeless dancer, very shy and stiff, but he was getting much better, even giving Miss Hope a little twirl every now and then. Yes, they were getting on really, really well.

I started drawing on one of the paper napkins, borrowing a biro from Simon's mum. I drew another wedding couple. The bride was wearing a long, slim, elegant dress. The groom was smiling. I drew a girl in a beautiful bridesmaid's dress too.

Dad and Miss Hope danced together a lot, right up to the end of the evening. Simon and Matthew kissed and hugged everyone goodbye, ready to drive off for their night flight to Boston.

'Right, Tilly, here's your wages for today,' said Simon, handing me an envelope.

I'd told them I charged five pounds, but there seemed to be several notes in the envelope.

'No, please, I don't want all this!' I said.

'You've earned it, sweetheart,' said Matthew. 'We absolutely insist!'

'And we've bought you a little present too,' said Simon, giving me a small blue leather box.

I thought it was going to be another necklace, but this time it was a silver bracelet with a heart charm. It fitted perfectly. I loved it so much I kept putting my arm up and down in the air so my bracelet could slide about elegantly.

'It's so lovely. Look, Miss Hope, isn't it the most beautiful bracelet?' I said.

'Yes it is. Really special. Though you'd better not wear it to school on Monday!'

'Oh, I want to show Matty and the others,' I protested – but not seriously, because I knew we weren't really allowed to wear jewellery to school.

To my great delight, Dad offered Miss Hope a lift home and she said yes. We got in the car, Dad and Miss Hope in the front and me in the back. I hadn't sat in the back seat for ages. I didn't mind at all.

I spread my pink silk skirts out over the seat so they wouldn't crease and sat there happily in the dark while Dad and Miss Hope chatted to each other. They weren't saying anything important, just talking about Simon and Matthew and the wedding, but the soft steady buzz of their words was so soothing I fell asleep.

I was so sound asleep I didn't even wake up when Miss Hope got out of the car, though I had a very hazy memory of her leaning over her seat and patting my shoulder. The next thing I knew, Dad was helping me out of the car, half lifting me as if I were a baby.

'Come on, sleepyhead,' he said.

'Where's Miss Hope, Dad?'

'She's gone home, silly.'

'Oh, I wanted to see where she lives. Is it a house?'

'She lives in a big old house, but I think she just has a garden flat.'

'What did you two say to each other when she went?'

'Mmm? Goodbye, of course!' said Dad.

'Did you kiss her?'

'What? No! For heaven's sake, Tilly, she's your teacher!'

'Yes, but you were dancing with her for ages.'

'I know, but it was a wedding. Everyone was dancing. *You* were dancing. Come on, let's dance you up to bed,' said Dad, opening the front door.

He clasped me tight and did a funny waltz with me down the hall, and then he two-stepped me all the way up the stairs.

'Oh, Dad, I do like it when you're funny like this,' I said.

'I do like it when you're chirpy too, little Till,' said Dad, giving me a kiss on the end of my nose. 'And it's all down to you that we've had such a lovely day.'

'Yes, it is, isn't it? So can I put another rent-a-bridesmaid advert in Sid's window?'

'No, enough is enough! You've had two fantastic weddings in one month. I bet very few girls are so lucky.'

Chapter Fifteen

I drew pictures of the wedding most of Sunday. I did a really big picture especially for Simon and Matthew, with us all in the Italian restaurant, clapping while they danced. I couldn't remember all the guests, so I mostly made them up, but I did quite good likenesses of Simon and Matthew, colouring their shirts very carefully, and of course I knew what Dad and I looked like. I drew me at the end of the table, so that I could show all of my bridesmaid's dress and my pink shoes. I also paid particular attention to Miss Hope, with her new hairstyle and her amazing red dress.

I did a little private drawing of Miss Hope and

Dad dancing together. I drew thought bubbles above their heads. Miss Hope was thinking: *Oh, Mr Andrews, I wish you were my boyfriend*, and Dad was thinking: *Dear Miss Hope, I think you look absolutely stunning.*

When I got to school on Monday, I ran to find Matty in the playground.

'Did the wedding go OK?' she asked.

'Yes, it was lovely, and Simon and Matthew gave me the most fantastic silver bracelet and it matches the silver necklace the Flowers gave me, so I've got two pieces of real jewellery now. But you'll never guess who else was at the wedding, Matty. Miss Hope! I hardly recognized her at first, she looked so different. She had her hair all long and curly, and she'd grown her chest and her bottom, but in a good way, and she wore ever such high heels that made her wiggle.'

'Don't be daft, Tilly! *Miss Hope?*'

'It's true, I swear it's true. I couldn't believe it was actually her, but it was, and my dad danced with her half the evening,' I gabbled. 'She looked so glamorous.'

Matty was looking over my shoulder. 'Glamorous?' she said.

I peered round. Miss Hope was crossing the

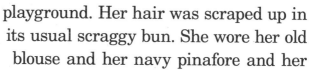 playground. Her hair was scraped up in its usual scraggy bun. She wore her old blouse and her navy pinafore and her flat moccasin shoes. She gave us a little nod – but she didn't come over. She didn't say, 'Oh, Tilly, you looked wonderful being a bridesmaid on Saturday.' Neither did she say, 'I had such a great time dancing with your dad half the evening.' She certainly didn't say, 'Now we're all such good friends you and your dad must come round for supper.' She didn't say anything at all, just carried on sloping across the playground and through the main entrance.

'There!' said Matty. 'I *knew* you must be mistaken. I knew Miss Hope would never wear a tight red dress and high heels.'

'It *was* her. I knew it was her. I recognized her by her moon earrings,' I insisted.

'Oh, Tilly, are you totally nuts? Heaps of ladies wear those earrings,' said Matty.

'Look, she was talking to us. And to my dad. And they danced together lots.'

Matty looked at me in an infuriatingly pitying way, her head on one side. 'You're telling stories,

Tilly, but I know they're not really lies. It's just what you'd *like* to have happened. It's not really wrong. Lewis does it all the time,' she said.

'Well, *I* don't! It was, *was* Miss Hope. Look, I'll ask her when we go into the classroom and then you'll see,' I said.

So when the bell went, I marched into school, pulling Matty with me. Miss Hope was sitting at her desk, peering at the register, adding up all the little ticks.

'Miss Hope, Miss Hope, did you enjoy the wedding on Saturday?' I said.

She frowned. 'Oh, Tilly, you've made me lose count!' she said, starting again at the top of the column.

'Sorry, but Matty doesn't believe me. You were at Simon and Matthew's wedding, weren't you?' I persisted.

'Tilly! Go and sit down,' said Miss Hope firmly.

'There!' Matty said, rolling her eyes.

I ground my teeth helplessly. I knew I wasn't telling stories. Although I was almost starting to doubt myself. I kept staring at Miss Hope. Her hair had been so different on Saturday. It was hard imagining her scragged-back topknot could ever be long soft blonde waves. And could the really bulky body underneath that dull pinafore ever display itself so glamorously in a bright red dress? Would her sensible flat feet ever squeeze into white high heels?

I drooped at my desk as our Maths lesson started, my numbers wavering as I blinked at the squares on my page. Miss Hope strolled round our tables, checking we were all working properly. She hovered over me.

'I think there's a little mistake in your working out,' she said. Then she bent closer. 'Yes, I did have a lovely time,' she whispered. 'But I don't like to talk about out-of-school things when I'm *at* school. OK?'

'Oh, it's very OK, Miss Hope. I understand now,' I said, as if I were talking about my arithmetic.

Miss Hope had whispered, but Matty was sitting right next to me and she had sharp ears. Her eyes were popping and her mouth was open.

'*See!*' I hissed, and gave her a little nod.

I hoped Miss Hope would come and whisper more things to me, but she just went back into teacher mode. The days went by and she didn't mention the wedding again. She didn't mention Dad either. I'd so hoped she'd talk about him, maybe even give me a little message for him.

Then, on Friday morning, Simon Perkins came running into our classroom, flapping the *Argus*, our local newspaper.

'Look! Look, Miss Hope! Page six. It's Tilly! *Her!*' he said. He tried to poke me in the chest but I stepped back sharply, because I hated getting anywhere near the fingers that spent so much time up his nose.

Miss Hope took the newspaper and peered at page six. 'Oh my goodness, it *is* you, Tilly, in your lovely bridesmaid's dress.'

Everyone came crowding round to see. It was a while before I could focus properly on the page. There was a big photo of Simon and Matthew and me. To my great irritation, I was actually pulling a silly face in this picture, my mouth open as if I were exclaiming 'Oh my!' but at least my dress looked beautiful.

The headline beside the photograph said:

KINGTOWN COUPLE RENT A BRIDESMAID!

'Wow! You're famous, Tilly,' said Matty, reading over my shoulder.

255

Two popular Kingtown men, Simon Smith, 45, headteacher at Larch Road Infant School, and Matthew Castle, 42, who owns Castle Books in Market Lane, tied the knot at Kingtown Registry Office on Saturday. They hired pretty-as-a-picture Matilda Andrews, 9, as their bridesmaid. Matilda had been given a bridesmaid's dress as a gift, and advertised herself in Sid's Newsagent's in Dudley Road.

'She's really made our day,' said Simon.

The happy couple and their little bridesmaid celebrated at La Terrazza in the High Street with a large gathering of family and friends of the two grooms.

'You could have said *I* gave you the bridesmaid's dress!' said Matty.

'I didn't realize they were going to put that in the newspaper!' I said, still stunned.

I told Dad that evening when he collected me from Matty's house. On Saturday morning we walked to Sid's to get our own copy of the *Argus*.

'Tilly's in the newspaper this week, Sid,' Dad said proudly.

'I know she is,' he said. 'It's been a talking point. Lots of folk have commented on it. Lucky job you popped in here for the *Argus*. I've got a letter for you, Tilly!'

'Oh good Lord, what is it this time?' said Dad.

'I bet someone else wants to rent her,' said Sid. 'She's obviously getting really popular. And so am I! I've had quite a few peering in the window, looking for that rent-a-bridesmaid card. I think I'm going to have to fish it out again. You can have a week's free advertising, Tilly.'

'I'm not sure I'm too happy about that,' said Dad. 'I'm starting to worry about all this publicity. Anyone might be trying to get in touch with my daughter. Let me have a look at that letter, Tilly.'

'It's addressed to me, Dad!'

We read it together.

Dear Matilda,

I read the article about you in this week's issue of the Argus with great interest. I'm getting married the last week in July and I'm planning on having several bridesmaids, plus two matrons of honour. I've had such difficulty finding a suitable design that will suit all of them. I'd set my heart on something

*traditional and pretty with lots of flounces –
but tasteful too. Your bridesmaid's dress
absolutely fits the bill! Please could you
ask your mother where she found it?*

*I loved reading about you advertising
yourself! You look so pretty in your dress.
I'd be thrilled if you would also be a
bridesmaid on my big day.*

*Yours sincerely,
Mandy Bygraves*

'Oh, Dad, *can* I be her bridesmaid?' I begged.
'It sounds like a really big wedding – lots of
bridesmaids and two matrons of honour! Oh please!
Just *one* more wedding.'

Dad gave a big sigh. 'All right. Just one more.
Though it doesn't sound as if this wedding will
be as much fun as the Flowers' or Simon and
Matthew's. Why does one bride need a whole
bunch of bridesmaids and two matrons of honour!
Perhaps she's going to have two bridegrooms too!'

I phoned up Matty when I got home. Angie
answered the phone.

'Hi, Angie, it's Tilly. I'm going to be a bridesmaid *again*!'

258

'Oh, sweetheart, I'm so happy for you! Who is it this time?'

'It's this lady called Mandy and she's having a great big wedding with lots of bridesmaids and she wants them all to wear dresses like mine, so please can I have the email and address of the lady who made my bridesmaid's dress?' I asked.

'Of course you can. Hang on a tick, I'll find them for you. She lives in Springfield Road but I'm not sure of the number.'

I waited, hanging onto the phone. I could hear Matty laughing in the distance and someone else talking. Was it Lewis? It didn't really sound like him.

'Here we are,' said Angie. She gave me the house number and the road and read me the email address, spelling it out twice to make sure I'd got it down correctly.

'Thanks so much. And thank you for giving me the dress in the first place!'

'You're very welcome, Tilly. I'm so happy that you're getting some use out of it! Matty told us about the piece in the *Argus*. Your fame is spreading!'

'Can I speak to Matty, please?'

'Yes, of course,' she said. I heard her calling, 'Matty, it's Tilly on the phone.'

There was a little pause.

'Hi, Tilly,' said Matty. She sounded funny. Friendly, but cautious.

'Hi, Matty,' I said. 'I could hear you laughing just now. What was funny?'

'Oh nothing. I was just messing about,' said Matty.

'With Lewis?'

'Mmm.'

That wasn't quite a yes.

'Do you want to come over and play?' I asked.

I heard Matty breathing. 'You never ask me round to yours,' she said.

'Yes, well, I'm asking now,' I said. 'And Lewis can come too, of course.'

'Well, thanks, but . . . I've got someone round at my house just now, actually,' said Matty.

'It's Marty, isn't it?' I said flatly.

'Yeah,' said Matty. 'Look, tell you what, you come round too. Then you can meet Marty – I just know you'll like her lots. Then we can all hang out together.'

'Oh, I've just remembered, Dad and I have got to go shopping,' I said. 'Sorry. Bye.'

I put the phone down and sat very still, staring at the carpet.

'We're going shopping, are we?' said Dad quietly.

I shrugged. 'Not really. It was just an excuse.

Matty's got that Marty round at her house.'

'You really might like her,' said Dad, who had obviously been listening.

'As if!' I said.

'OK. Well, *we* really might like a shopping trip. Come on, kiddo. Let's go!'

'Shopping like going to Sainsbury's?' I said.

'As if!' said Dad, imitating me. 'Shopping like going to the Flowerfields Shopping Centre and finding you some new bits and bobs. Hairslides and felt pens and story books. And I'd better look for a new shirt and tie if I'm going to a really posh wedding. I spilled tiramisu all down my front at Simon and Matthew's do. Now that was what I really call a good wedding!'

'Because you hooked up with Miss Hope!' I said daringly.

'Tilly! I hate that expression! And it's all nonsense anyway. Miss Hope is your teacher. Of course I'm going to be sociable with her. She's a very nice lady, but that's all. Now, don't be silly.' Dad was so brisk that I believed him.

He was still a bit huffy with me when we set off for Flowerfields, but we both had a strawberry milk-shake and a cheeseburger and fries, and cheered up.

'Now let's shop until we drop,' said Dad.

I chose two small rosebud hairslides from Claire's, a new set of felt tips from Smiggle and a Puffin Classic called *A Little Princess* from Waterstones. Dad chose a pale blue shirt with a flowery tie from Pink.

We watched the DVD of *Inside Out* in the afternoon and had baked potatoes for our tea.

'It's been a great day, Dad,' I said when he came to kiss me goodnight.

'I'm glad you enjoyed it, poppet,' he said. 'Don't read too late, will you?'

'Just ten minutes,' I said, but *A Little Princess* proved surprisingly easy to read. It was so gripping I raced through chapter after chapter. I loved reading about Sara's beautiful pink party dress – and was horrified when Miss Minchin said she had to change into an old black dress because she'd just got news that her father had died.

I stopped reading then and tried to go to sleep. It was really late now but I couldn't help worrying about my own dad. What would I do if *he* died suddenly? It was such a terrible thought that I had to put the light on to stop myself imagining all the different ways Dad might die.

I was in such a state that I even imagined he might be dead already, felled by a sudden heart attack in his armchair downstairs. I sat up, listening hard. I couldn't hear the buzz of the television. Perhaps Dad had got up to switch it off, tripped over something – oh no, had I left my pack of felt tips on the floor? – and was now sprawled lifeless on the carpet?

I had to go and check. I got out of bed, my legs so trembly I nearly keeled over. I slipped quietly along the landing, hugging myself, so scared I didn't even dare call out.

Then I heard Dad's voice and went limp with relief. He wasn't talking to me. Was he talking to himself then? Then I heard him laugh softly. He was on the telephone!

I crept down the stairs, listening.

'That's so sweet of you, Sarah,' he said.

Sarah?

Who on earth was this Sarah? And then I remembered the posh ballpoint pen Miss Hope had lent me because I'd forgotten to bring any pens on my first day at this new school. The silver part had been engraved in tiny swirly writing.

Sarah Mary Hope.

Chapter Sixteen

Mandy Bygraves wasn't quite as nice as the Flowers or Simon and Matthew. She lived in such an immaculate house that Dad and I had to leave our shoes at the door when we went round to visit her.

'I hope you don't mind. It's just that I have a thing about muddy carpets,' she said, as if Dad and I had been wading through a boggy field instead of walking in sandals along a dry pavement.

Mandy left her own pinky-beige high heels standing to attention at one side of the door. Her fiancé, Ian, had his own little mat for his brown brogues, though they were as highly polished as a conker. He padded around the house in gleaming white deck shoes, while Mandy wore amazing pink high-heeled mules with fluffy swansdown at the front. I might not have liked Mandy very much, but I *loved* her slippers. I wondered if she'd let me try them on. I kept gazing at them longingly but she didn't take the hint. Perhaps she was scared I had verrucas.

She led us into her living room. It was spectacularly clean and neat, with a cream sofa with two fat purple cushions, and a matching pair of cream chairs. There was a large porcelain leopard on either side of the electric fire, while china Siamese cats marched two by two along the mantelpiece. There were no real cats, large or small, probably because they'd scratch the furniture or shed hair on the sofas.

Mandy seemed worried by my hair too, actually lifting it up and twirling locks around her fingers, frowning.

'Your dad will have to drive you round to my place early so

that your hair can be styled properly to match all the others,' she said.

She wasn't too keen on my pink shoes either. I'd taken them to show her in their special shoe bag.

'I'm ordering satin shoes for the other girls. I think we'd better order an extra pair for you, Tilly. These are rather cheap and cheerful, if you don't mind my saying,' she said, holding them at arm's length.

I *did* mind her saying.

She didn't even like my beautiful raspberry-pink silk bridesmaid's dress very much, even though it was the whole reason she'd got in touch with me! She got it out of its special cellophane bag and examined it minutely.

'Yes, it's a lovely design, of course. Mrs Michaels is going to make five more, exactly this style and shade, and two for my matrons, slimmer fitting of course, and lower cut. But this dress isn't quite up to scratch any more. Those decorative rosebuds have gone out of shape. They look more like little pink cabbages now. I think all the decorative twiddles need to be replaced. And have you had it dry-cleaned?'

'Yes, and it cost a fortune too,' said Dad.

'Mmm, well, I don't think you went to an expert

in silk even so. It's gone a bit limp, hasn't it?' said Mandy, rubbing a fold doubtfully.

'I don't think so. Tilly's looked after it very carefully,' said Dad. 'Look, perhaps it might be more sensible for Tilly to bow out now. You're having your dresses made for the other little girls. You don't really need Tilly too. You don't mind too much, do you, Tilly?'

I shrugged awkwardly, not really sure. I badly wanted to be a bridesmaid again, especially at a big wedding, but I didn't fancy Mandy forever picking holes in my appearance on the big day.

'Oh, but I must have Tilly! I've only got five little girls for bridesmaids. I must have a sixth for symmetry. Besides, she's the little celebrity rent-a-bridesmaid. She's the talking point. Ian's got a friend who works for one of the London television news programmes. He's bigging it up to one of the producers and they've more or less promised to send a camera crew to do a little feature on the day. Just think, Tilly, you'll be on television! At *my* wedding!'

I blinked. Television!

'I think Tilly can do without her fifteen minutes of fame,' Dad started, but then he saw my face. 'So you want to after all, Tilly?'

I nodded emphatically.

'All right then,' he said.

'I should think so,' said Mandy, a little affronted. 'But, as I say, we need to freshen up the original dress a little, and check the colour hasn't faded, plus add new rosebuds. Can you take her round to Mrs Michaels now with the dress?'

'No!' I said.

They stared at me.

'Tilly,' said Dad.

'I don't want to,' I said.

They were both frowning now. They didn't understand. I wasn't meaning to be rude or awkward. I just couldn't stand the thought of meeting Mrs Michaels. I especially couldn't stand the thought of meeting Mrs Michaels's daughter Marty.

But I couldn't get out of it. I begged Dad to take the dress to her house for me while I stayed in the car, but he said I was being silly.

'Mrs Michaels will want to see the dress on you, Tilly, even I know that,' he said.

'I can't bear the idea of going there. I don't like her,' I said.

'You've never even met her. And I think you'll probably like her very much if she makes such beautiful dresses,' said Dad.

'Well, she might be all right, but I absolutely definitely know I totally dislike her daughter,' I said.

'Isn't she the one Matty sometimes plays with?' said Dad. '*She* must like her.'

I rolled my eyes, unable to believe he could be so tactless.

'Tilly! I hate it when you pull that face. You're getting a bit above yourself, young lady. Now, we'll go round to this Mrs Michaels's house straight away – you can give her a twirl in your dress, she can prink about with the frills and sew on a few rosebuds or whatever, and then we can go home. Then after Mandy-fussy-knickers-Bygraves's wedding I think we'll definitely call it a day on being a bridesmaid,' Dad said sternly.

He drove us round to the house in Lingfield Avenue. I expected it to be bizarrely horrible, picturing it like a yellow bouncy castle with a red-nosed clown girl hanging out of the window blowing raspberries at passers-by. It was a surprise to see it was a perfectly ordinary semi-detached house with a pretty garden, all lavender and roses.

'Please you go by yourself, Dad,' I tried again, handing him my bridesmaid's dress.

'For goodness' sake, Tilly, stop this nonsense,' said Dad.

I had to get out of the car, open the green gate and go up the crazy paving to the front door. Dad knocked while I hung back. I heard someone calling inside and then the door opened.

The girl standing in the hallway was one of the prettiest girls I'd ever seen. She had long straight shiny brown hair, so soft and silky it fell smoothly past her shoulders without a single tangle or unruly wisp. She had big blue eyes in a lovely pink-and-white face. She was wearing a pink T-shirt with bluebirds flying across it, immaculate blue jeans and pink sequin trainers. She didn't look like a real girl at all. She seemed perfect in every way, like a big beautiful doll on a glass counter in a toy department.

'Hello,' she said politely.

'Hello,' said Dad. 'We've come to see your mother about a bridesmaid's dress. I'm Mr Andrews and this is my daughter—'

'Tilly!' she said, smiling. 'Matty told us all about you.'

'*You're* Marty?' I gasped, utterly astonished.

She looked appalled. 'I'm not *Marty*!' she said. 'I'm Melissa, her big sister. I'm not a *bit* like Marty!'

'Thank goodness!' said a voice behind her. Another girl pushed forward. 'Hi, Tilly. *I'm* Marty.'

She was sooooo different from her sister. Marty's hair was a great fuzzy cloud of curls. She had blue eyes, but hers were crinkled and mischievous. 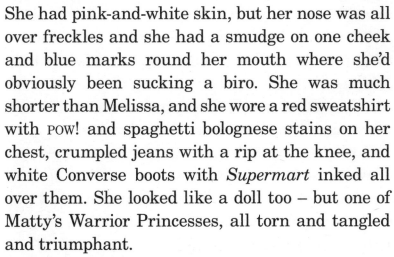 She had pink-and-white skin, but her nose was all over freckles and she had a smudge on one cheek and blue marks round her mouth where she'd obviously been sucking a biro. She was much shorter than Melissa, and she wore a red sweatshirt with POW! and spaghetti bolognese stains on her chest, crumpled jeans with a rip at the knee, and white Converse boots with *Supermart* inked all over them. She looked like a doll too – but one of Matty's Warrior Princesses, all torn and tangled and triumphant.

'Come in!' she said, taking my hand and pulling me inside, as if we'd known each other for years. 'You've got Matty's yucky pink bridesmaid's dress, haven't you – the one with all the flounces. Still, it looks much better on you than it does on her. She looked totally hilarious. Mind you, all my mum's dresses are total frilly disasters.'

'That's enough, Marty!' A lady who was clearly Marty's mum seized hold of her and jokingly put her hand over her mouth. 'Excuse my younger daughter! Do come into my workroom, both of you. Melissa, can you pop the kettle on? And, Marty, make yourself scarce upstairs, young lady.'

'Oh, Mum! Can't I stay and talk to Tilly? I want to get to know her. She's Matty's best friend,' said Marty.

'Well, let me see Tilly in her dress and work out how to make it look like new – and *then* you can go and play together for a bit, so long as her dad doesn't mind,' said Mrs Michaels. She smiled at Dad, who was looking bemused. 'My husband's in the living room, watching the big match on the telly. Perhaps you'd like to join him, while Tilly and I get on with the girly stuff?'

Dad's not really into football but he looked relieved all the same. Melissa brought him a cup of tea and me an orange juice.

'I really should be offering you both champagne,'

said Mrs Michaels. 'I was so delighted to see that little piece in the *Argus*. And it's had such brilliant repercussions! I've had three different bridesmaid orders already, not to mention multiple dresses for Mandy Bygraves! Thank you so much, Tilly, for being such a brilliant advert. Any time you'd like a new party frock you just have to say the word and I'll make you one for nothing. Now, dear, you pop behind the screen and put your dress on, and let me have a good look.'

Dad escaped to the living room while I put my dress on very carefully. I took my shoes off before stepping into it, just in case I got it dirty.

'What a careful, sensible girl you are,' said Mrs Michaels approvingly, seeing my stockinged feet. She turned me round, squinting at me. 'I don't know what Mandy was moaning about. Your dress still looks perfect to me. You've taken great care of it. And I wouldn't imagine young Matty handed it over in pristine condition. She's a messy little monkey, almost as bad as my Marty.'

'It was ever so kind of her to give it to me. It's the most beautiful dress in the world,' I said.

'Yes, it did turn out rather well, even if I say so myself,' said Mrs Michaels, fluffing out the frills. 'And it's such a lovely shade of pink too. It really suits you. You've got exactly the right colouring. And you're the right size too. It's going to be a bit of a nightmare sorting out those Bygraves nieces. I think their mothers must give them ten meals a day – and another ten all through the night. It's going to be hard work getting those girls to look a picture, but I'll do my best.'

'Mandy Bygraves wants me to have new rose-buds,' I said.

'Yes, I suppose yours have got a bit squashed. I've been fashioning a whole flower bed of them for all the finished frocks. Whip your dress off and I'll sew some fresh ones on for you. It'll only take twenty minutes. You pop upstairs and play with our Marty. Off you go,' said Mrs Michaels.

When I'd changed back into my ordinary school uniform, I went hesitantly up the stairs. Marty wasn't at all how I expected. I didn't detest her. I actually quite liked her. Astonishingly she seemed to like me too. And she knew Matty and I were best friends. Maybe she wasn't trying to take her away from me after all. But even so, I still felt shy. Maybe she'd change the moment we were together in her bedroom? Sometimes girls were all nicey-nicey in front of other people, but then they turned on you in private.

I got to the top of the stairs and hovered on the landing. Maybe I'd just stay there, very still and quiet, until Mrs Michaels called to say my dress was ready. But then Marty herself peered out of her bedroom and did a delighted double take when she saw me lurking.

'Hi, Tilly! I was just going to see if you'd stopped all the boring dressy stuff so you could come and play – and here you are! In you come!' She seized hold of me and pulled me into her bedroom.

It was immediately clear that it wasn't just Marty's bedroom, that she shared it with Melissa, like Matty had said. One half of the room was excessively neat and beautiful, with a glass-topped dressing table and a bright pink stool and a black furry rug. A ballet dancer ornament twirled on the shiny surface, together with a white plaster arm with rings on every long white finger and bangles adorning the wrist. There were posters of pop stars and YouTubers and fashion models pinned on a cork board with geometric neatness.

Bunk beds took up the whole of one wall. The bottom bunk had a carefully arranged duvet, with

275

a fluffy white cat nightdress case. The top bunk was a terrible mess, with weird soft toys climbing all over it, and a big snake made of old tights swinging headfirst from the bedpost.

It didn't take even a split second to work out which sister had which bunk. Marty's side of the room was in chaos, with old clothes and trainers and art things and Lego and half a Coco Pops packet spilled all over the carpet. I had to pick my way through the rubble, pausing to admire her posters. They were all inventive comic strips, with a girl with exploding curls flying through the air, *Supermart!* emblazoned on her scarlet catsuit.

'Wow!' I said. 'She's you! Who did them for you, Marty?'

'No one. *I* did them,' Marty said proudly.

'They're brilliant. I absolutely love this one of Supermart on the moon! And here she is as a cowboy – oh, and I love the circus one too. You're so clever,' I said.

'Do you really think so?' Marty asked. 'All my family think they're totally weird. Especially Melissa. Though that's maybe because I gave Supermart a bossy big sister called Mighty Fart.' She burst out laughing and I did too.

'I bet Matty loves them,' I said.

'Yeah, she does. But she told me you can draw heaps better. She says you're absolutely ace at drawing, especially monsters. Hey, will you draw some for me?' She scrabbled on the floor for her large drawing pad and found several loose crayons under the bed.

Matty said I drew heaps better!

'I can't draw anywhere near as good as you,' I said modestly. 'But I did use to love drawing monsters. I'm not supposed to draw them any more though.'

'Why?'

'Oh, because . . . It worries my dad. I used to draw all sorts of scary stuff, see, after . . .' I let my voice tail away.

'After your mum?' said Marty.

I tensed. Had Matty told her? It was my biggest ever most dreadful secret.

'What did Matty say?' I asked, my voice going wobbly.

'Matty said you didn't have a mum. That must be so sad. When did she die?'

I breathed out. Matty hadn't told. She really *was* a true best friend. Somehow it made it easier to tell Marty myself.

'My mum isn't dead,' I said, picking up Marty's snake and winding him round and round my arm. 'She just left.'

'*Left?*'

'Yes, because – because she's not really like other mums.'

'You mean she doesn't care about you?'

'She does! She just doesn't want to be tied down. She's an artist. She needs to be free,' I said. 'That's what Dad told me.'

'But she's not free. She's got you and your dad,' said Marty, shocked.

'It's hard to explain,' I said. That's what Dad had said too.

'So she just left and never came back?'

'No! No, she's come back heaps of times. Well, several. And she sends birthday and Christmas presents. She's still my *mum*, but she just doesn't live with us,' I said, winding Marty's snake tighter and tighter around my arm.

'So where does she live then?'

'I'm not quite sure where she lives now. Somewhere abroad, I think.'

'But you can still phone her and email her and Skype her?' Marty went on relentlessly.

'Look, it's none of your business,' I said.

Marty blinked. 'You're right. It's not. Sorry.' She unwound her snake and mimed wrapping him round her neck and pulling him tight. 'I should learn to shut up and stop being so nosy.'

'It's OK,' I said. 'I like your snake.'

'Do you really? He's called Basil and I love him to bits. I made him all by myself. Melissa thinks he's revolting. She hates all my animals but I think they're cool. I don't go on about them at school in case they call me a baby – you know what people can be like,' said Marty. 'Matty understands though, doesn't she?'

'We play Warrior Princesses,' I said.

'That sounds seriously cool,' said Marty.

I took a deep breath. 'Maybe we could all play it some time,' I suggested.

'Oh, wow, yes. Great,' said Marty.

'Look, tell you what,' I said, squatting on the crowded floor and grabbing the drawing pad. 'We could do a picture together now. You do Supermart. And I'll do some monsters. I've missed drawing them. It'll be fun.'

So we sat side by side and I invented some brand-new monsters with staring fish eyes and extra little dangly limbs and enormous slimy warty bodies with long bare pink tails, and Marty drew Supermart kicking and punching and stamping on them all. We described what was happening as we drew and coloured. I kept inventing brand-new monsters and Marty imagined ever more painful ways of squashing them. We were so absorbed that we didn't hear Mrs Michaels calling. We didn't hear Melissa yelling to us halfway up the stairs. We only looked up when Dad and Mrs Michaels came into the bedroom, shaking their heads at us.

'What are you two up to? Didn't you hear us calling? What's that you're drawing?' Mrs Michaels asked.

'Just a game,' said Marty, closing her drawing book quickly.

'I bet it's something to do with your silly old Supermart cartoons,' said Mrs Michaels, sighing. 'You could be quite good at art if you'd only draw something properly.'

'Oh, Mum, you don't half nag,' said Marty – but she suddenly jumped up and put her arms tight round Mrs Michaels's waist.

'That's right,' said Mrs Michaels fondly. 'Naggle, naggle, naggle, all day long. And with good reason!'

I had a lump in my throat watching them. I cuddled my dad lots, but it wasn't quite the same as cuddling a mum. I remembered how soft my own mum felt, and the beautiful rosy smell of her perfume. For a moment the ache for her was so bad I thought I'd crumple up amongst all the rubbish on Marty's carpet – but Dad put his arm round me, keeping me upright.

'Come and see what a lovely job Mrs Michaels has made of your dress, Tilly,' he said gently.

I tried on the bridesmaid's dress. Mrs Michaels had not only sewn on new rosebuds, she'd sprayed my dress and ironed it so that the skirts stuck out beautifully and it looked brand new.

'There, you'll do me proud now,' she said. 'Let's take a few photos of you, sweetheart. My husband's got a fancy camera. Will it be all right if I use a photo on my website, Mr Andrews?'

'We'd be proud, wouldn't we, Tilly?' said Dad.

'But my hair isn't right. Mandy Bygraves says I've got to have it properly styled,' I said.

'Silly woman. I like little girls to look natural,' said Mrs Michaels. 'Tell you what, I'll get our Melissa to brush it for you – she's got a knack with hair.'

Melissa did my hair, letting it hang loose, with just one little plait wound with more tiny rosebuds – and she gave me pale pink lipstick too!

'I expect you'd like some lipstick too, Marty,' she joked, waving the lipstick near her mouth.

'Yuck!' said Marty, and sucked her lips safely inside her mouth.

I *loved* the lipstick. It even tasted wonderful. I stood on top of Mrs Michaels's work table and turned round and round, holding out my skirts, while Mr Michaels snapped me at every angle.

'You'll be Madam Mandy's prettiest bridesmaid, no doubt about that,' said Mrs Michaels.

Chapter Seventeen

I woke up early on the day of the wedding. I lay cuddling Stripy, rehearsing in my head exactly what I had to do. Mandy had put all us bridesmaids through our paces several times, making us keep exactly in step, pointing our feet, our heads held high. The others didn't listen properly and barged into each other, which made Mandy very snappy.

'For goodness' sake, you'll wreck the whole wedding if you carry on like that on my big day,' she said.

She was particularly fierce with Lovejoy, the bridesmaid twinned with me. She was as tall as me, though she was two years younger and kept getting the giggles.

'Do stop that silly chortling, Lovejoy,' said Mandy severely.

'I can't help it, Aunt Mandy. We all look so daft mincing about like this,' said Lovejoy.

'I'm trying to help you look dainty, not daft. Though that's a big ask in your case, Lovejoy,' said Mandy.

Lovejoy simply giggled again, but her mum looked furious.

I couldn't help feeling there were going to be several big arguments by the time the wedding was over. I didn't really care, just so long as the wedding itself went splendidly. I had loved the Flowers' wedding. I had loved Simon and Matthew's wedding too. But this was a big-time wedding, with Mandy in a fairy-tale princess white wedding dress and Ian in top hat and tails, and the two matrons of honour and six girls in raspberry-pink frills. We were even arriving at the church in style. I had to be at Mandy and Ian's house at eleven to have my hair done, and then me and my dress had to pass a close inspection. At half past twelve all us bridesmaids then had to pile into a pink limousine! Mandy gave us strict instructions that we weren't allowed to mess about or act rowdy, and we absolutely mustn't crease our bridesmaid's dresses under pain of death. I rather expected that Lovejoy at the very least would be enduring this pain when we arrived at the church, but that was her lookout.

I was determined to enjoy this last chance to be a bridesmaid no matter what. I wondered if the television crew really would turn up. Dad had said that this was wishful thinking on Mandy's part and that a real news team wouldn't ever turn up just for a wedding.

'Not even if there's a rent-a-bridesmaid?' I asked.

'Not even,' said Dad, shaking his head at me sympathetically.

I realized he was right but I couldn't help hoping all the same. It would be so wonderful if I was actually on television in my raspberry-pink bridesmaid's dress. Matty might actually regret giving it to me! Cathy and Amanda and all the other girls in my class would be so impressed. And all the girls at my old school too. And maybe, just maybe, Mum might happen to turn on her television just at the right moment and see me!

I looked pretty in my bridesmaid's dress – everyone said so. Much prettier than normal.

Much, *much* prettier than I used to be. My hair was still a bit thin and wispy, but I liked the way it looked after Melissa had styled it, and maybe it would look even better after Mandy's hairdresser had sorted it out. My dress would look brand new and I'd be wearing snow-white socks and new shoes that Mandy was buying specially.

It was mean to say it, but I wouldn't be able to help looking the best bridesmaid, especially as I was the only one who'd be holding her head up high and walking daintily.

Mum would look at me and then suddenly rush to her television and freeze-frame it. She'd stare at me, her heart beating. 'My Tills,' she'd murmur. 'My own little girl.' She'd have tried to put me right out of her mind but now she'd look at me, transfixed. She'd see I wasn't just much prettier. I was much more grown up too. Too old to cling to her or cry or need her to do anything for me. I could help her, make her cups of tea, chat to her like a grown-up. We could be like two special friends. She'd see that she might *like* living with me now. She'd realize just how much she'd missed me and Dad.

She'd start the television again and watch the clip of the wedding, and this time she wouldn't scoff and say weddings were naff. She'd see how wonderfully romantic they were. She'd imagine herself in white lace, with Dad at her side – and me as their bridesmaid in a raspberry-pink dress.

I'd been so silly to think that Miss Hope and Dad would get together. They barely knew each other. They had never fallen in love, lived together, had a child. They weren't a family. I liked Miss Hope and Dad obviously liked her too, but we didn't *love* her, not the way we loved Mum.

It was a shame about Miss Hope all the same. She could be a guest at Mum and Dad's wedding, wearing her red dress with the white belt, and she'd smile bravely and throw confetti over Mum and Dad but there'd be wistful tears in her eyes.

Still, Mr and Mrs Flower and Simon and Matthew would be guests at the wedding too, and they'd comfort her, and you never knew, Miss Hope might well meet someone else at our wedding and dance the night away with them, forgetting all about Dad.

No matter how lovely Miss Hope was, she could never be as special as Mum. Mum and Dad and I belonged together. And now, after waiting such a terribly long time, it looked as if all my wishes might actually come true.

I was in such a happy daydream that I jumped when Dad came into my bedroom holding a tray.

'I thought the special bridesmaid might enjoy breakfast in bed,' he said. 'How's my girl? Have you got butterflies in your tummy? This is clearly the wedding of the century, according to Mandy Bygraves . . . When you've finished your toast and honey you'd better hop in the bath and scrub for England because I dare say Mandy will be inspecting you carefully.'

Dad seemed in a very jolly mood. Had he been daydreaming too?

'Dad, about these television people . . .' I said tentatively.

'Tilly, it's not going to happen,' said Dad, though he sounded hopeful.

'It might,' I said.

And it did, it did, it did! Dad dropped me off at Mandy's and then made a hasty retreat, saying he'd meet me at the church. I didn't blame him. The house was packed tight with females, big and small, and they all seemed to be screeching their heads off. Mandy was squawking the loudest, running around in her petticoat and wedding veil snapping at the bridesmaids, her phone clamped to her head as she furiously complained about the pinkness of the roses just delivered by the florists. There was a smaller, fiercer, wrinklier version of Mandy also shrieking down her phone, clearly Mandy's mum. Then there were the two best-friend matrons of honour, only they seemed more like worst enemies now, arguing bitterly about who was going to dance first with the best man. Four of the bridesmaids in various states of undress played chase all over the house. Lovejoy was only wearing knickers and wasn't a pretty sight. The fifth bridesmaid was wailing and struggling to escape because she said the hairdresser's tongs were too hot, and the hairdresser herself was practically beating her about the head with her hairbrush to get her to stay still.

I could see why the fifth bridesmaid was moaning when it was my turn to get my hair styled, but it was fascinating too, watching in the mirror as my straight hair was turned into crinkly cascades. I shook my head experimentally to see what it felt like.

'Don't do that! You'll shake all the curl out, silly,' said the hairdresser. 'Oh dear heavens, I can't wait to be back in a proper salon. You bridesmaids! It's more like a bear garden than a wedding.'

But at half past eleven we were miraculously all ready, hair curled and decorated with fresh rosebuds, new shoes still unscuffed and raspberry-pink dresses immaculate.

'Oh, Mandy, come and see. They look adorable!' said Mandy's mum. 'They'll do you proud.'

Mandy peered round her bedroom door. She was in the middle of having her make-up done, so she had one very fierce eye and eyebrow and one that seemed barely there by comparison, so she looked like a pirate – but she gave us a sudden beaming smile.

'You look lovely, girls,' she said. 'Now, no mucking about in the limo, remember! Just sit still and don't crease your dresses.'

We couldn't help playing about a bit, pretending we were movie stars quaffing pink champagne to match our dresses. Lovejoy pretended she was a drunk movie star and flopped about and then mimed copious vomiting, which made the rest of us start to feel sick for real – but we got to the church without further disaster.

There were guests going in, quite a lot of onlookers gathering around the little railings – and a van parked opposite with several men carrying unwieldy equipment, and a lady in a smart blue suit.

'OMG!' said the oldest bridesmaid. 'Look! It's the telly!'

All the bridesmaids struggled frantically to get out of the limo, crushing each other as well as their dresses.

'Fancy, the television people coming to film Aunt Mandy!' said Lovejoy, jumping out and capering wildly.

A lady in black with a clipboard came running up to her. 'Ah! *You* must be the little rent-a-bridesmaid!' she said. 'Come over here, dear. We'd like you to do a little piece to camera before the wedding gets started.'

Lovejoy looked bewildered, but followed her obediently. I was so shocked I just let her.

'Tilly! Hi, Tilly!' It was Marty. She came running up to me. 'Hey, Mum insisted on coming to see all her dresses on show and, guess what, the television crew have interviewed her. She's ever so thrilled. They want to interview you too. They're over there.' Marty gestured and saw Lovejoy grinning inanely at the cameraman. 'What's *she* doing? It's not about *her*!'

Marty charged over to the television people. 'Stop! You've got the wrong bridesmaid. *She's* not Tilly.'

The lady in black frowned. 'You're *not* Tilly?' she demanded of Lovejoy.

'I never said I was,' said Lovejoy, truthfully enough. 'But I am a bridesmaid – honestly.'

'But this is the actual rent-a-bridesmaid!' said Marty, pulling me over to them. 'This is the one you want. Tilly. She's my friend.'

'Hello, Tilly,' said the lady in black. 'At last! Where's your mum, dear? I'd like her permission to interview you.'

'She hasn't got a mum,' said Marty.

'I have, but she's not here,' I said. 'But I've got a dad.'

I looked around wildly – and there was Dad, elbowing his way through the crowd of onlookers.

'Oh, Dad, please can I be on television?' I pleaded.

'Oh Lord, what next? I never thought— Oh well, yes, I suppose so,' said Dad.

The lady in black got him to sign a piece of paper on her clipboard and then took me to the pretty woman in blue.

'This is Jasmine, our presenter. She's going to ask you a few questions. Just talk straight back to her – don't stare at the camera.'

'It won't take very long, will it?' I asked anxiously. 'Mandy won't like it if her wedding is held up.'

'Ah, sweet,' said Jasmine. 'Don't worry, darling, we'll be quick as a wink. Then we'll film you with all the other bridesmaids going into church and stick around for a little shot when you all come back out with the bride and groom. OK? Stand up straight then – and how about a nice big smile, because it's a really happy day, isn't it?'

It might actually be the happiest day of my life if all my daydreams came true – so I smiled and smiled.

'When you're ready,' said the cameraman.

'Now, Tilly, you're the little girl who's the rent-a-bridesmaid,' said Jasmine. 'Tell us how you got the whole idea.'

'Well, my best friend Matty gave me her own bridesmaid's dress, this one, and I just loved it so much,' I said. 'Only no one

293

I knew was getting married, so we thought I might advertise to see if anyone needed a bridesmaid. So I put an advert in Sid, our newsagent's, window.'

'How very enterprising,' said Jasmine. 'How much do you charge then, Tilly?'

'Not very much. In fact you don't really have to pay me anything. I'm happy to be a bridesmaid for free, though everyone's insisted on paying me so far because they thought I did a good job,' I said proudly.

'So this isn't your first bridesmaid rental?' asked Jasmine.

'No, it's my third. I was Mr and Mrs Flower's bridesmaid – they're this lovely elderly couple and they're almost like a gran and grandad to me now. And then there's Simon and Matthew – I was their bridesmaid as well, and they're lovely too, just like uncles, and they both danced with me at their reception,' I said.

'And now you're a bridesmaid at Mandy and Ian's wedding and I expect that will be lovely too,' said Jasmine.

'Well, I hope so, because it's ever such a big posh wedding,' I said.

For some reason that made Jasmine and all the people listening laugh.

'Well, we'd better let you line up with the other bridesmaids now, because I think the bride's limo has just arrived,' said Jasmine.

Mandy was struggling out of the car, fussing about her beautiful white dress, moaning at her two pink matrons of honour because they weren't helping her properly. Then she suddenly spotted the camera. Her tight mouth stretched into a serene smile, she stepped forward, smoothing her lace, and fluttered her fingers at her assembled bridesmaids, not even frowning when Lovejoy lumbered forward to greet her and trod on her hem.

The crowd gave a little cheer – but when I darted over to stand beside Lovejoy they gave me an even bigger cheer! I couldn't believe it. I couldn't help turning round, wondering if they were cheering someone else entirely, and they laughed. Lots of them waved and the cameraman hurried forward to get a clear picture of me. It was almost as if it were *my* wedding.

It was much more solemn inside the church. The organ music made the back of my neck prickle. We stepped slowly and gracefully up the aisle behind Mandy and her father, even Lovejoy keeping in step, and then sat quietly without fidgeting while the vicar conducted the wedding service.

It was the first time I'd heard all the proper old-fashioned church words and I thought they sounded beautiful. Mandy and Ian stood together, looking at each other as they recited their vows. Mandy suddenly looked much younger and softer and Ian had tears in his eyes. He was trembling so much he found it hard to put the gold wedding ring on Mandy's finger.

I imagined Dad putting a ring on Mum's finger to keep her safely married to him until death did them part. I gave a big sniff, because no one can look a beautiful bridesmaid with a runny nose.

Ian kissed Mandy and there was a little sigh all over the church, and I peered around looking for Dad, wondering if he were daydreaming about Mum too. He did look a bit sad, but when he saw me staring he blew me a kiss and gave me a thumbs-up sign.

The wedding was over so quickly. Mandy and Ian processed back down the church, the matrons of honour behind them, and then us six bridesmaids. Everyone smiled at us, and Lovejoy pranced about a bit for their benefit, even dropping a curtsy every now and then. I gave up trying to control her and walked on solemnly, clutching my little rosebud posy.

Then we were outside again, with the crowd throwing confetti and rose petals. The television crew was still there, and Jasmine talked to Mandy and Ian. Mandy kept tossing her head and smiling in a showy fashion, not knowing that a piece of bright pink confetti had landed on the tip of her nose looking like a very big spot. Ian looked at her fondly and blew gently so the confetti drifted away.

I suddenly felt all tearful again and had to swallow hard to stop myself crying, which was just as well, because Jasmine turned to me.

'Let's have your professional opinion on the wedding, Tilly. Was it a lovely wedding?' she said.

'Oh yes, it was beautiful,' I said.

'I expect it will be hard to beat,' said Jasmine. 'So have you got another wedding lined up?'

'Not yet,' I said. 'But I'm hoping.'

'You sound as if you've got someone in mind,' said Jasmine, laughing.

'Oh, I have,' I said, carried away. 'I wish I could be the bridesmaid at my dad's wedding.'

The people around me all went 'Aaah!' Jasmine looked momentarily at a loss for words, and then she patted me on my silk shoulder.

'That's so sweet,' she said.

Then she looked away from me, and said straight to camera, 'Well, this is a happy day for everyone here, especially our little rent-a-bridesmaid Tilly. This is Jasmine Symes for London Local.'

Then she smiled and said goodbye to me and went to sit in the van while the camera guys started packing up their equipment.

'Hey, you were so cool, Tilly!' said Marty, sounding really impressed.

'You were a beautiful advert for my dresses,' said Marty's mum.

'You look lovely, though I like the way *I* did your hair more than all those curly-whirlies,' said Melissa.

Dad patted me on the back and said, 'Well done, Tilly,' but he didn't say any more. He didn't comment on my wish. He didn't say very much all the long afternoon at the wedding reception. I couldn't sit with him while we were having the meal. I had to sit with Lovejoy and all the other bridesmaids at a special table just for us.

We had smoked salmon with fiddly bits of greenery, then chicken in a white sauce with sauté potatoes and asparagus, and then Mandy's favourite pudding, banoffee pie. It's *my* favourite too, so it was a lovely meal, but it was a bit boring sitting with the other bridesmaids because they all knew each other and chatted together and I got a bit left out.

I talked to Lovejoy some of the time, but then she gestured wildly with her fork while she was eating and spilled chicken and white sauce all down the front of her dress. She didn't seem that worried but I couldn't bear to look at her bodice after that because it was clear her dress was ruined.

There were a lot of very long speeches. Lovejoy yawned loudly through most of them. We all perked up a little when the best man toasted us bridesmaids and said we looked like little pink roses. Then he gave us each a present. It was a silver bangle with roses engraved around it. So now I had a silver necklace with a flower pendant, a silver bracelet with a heart, and this new silver bangle. I was going to have to find an old chocolate box in which to keep all my special bridesmaid jewellery.

Then when the meal was all over the best man danced with each of us bridesmaids in turn. He didn't do *proper* dancing, he just messed about whirling us round and round, but it was quite good fun. Then Dad came to dance with me. He said he hoped I was having a good time. I said I was, and that I hoped *he* was too. He smiled at that but he still looked very serious.

I was sure I knew why. He was daydreaming about Mum too, wishing and wishing that she would come back and we could have our own wedding. We were both getting very tired by this time.

'I think I might whisk you home to bed,' said Dad. 'Or do you really want to stay on at the wedding to the bitter end?'

I protested a little, but I really didn't mind leaving early. It was a very grand reception in a huge marquee lit by fairy lights with a proper band instead of a disco, but somehow it was nowhere near as much fun as the other two receptions. We had to go and say goodbye to Mandy and Ian and thank them for having us.

'Well, thank you for coming,' said Mandy. 'You were quite the little star of the show, Tilly. You absolutely hogged all the television coverage.'

I'd thought she'd be pleased but she was clearly irritated. Still, Ian thanked me properly and insisted on giving me a special envelope with *Tilly's*

Fee written on the front in fancy italic handwriting. It seemed rude to open the envelope in front of him, but when I peeped in the car, I saw it was a fifty-pound note!

'Look, Dad! I've never had so much money in my life! Should I give it back? It's too much, isn't it?' I said.

'It's much too much. But I suppose you can keep it. Mandy and Ian seem to have lots of money. And they did have their wedding televised because of you,' said Dad. 'Though poor Mandy obviously felt they didn't pay enough attention to her.'

'It was nearly all about me, wasn't it?' I said. 'Imagine, everyone watching me on television!'

'I wouldn't get too excited. I don't think they always show all the news items they film,' said Dad. 'But we'll see when we get home. We'll watch it on iPlayer.'

They *did* use it, though I started to fear that Dad was right, because my wedding item was right at the end of the news, just before the weather forecast. They showed my entire interview, and at the end, after I'd said the bit about wanting to be a

bridesmaid for my dad, the presenter in the studio put her head on one side and said, '*Sweet!*'

'Oh, Dad! Was I really sweet?' I asked.

I looked round at Dad. I hoped he'd be smiling but he looked even more serious.

'Oh, Tilly,' he said.

'I'm sorry! I didn't mean to make you sad, Dad. But maybe Mum will be watching and she'll come back and it will really happen,' I said.

'Tilly!' Dad took me by the shoulders and looked straight into my eyes. 'Please don't, sweetheart.'

'It could happen,' I insisted.

'No. Not now. Mum's obviously made a new life for herself. And we've made a new life for ourselves too. I thought you were starting to be happy again.'

'I *am* happy, Dad. But think how even happier we'd be if Mum came back,' I said.

'It's not going to happen,' Dad said firmly. 'Get it into your head, Tilly, once and for all.'

Chapter Eighteen

IT'S NOT GOING TO HAPPEN. IT'S NOT GOING TO HAPPEN. IT'S NOT GOING TO HAPPEN.

I tried and tried to get it into my head. I imagined inside my skull, where all the weird grey coils of my brain were stuffed in tight. I thought the words IT'S NOT GOING TO HAPPEN – imagined them written in red felt tip round and round every bit of my brain. I could *see* the scarlet. I blinked my eyes quickly to make it seem as if the words were flashing on and off inside my head. I tried sooooo hard, but it didn't work.

Inside all the brain coils there was a tiny screen

for ever switched on, showing the same film over and over. I watched it on and off throughout the night, whenever I was awake. Which was a lot.

It was still playing the moment I got up. When I looked in the mirror to brush my hair, I couldn't even see myself properly. I just watched the screen inside my head.

It was Mum and Dad and me. Mum was wearing a long white dress, but not a great long flouncy affair like Mandy's. Mum's was a soft, flowing, silky princess dress, maybe with embroidery on the bodice and all round the hem. Flowers? I peered harder at the screen. No, they weren't flowers; they were little birds. Bluebirds, for luck. They circled

Mum, flapping their tiny wings, making her feel so lucky and safe and happy that she'd never ever need to run away again.

Dad was wearing a blue shirt to match, and his best grey suit, and a new blue and silver tie that I'd bought him specially because I loved him so much, and he'd never ever run away.

I was wearing a beautiful bridesmaid's dress, but it wasn't raspberry pink! I needed a brand-new bridesmaid's dress for my mum and dad's wedding. The raspberry-pink dress had been worn three times already. No, four, because Matty wore it first of all.

Mrs Michaels had made me a new bridesmaid's dress for nothing, because I'd brought her in so much new business. It was sky blue, the purest bluest blue, made of the softest silk, with such a full skirt that I needed three frilly petticoats to flounce it out properly. When I twirled round fast, the skirt and petticoats whirled right up to my waist, but it didn't matter because I had specially made sky-blue knickers to match. I wore blue shoes too, suede ones just like that funny old song Dad sometimes sang when he was happy.

I wore my silver flower necklace and my silver bracelet and my silver bangle, and Mr and Mrs

Flower and Simon and Matthew and Mandy and Ian all nodded and smiled. Mrs Flower had made Mum's wedding cake, three layers of sponge with thick cream, and white icing on top, and silver bells for decoration. Matthew gave us a set of books to take on our honeymoon. He'd let us take our pick from his shop. Mum chose a big art book, Dad had an adventure book and I picked out an old volume of fairy stories and they all ended happily ever after.

Mandy didn't give us anything, perhaps because she was still a bit mad at me for being on television for three minutes when she was only on for twenty seconds. I timed us both.

Mrs Michaels and Melissa and Marty were there, waving. Marty and Matty were chatting away together, but I didn't mind, because I knew Matty was my best friend for ever, with Lewis second. And I liked Marty so much now that I decided she could be my third best friend. Cathy and Amanda were bumped right down to joint fourth. They were there – my entire class was there. Miss Hope was there too, and that was the only worrying part, because I wanted her to have a happy ending too. She was smiling and waving at us, but I could see she was really sad.

I wished for a moment that Dad came from one of those cultures where a man can have two wives. He could have Mum as his best wife for ever and Miss Hope as his second-best wife. Then I could have two mums, and that would be magic, because at least one would be there all the time.

I wanted to draw the wedding. My hand itched to start the moment I'd had breakfast, but Dad was hovering, keeping an eye on me. I knew it would upset him if I drew my fantasy Mum-and-Dad wedding. I wondered about drawing a bride and groom and bridesmaid with no features, pretending it was just an imaginary wedding, but Dad wasn't daft.

I could draw Mandy and Ian's wedding, but surprisingly it hadn't been as much fun as I'd hoped, even with the television people. It just seemed too much of a bother to try to reproduce everything, and if I did all six bridesmaids and the two matrons of honour, I'd use up all the ink in my pink felt tip.

So I didn't draw at all. I just fiddled around with the felt tips in their big tin, arranging them in different colour combinations and then running my finger up and down them, playing them like a musical instrument.

Dad put down his Sunday newspaper. He hadn't really been concentrating on it anyway.

'Let's do something together,' he said. 'We could . . . go to the zoo?'

'I don't think I like zoos any more,' I said.

'OK. Then how about a walk in the park?'

I shrugged.

'Tell you what, I'll take you swimming!'

'But you don't really like swimming, Dad. Not like Mum,' I said. I wished I hadn't said it the moment the words were out of my mouth.

'We could ring up Matty and her family and see if they want to go,' said Dad.

'They don't go swimming on Sundays. They have a big family roast lunch – chicken or roast beef with Yorkshire pudding, and a real homemade pudding too, sometimes at their house, sometimes at their granny's,' I said.

'Well, tell you what, why don't we whizz out to Sainsbury's and get all the stuff for a *little* family roast lunch. We can choose whatever we want,' said Dad.

'But we always have pizza on Sundays,' I said.

'So we'll have a change and go for a roast.'

'But we don't know how to cook it.'

'We'll work it out. I can look up recipes on the internet. We'll have a real cooking session. Let's give it a go, Tilly,' said Dad.

He looked so eager that I said yes, even though I didn't really fancy shopping or cooking, not just the two of us. I so badly wanted it to be the three of us. I seemed to have forgotten how to be happy all over again.

We went round Sainsbury's together. It took ages, because Dad kept asking me what I wanted and I couldn't really decide. It was especially hard deciding on which roast, because they all looked so horrid. The chickens were all white and pimply and the beef was much too red and raw.

'All food looks weird raw,' said Dad. 'Come on, decision time, Miss Tilly Andrews.'

'Well, I think I like chicken best, but I also love Yorkshire pudding, so maybe the beef,' I said, dithering.

'We'll have chicken *and* we'll make Yorkshire puddings,' said Dad.

'Are they supposed to go together?' I asked doubtfully.

'Who cares? If we want them together, then that's fine. Now, veg. And some potatoes so we can roast them. You put your thinking cap on and decide what pudding you'd like.'

'Well, my favourite's banoffee pie.'

'Then that's what we'll go for. I'll look up the recipe on my phone to see what ingredients we need,' said Dad. 'Bananas, obviously, but I'm not sure about the other stuff.'

'We've only just had that at Mandy's wedding,' I pointed out.

'So we'll have it again. There are no rules that say we can't have banoffee pie every single day for the rest of our lives.'

'Promise?' I said, though I knew Dad was only joking.

He was trying so hard to make everything fun, though perhaps deep inside he felt as flat as I did. But I cheered up a little and tried hard too – and when we got home and started unpacking everything and assembling recipes and putting on tea towels as aprons, it really did start to be fun.

I left the chicken to Dad, especially when it came to pulling out its innards and stuffing it. He prepared the vegetables too, because we didn't have a proper peeler and he wouldn't let me use the sharp knife. But *I* did the pudding all by myself.

It was easy peasy. I crushed up a
lot of biscuits and put them in a
tin. I sliced bananas, and poured
a tin of special caramel over
them. I whipped all the cream
and spread that on, and
then I crumbled a chocolate
flake into little bits and
sprinkled that on top. My
arm ached from all the
crushing and whipping, but it was totally worth it.

'Pop your banoffee pie in the fridge to chill it,
and then you can get started on the Yorkshires,'
said Dad.

They were quite easy too, though my arm ached
all over again beating the eggs and flour and
milk together. There was a lot of washing-up to do
afterwards. When you have a takeaway pizza,
there isn't any washing-up at all. But we turned
the washing-up into a game, singing the names of
all the plates and pots and pans in great trills, as
if we were opera stars.

'Here is a p-l-a-a-a-t-e, *cara mia!*' Dad sang,
gesturing wildly.

'T-h-a-a-a-n-k you, oh, my papa!' I sang back,
flapping my tea towel with a flourish.

The chicken started to smell very good in the oven. Much better than pizza.

'Let's set the table properly. You shouldn't eat a proper roast meal on a tray,' said Dad.

I laid out knives and forks and spoons on the kitchen table, like in a restaurant. I polished two glasses. We didn't have any fancy napkins, but I carefully folded two pieces of kitchen towel to use instead.

'They have flowers in restaurants,' I said. 'But we haven't got any vases – or flowers either.'

'We could use a jam jar,' said Dad. 'And if you run out into the front garden, you could pick some of our flowers.'

'We haven't got proper flowers in our garden,' I said.

'OK, OK, so I'm not a very diligent gardener. But you could cut some lavender off the bush, and then there's all that purple creeping stuff – that would look quite pretty in a jar,' said Dad.

'Yes!'

I got the scissors and ran down the hall and out of the door. We only had a very small garden at the front, and the back was mostly yard and my old trampoline. But Dad was right – the lavender and the little purple flowers looked good together, and I picked some of the taller daisies in the grass.

When I straightened up, I saw that there was a lady watching me from the pavement. She had long black hair and very red lips and a big black dress and purple boots. I loved the way she looked. I didn't know her but she looked strangely familiar.

'Tills?' she said.

I dropped all the flowers I'd just picked. I nearly fell on the grass myself. It was Mum! But it couldn't be Mum. Mum had dark-blonde hair and she didn't wear red lipstick and she was very thin. This lady was very large underneath her dress.

'Oh, Tills, don't you recognize me?' she said.

It *was* Mum, but she looked so different that she seemed like a stranger. She *was* a stranger, yet she still had Mum's voice. But when she held out her arms, I ran straight into them, and when I was pressed against her, I smelled her wonderful rosy perfume and knew it really *was* Mum.

'That's my girl,' said Mum, sounding choked.

When I looked up, she had tears in her eyes. 'My Tilly,' she said.

'Are you my actual real mum?' I asked.

'How many other mothers have you got then, you soppy date?'

'But you look so different!' I said, craning my neck back to have another look at her.

'Oh, my hair. Yes, I got fed up with all that mouse. I decided to dye it black. It looks more dramatic, don't you think?'

'Yes, it looks lovely,' I said, though I didn't really like it, not on her.

'Maybe you'll fancy dyeing *your* hair when you're a bit older,' said Mum, running her fingers through my mousy hair. 'Still, it looked lovely at that wedding, all curly. Shame it's gone straight already.'

'You saw me? On the television?'

'Yes, I did. I couldn't believe it was you at first. You've got much bigger!'

So had Mum, but I didn't think it would be tactful to say so.

'Then they said your name,' Mum went on. 'And I just burst into tears. My little girl, all grown up and a bridesmaid on the television.'

'Did you like my bridesmaid's dress?'

'Well, I'm not that keen on pink, but you did look very pretty in it.'

'It's not ordinary pink – it's raspberry pink,' I said. 'Oh, Mum, I just *knew* you'd see me on the television and come and find me.'

'It took some doing. I drove to the old house and the people there said you'd moved nearly a year ago.'

'We couldn't tell you because we didn't know where *you* lived. I thought you were abroad somewhere,' I said.

'Well, I was. For a bit. I've been all over the place. And I came back to see you, lots and lots of times – don't you remember?'

Three times. Was that lots? Didn't *she* remember properly?

'I was always thinking of you, Tills. Sometimes it practically drove me mad. You mean the world to me. You know that, don't you?'

'And you mean the world to me too,' I said, clinging to her. 'Oh, Mum, you are real, aren't you? I'm not just making you up? Sometimes I make you up so that it *is* almost real. And this is so exactly the way I've been imagining it would be. Oh, come and see Dad. He'll be so happy to see you!'

'Will he?' said Mum. 'But hasn't he got a new lady now?'

'Oh, Mum, as if! Come on!' I grabbed her by the hand and pulled her up the path and through the front door. 'Dad, Dad, Dad! We've got a surprise visitor! And look who it is!'

'Sarah?' called Dad from the kitchen.

'Sarah!' said Mum, raising her eyebrows. 'Oh! So that's her name.'

'Mum, she's just my teacher,' I said quickly. I felt a bit queasy as I said it. Miss Hope was far more than just a teacher. But I didn't want to explain about her to Mum, just in case it spoiled things. Not when all my dreams had come true at last. I still couldn't believe it.

I knew you were supposed to pinch yourself if you thought you were dreaming. As Mum followed me down the hallway, I nipped at my wrist where it was stick-thin, digging my nails in so that it really hurt. It wasn't a dream. It was all really happening.

'It's Mum, Dad,' I called, because I was worried he wouldn't recognize her either.

He came to the kitchen door. Then he stood totally still, staring at Mum. I waited for the bells to chime, the birds to start singing, the air to be thick with little cherubs with wings. But Mum and Dad didn't embrace, didn't kiss, didn't even say anything. They just stood there, looking at each other.

Dad swallowed so hard I could hear it. 'So I assume you saw Tilly on the television?' he said eventually.

'Yes, quite by chance. I don't even usually watch the London Local news. You should have told me,' said Mum.

'How, exactly, when I don't have a clue where you're living?' said Dad. 'So I take it you live in the London area now?'

'North London. I've done quite a bit of driving around this morning, trying to find you both,' said Mum. 'But here I am now. And something smells good. Can I come to lunch?'

'Oh, Mum, it's like we knew! We never bother cooking on a Sunday, but today we're doing a proper roast. I did the Yorkshire puddings and I've made a banoffee pie all by myself, look!'

I ran to the fridge and pulled out the plate of pie. My hands were trembling. The plate was cold and I lost my grasp of it. In terrible slow-motion moment I saw it tilt in the air, and then my banoffee pie slid over the side and cascaded onto the floor like a clotted waterfall.

'Oh, my pie!' I cried, and burst into tears.

'Oh, Tilly,' said Dad, moving towards me – but Mum got there first.

'Poor old Tills,' she said, and she sat on a kitchen chair, pulling me up onto her lap. 'There now, darling, it was only a silly old pudding. We can make another. Don't cry so.'

But I couldn't stop crying now I'd started. I sobbed and sobbed, leaning against Mum's soft bulk, while she patted me on the back and made little hushing noises. It brought back so many memories that I was stuck, unable to stop. I could hear Mum and Dad talking to each other, but their voices were muffled. All I could hear was my ugly gulping cries and the voice in my head going *Mum-Mum-Mum*.

'Here, Tilly, drink this,' said Dad, giving me a glass of cold water. He put my hot hands round the cool glass and made me drink.

I hiccupped at first, and could barely swallow, but he made me keep on sipping until the sobs died away.

'There now,' said Mum. 'That's better. What was the pudding anyway?' She peered at the horrible slop on the floor. 'It smells of bananas. Well, that's OK, because I can't stand bananas.'

'It was banoffee pie, Tilly's favourite,' said Dad, getting down on his hands and knees with a big spoon and cloth and bowl, attempting to clean it up.

'Rubbish!' said Mum. 'Tilly's favourite is *my* favourite, strawberries and cream. Isn't it, Tills?'

'Well . . . it used to be,' I mumbled.

Not long after Mum left us Dad had given me a very big bowl of strawberries as a special treat, with lots of whipped cream on top. I'd bolted them down and then I was almost immediately sick all down myself. I've never been able to face strawberries since.

I couldn't help feeling a bit sick now, especially as the chicken smelled so strongly.

'Just got to pop to the bathroom,' I muttered, wriggling off Mum's lap.

I made a bolt for it, terrified of being sick in front of Mum. I wasn't properly sick, though a lot of nasty liquid came into my mouth and I had to keep spitting it out. I looked in the bathroom mirror afterwards and nearly died. I looked absolutely terrible – bright red in the face, and red in the eyes too. I had a disgustingly runny nose!

I mopped at myself frantically and tried brushing my hair, winding it round and round my finger to try to make it go curly again.

'Tilly? Are you all right?' Dad called softly, from outside the bathroom door.

'Yep, fine, Dad,' I said quickly. 'Sorry I was such a baby. Just coming!'

I rushed out of the bathroom. Mum wasn't in the kitchen. I felt sick all over again.

'Where's Mum? She hasn't gone already, has she? Is it because I was so stupid?' I gabbled.

'No, no, calm down, lovey. Mum's just having a little wander around,' said Dad.

'Oh thank goodness! Oh, Dad, isn't it weird? I just *knew* Mum would come back – and it's all because of my bridesmaid's dress! It's the most wonderful magic dress in the whole world. This is the happiest day of my life. Isn't it yours too?' I said, hanging onto his hand.

'Darling, I know you're happy to see Mum, but—'

'Happy-happy-happy!' I shouted quickly. I didn't want to hear him say anything else. Especially not any sentence with a 'but' in it. I pulled my hand away and ran to find Mum.

She was upstairs in my bedroom, actually sitting on my bed. She was cuddling Blue Bunny.

'Oh, darling! Here's dear old Stripy,' she said, rubbing her cheek against Blue Bunny's ears.

I stared at her. How could she possibly mistake Blue Bunny for Stripy? Blue Bunny was twice the size, with long ears and a fluffy tail. I didn't even *have* Blue Bunny when Mum lived with us at the old house.

I opened my mouth to point this out, but thought better of it. I didn't want Mum to think I was arguing with her. I sat down slightly awkwardly on the bed, right beside her, wanting us to be as close as possible.

'Ooh, don't squash me!' Mum said in a baby voice, making Blue Bunny's head bob about in an unnerving way.

I remembered I used to love it when Mum made my toys talk. But now it seemed peculiar, especially as she had given him the wrong sort of voice. I smiled politely all the same and eased along the bed a little.

'Sorry,' said Mum. 'Are you a bit old for babyish stuff now? I can't believe how much you've grown up in just a few months!'

Eighteen months. Maybe twenty.

'But you're still my little girl?' Mum asked.

'Of course I am,' I said quickly.

'I've missed you so, my little Tills,' said Mum.

Then why didn't you come and see me more?

I didn't say it out loud, but she seemed to hear the words inside my head.

'It's been . . . complicated,' she said. 'And I've moved around a lot. And I've been ill, actually.'

'Did you have chicken pox? I did, just before we moved here,' I said. 'I've still got scars on my tummy because I scratched them.'

'Poor baby. No, I was more sick in the head. You know, I went a bit bonkers. *Probably* because I was missing you.'

'And Dad?'

'Yes, and your dad too,' said Mum. 'But I needn't have worried so. You two seem absolutely fine and you've made a lovely new life together.'

'Well, it *is* lovely now you've come back,' I said.

'Oh, Tilly, don't. You'll make me cry.' Mum got a mirror out of her handbag and dabbed at her eyes. Then she put a fresh smear of scarlet on her lips. 'Want to try some?' she said, offering me the lipstick.

'Yes, please!'

'Hold still then,' said Mum, and she turned my ordinary mouth into a startlingly bright cupid's bow. 'There now!'

'Doesn't it look a bit funny on me?' I asked anxiously.

'Don't you like my lipstick then?'

'On you, yes, it looks lovely.'

'I thought I needed a bit of brightening up. My face looks so pale now I've dyed my hair black.'

'Do you remember Aunty Sylvie? She's got blue hair now!' I said.

'No, it was bright pink last time I saw her. And before that she went through a weird grey phase, like she was an old lady,' said Mum, laughing.

I laughed too, but my heart was thumping. So she'd obviously seen Aunty Sylvie twice this last year, or at the very least been in touch with her. She hadn't bothered to get in touch with Dad and me. Not even the quickest phone call or a one-line email.

There was a little silence. Mum bit her lip, smudging some of the scarlet gloss.

Then Dad called, 'Tilly, why don't you come and make some of those little fairy cakes for pudding? They can be cooking while we eat the chicken. It's nearly ready, and your Yorkshire puddings are rising beautifully.'

Mum raised her eyebrows. 'My, it sounds as if you're a clever little cook now. I can't cook for toffee. Who's been teaching you? This school-teacher friend?'

'No, Mrs Flower. I was her bridesmaid. She's like my granny,' I said.

'Don't be silly. Your granny lives in Spain,' said Mum.

'Yes, I know, but I don't see her, and my other granny's dead, so I've got Mrs Flower now and she's lovely. Come and watch me make cakes, Mum. I'll let you lick the bowl if you like – that's the best bit,' I said, grabbing Mum's hand and pulling her to the door.

She stood up and rubbed her back. For a moment she looked quite old, a plump dark-haired stranger – but then she started doing that funny Dorothy dance from *The Wizard of Oz*, singing the song about follow, following the yellow brick road all the way along the landing and down the stairs.

She sat at the kitchen table and did a little sketch of the room while I made the cake mixture and Dad cooked the vegetables. It was so cosy, all of us busy. I willed the kitchen clock to stop ticking so that we could stay trapped there for ever, drawing and stirring and cooking, my family.

Dad carved the chicken and dished up the roast potatoes and the beans and carrots and my lovely golden Yorkshire puddings. I put my cakes in the oven and then we all sat down to eat at the table. Dad had to open the window because it had got so hot and steamy, and it was as if he'd let some of the happiness out because he started asking questions as we ate.

'So where are you living now, Laura?' he said, with a little edge to his voice.

No, Dad. Don't ask. It doesn't matter. Mum's living here *now.*

'Oh, the other side of London.'

'And are you still painting?'

'Not so much. I'm designing more. Wallpapers, stationery, stuff like that.'

'We've got your paintings stored away in the attic if you want them.'

'Not really. They were all a bit dark and intense. I'm in a happy place now,' said Mum.

'Well, good for you.'

We ate silently for a minute.

'Tilly's very good at drawing now,' said Dad.

'Are you? Show me, darling,' said Mum.

'Well, let her finish her chicken first.'

'Oh, Tills, I can't wait to see them!' said Mum.

I slid off my chair and ran to get my drawing pad from upstairs. Then I leaned against Mum as she turned the pages, pointing and remarking every so often. She smiled at all the wedding pictures. She didn't seem to notice that she was very often the bride. Surprisingly, Mum liked the monster drawings most of all.

'I didn't know you had such an amazing imagination, Tills. These are really, really good,' she said.

'Do you really think so, Mum? No one else likes my monsters.'

'Well, I do. Here, I'll swop you this monster picture here for my sketch. Is that a bargain?' Mum asked.

'You bet!' I gave her the monster picture and held out my hand. Mum's sketch was much better than anything I could do. There was Dad with his back to us, standing at the stove. She'd drawn it so that steam seemed to be coming out of his head, not just from the boiling pots. She'd drawn me at the front of the picture, making my cakes, stirring the mixture earnestly with my hair in my eyes.

'But you haven't drawn yourself too, Mum!' I protested.

'Well, I can't see myself, can I? Not if I'm sketching,' she said.

'Couldn't you add yourself into the picture even so?' I said.

'All right, give it back then.' Mum drew a rectangle round her sketch, making it like a page in a book, and then she added a pen held by a hand. 'There, that's me, drawing us,' she said, pointing to the hand.

'I wanted all of you in the picture,' I said.

'Eat your chicken, Tilly. It's getting stone cold,' said Dad.

'You're saving yourself for your cakes, aren't you, Tills?' said Mum, winking at me. 'Me too!'

She scraped all her chicken and vegetables to one side of her plate, but picked up her Yorkshire pudding and nibbled at it. 'Mmm, delicious,' she said. 'Pudding and cakes, that's what a girl likes.'

'Very nutritious. You're a great example to Tilly,' said Dad sarcastically.

I fidgeted uncomfortably. I didn't know whether to leave my chicken too and eat the Yorkshire pudding, copying Mum – or whether to carry on eating properly. I didn't really feel like eating anything. My tummy felt as if it were shut.

'I'd better check my cakes. I don't want them to burn,' I said quickly.

They were pale gold and looking perfect. 'Just right!' I said, reaching for a tea towel to take them out.

'Watch out. Use the oven gloves and mind your arms on the bars of the oven. Here, better let me do it,' said Dad.

'Oh, don't fuss so. Tills can do it herself, can't you? You're practically grown up now, aren't you, darling?' said Mum.

I hovered, not knowing whether to try to take the cakes out myself or not. Dad handed me the oven gloves and let me do it myself, but his hand was over mine, just in case. I needed his help because I'd gone a bit trembly. It wasn't quite the way I'd imagined. Mum and Dad weren't exactly arguing but they weren't acting all lovey-dovey either.

'I'm going to ice my cakes and then I'll decorate them. I'll put little pink hearts on them,' I said.

'Better let them cool down a bit first,' Dad muttered.

'They'll be cool enough by the time she's made the icing,' said Mum. 'Come on, Tills, let's do it together.'

Mum poured icing sugar into a bowl. She was a bit careless and clouds of white sugar rose in the air, like a tiny snowstorm. She just giggled.

'Let's add a few drops of lemon juice to the water, to stop it being overly sweet,' said Mum. 'There, I know all about baking too, Tills. Let's get stirring then.'

Mum had a turn, and then, when the icing sugar stopped being so stiff, she handed the spoon to me.

'You have a go now. That's my girl. Stir, stir, stir. And you can make a wish if you like.'

I closed my eyes to make my wish, the most important wish in the world.

'Stop it, Laura!' Dad said, so sharply it made me jump. 'You know very well what she's wishing.'

'She can wish for anything she wants,' said Mum.

'But it's not going to happen, is it?'

'Yes it is! I'm going to make sure I see Tilly lots and lots now. In fact, I'm going to have her to stay with me sometimes.'

'No, Mum! You stay *here*,' I said. 'With Dad and me.'

'Well, it would be a bit squashed, wouldn't it, if your dad's going to marry this girlfriend of his,' said Mum.

'I *said*, he hasn't got any girlfriend.'

'Then how are you going to be his bridesmaid? You said it last night on television!'

'But that's when Dad marries *you*,' I said.

Mum stared at me. 'But of course *I* can't marry your dad! Come on, Tills, you're not a baby. Surely you understand the situation? Don't look so upset. I meant what I said – you can come and stay with me sometimes, especially when your sister's born.'

'My *sister*?' I had to hold onto the edge of the table to stop myself falling.

'I had a scan so I know it's a little girl,' said Mum.

It felt as if I'd breathed in all the icing sugar. I was so choked I could hardly speak. 'You're going to have a baby?'

'Oh, darling, surely you realized? I'm eight months gone and starting to look like a tank,' said Mum, patting her tummy.

I stared at her. I stared at Dad. For one mad moment I thought Mum and Dad were having another baby together in spite of everything, and we could still be a proper family – Mum, Dad, the new baby and me.

'Oh, Dad!' I said.

Dad looked at me very sadly. 'It's not my baby, Tilly,' he said gently.

'Oh!'

'Don't give me that old-fashioned look, Tills!' said Mum. 'It's all perfectly legitimate! Tim and I even got married.'

The room was swirling round and round. It seemed to have spun me into a new terrifying world where nothing made sense.

'You got *married*?'

Mum shrugged. 'Yep.'

'But I thought you never wanted to get married!' I said.

'I know, I know. I didn't even plan it. But we were on holiday, staying with Tim's folks in the Caribbean, and it just suddenly seemed a lovely romantic idea to have a beach wedding,' said Mum.

'Did you have a long white wedding dress and a veil?' I whispered.

'No, I wore a silk sarong, with flowers in my hair,' said Mum. She searched in her bag and brought out her mobile phone. 'Here, want to see?'

I stood beside her, my fists clenched.

331

Mum flicked through photos hurriedly. 'Ah, here we are!'

I stared at the photo. The sun was just setting, casting a pink glow over everyone on the beach. There was Mum, her new black hair threaded with pink and yellow flowers, wearing a loose silky dress, her feet bare on the sand. There was this Tim, a foolish-looking man wearing white shorts with a white shirt flapping in the breeze. And there was a girl about my age in a matching silk dress holding a posy of pink and yellow flowers.

I pointed to her, suddenly unable to speak.

'That's Maya, Tim's little niece,' said Mum.

'Your bridesmaid?' I croaked.

'Well, yes. Oh, Tills darling, I'd have much preferred to have you as my bridesmaid, of course I would, but you weren't there,' said Mum.

Why didn't you invite me? Why didn't you tell me you were getting married to someone else? Why didn't you think of me? Why didn't you ever come and see me? Why did you have to wait until you saw me on television?

I didn't ask any questions out loud. I could see there wasn't any point. I hardly said another word as I spread the icing on my cakes. Dad was right: they hadn't cooled down enough. The icing went all runny, and when I tried to stick the hearts on they slipped sideways. My cakes looked a mess.

'Oooh, delicious!' said Mum and ate one straight away, gobbling it down and then licking her shiny red lips. 'Aren't you having one, Tills?'

I knew if I ate a cake I'd probably be sick. 'I'm a bit full up,' I mumbled, though I'd hardly eaten anything.

'Oh well, I'll have another, seeing as I'm eating for two,' said Mum. 'And then what shall we do? Shall we all play a game together? Or watch a favourite film. *I* know, let's watch *Frozen* and sing along.'

So that's what we did, even though I'd long ago stopped being obsessed by *Frozen*. I didn't sing either. Neither did Dad. But Mum did, remembering nearly all the words. She even did the right gestures. She laughed when she saw me watching her.

'See, I remember everything,' she said.

It was as if she'd frozen me in time. She didn't really know anything about me now. And I didn't know anything about this dyed-haired red-lipped stranger mum who had a baby under her black dress who was half my sister.

'Why did you leave me, Mum?' I asked as the credits rolled on the film.

333

Dad switched the DVD off. The room was very quiet. I could hear the sound of my own breathing.

'I didn't leave *you*, Tills. I left your dad,' said Mum. 'It just . . . wasn't working between us any more. I felt so trapped.'

'But why didn't you take me with you?'

'Well, I thought about it. I wanted to. But – but I thought it would be kinder to you to let you stay with Dad. He's not so up and down as me. I knew he'd look after you well.' She looked at him. 'You've done a good job, Michael,' she said.

Dad just nodded. He was looking at me worriedly.

'But you could have come to see me more.'

'I *did*. At first.'

'So why did you stop? Why wouldn't you let me know where you were? Why couldn't I even phone you?' I was heaving the words out now, as if I were being sick. I couldn't choke them back.

'Oh, darling, don't get so upset. I thought it was for the best,' said Mum. She got up and tried to put her arms round me, but I struggled away from her this time.

'I missed you so,' I said.

'And I missed you, Tills, terribly. But I thought it best not to keep on coming back because it was so painful for both of us.' Mum was nearly crying

334

now. She dabbed at her eyes, careful of her black eyeliner. 'And, you see, I was right. We're both getting upset. I think I'd better go now. I'll call a cab.'

She waited, perhaps hoping I'd argue with her. I clamped my lips together. I curled up very tight on the chair, my arms wrapped round my legs, my head resting on my knees. I shut my eyes too.

I stayed like that while Mum called her cab, and then she and Dad made awkward conversation. They weren't getting at each other now. They were careful with each other, Dad patiently answering all Mum's questions about my new school and my friends and the other weddings where I'd been a bridesmaid.

'So you're not getting married after all?' asked Mum.

'No I'm not,' said Dad.

'I must admit, I was very curious to see who it was. Well, I'm sure you'll meet someone else soon. Someone who'll make you happy. I'm truly sorry it didn't work out for us. And I'm truly sorry it's been so hard on you, Tills,' said Mum.

I didn't answer her. I didn't even look at her. I shut my eyes. I wished I could shut my ears too.

Dad offered to make Mum a cup of tea while she was waiting. She accepted and also ate another of my cakes.

'Mm, delicious,' she said again.

Then she was texted to say the cab was here.

'Goodbye then.' She came and stood beside me and tried to cuddle me, but I stayed as wooden and unbending as the chair. She kissed my head instead.

I peeped as she said goodbye to Dad. They kissed too, but just on the cheek. It was hard now to imagine they were ever a couple who kissed properly. He went with her to the door. I heard it open. And then I hurled myself off my chair, stumbled, staggered out of the kitchen, down the hall, past Dad in the doorway, and along the path.

I caught Mum just as she was getting into her cab. 'Mum!'

'Oh, Tills!' Her arms went round me and we hugged as if we could never let go. But after a few seconds Mum gently unpeeled my arms and got into the car. 'Goodbye, darling. I'll come and see you soon, I promise. With your baby sister! Take care now. Love you lots.'

Then she shut the cab door and they drove off. I was left staring after her. After a while Dad came and put his hand on my shoulder and steered me back into the house. The kitchen was still thick with the smell of chicken and cakes. I ran upstairs and threw myself down on my bed.

Dad followed me. He sat on the edge of my bed and patted my back while I sobbed and sobbed. When I stopped crying and reached that awful gulpy stage, he went and got tissues and a cold flannel and mopped me up.

'She said she loved me lots,' I whispered.

'She does, of course she does,' said Dad.

'But not enough to stay.'

'She's got her new life now, Tilly. And we've got ours,' said Dad.

He was very kind and gentle for the rest of the afternoon and evening. I wasn't at all hungry, but he made me a small chicken sandwich and I nibbled at it to please him.

I couldn't settle down to anything. I tried drawing. I drew my new mum with her black hair and a tiny baby sister inside her, and her horrible new husband with a big smirk on his ugly face. Then I scribbled all over him. I scribbled all over Mum too. That meant that the baby disappeared under all the black too. I felt bad then. It wasn't the baby's fault.

I'd always wanted a sister. This one would only be my half-sister, but a half was better than none. I'd *make* Mum keep in touch so I could watch out for my sister. And if Mum ever went off and left my sister, then I'd look after her.

I drew my sister all over again. I drew her as a little girl, not a baby. But I tried too hard, giving her lovely long thick fair hair and a heart-shaped face with a big smile. She was much prettier than me, even when I was wearing my bridesmaid's dress. Mum would never dream of leaving a little girl like that.

I scribbled all over her quickly and then felt guilty. I had another little weep.

'I think you're worn out, Tilly,' said Dad. 'Come on, how about a nice hot bath and then bed? I'll read to you. Would that be nice?'

I had my bath. I got into bed. Dad came and tucked me up and then read me his old copy of *Winnie-the-Pooh*, doing all the different voices. I kept closing my eyes so he settled me down, gave me a big kiss and turned out the light.

I might have gone to sleep for a little while, but then I woke up, feeling hot and sick. For a moment

I thought Mum's visit had been a bad dream. Then I remembered it had actually happened and felt worse.

I felt for Stripy but he wasn't enough. I wanted Dad. I ran into his bedroom – he wasn't there. I saw the light on downstairs in the living room and ran downstairs.

'Tilly?' Dad called.

I burst in ready to go and jump on his lap. He was on the phone. For a second I thought it might be Mum phoning, saying she'd made a terrible mistake, that coming to see us had changed everything, and could she come back and stay with us for ever. Then it would be Mum and Dad and me and my new sister, and we could still be a family in spite of everything.

'Just a minute, Sarah,' Dad murmured into the phone. His voice was soft and warm.

Why wasn't Dad as miserable as me? Didn't he care about Mum any more? Didn't he even care about me?

I suddenly snatched the phone.

'Leave my dad alone!' I shouted into it. 'He's mine, not yours. Go away!'

Chapter Nineteen

I thought Dad would be furious with me but he simply took me back to bed and waited for me to stop crying again.

'I don't think you're really angry with Miss Hope,' he said quietly. 'I think you're angry with Mum.'

'I'm angry with all of you! I hate all grown-ups. Why do you have to make such a mess of your lives? Why can't you stay together and love each other?' I shouted into my pillow.

'I wish we could,' said Dad. 'But sometimes people change. Or they meet someone new. You were friends with Cathy and Angela when you first started your new school, and then Matty came along and you became her best friend instead.'

'Cathy and Angela didn't mind. And I'm always going to be Matty's best friend. It's not the same at all. Children are allowed to have all different friends. But mums and dads are just meant to have each other,' I said sternly.

'Yes, I know that's the way it's supposed to be. And lots and lots of couples – most of them – *do* stay together. But sadly not Mum and me,' said Dad.

'You don't even sound as if you mind much any more,' I said.

'Well, perhaps I don't. I can see that Mum and I don't really have a thing in common. Maybe we should never have got together in the first place. But I'm very glad we did, because we've got you.' Dad bent down and kissed me.

'You won't ever leave, will you, Dad?'

'Never ever.'

'Even if you and Miss Hope hook up properly?'

'Don't use that horrible expression! But even if, you'll always come first, Tilly.'

'And you don't mind that I shouted at Miss Hope on the phone?'

'Of course I mind! It was very rude and naughty of you. But I understand. Now, go to sleep. You're worn out,' said Dad.

He patted me on the back and walked to the door.

'Dad?'

'Now what?'

'Dad, what do you think Miss Hope will say to me tomorrow? Do you think she'll be very cross?'

'Well, you'll have to wait and see,' her said. 'I hope you'll say sorry to her.'

I worried about it half the night. I felt exhausted the next morning. I had a headache from all the crying and my throat felt sore and scratchy.

'I don't feel very well, Dad,' I said. 'I don't think I'd better go to school today.'

'You've got to go to school, sweetheart,' he said. He was sitting at the kitchen table, drinking a cup of coffee.

'But I'm *ill*. It's all right – you don't have to take time off work. I'll just stay in bed and go back to sleep. I'm *tired*, Dad. Look, I've got really dark circles under my eyes,' I whined.

'So you have. My daughter, the panda. Shall I ask the ladies at breakfast club to give you some eucalyptus leaves for breakfast?'

'Oh, Dad! You don't half get on my nerves sometimes,' I said, trailing off to pack my school bag. Then I ran back to him and climbed on his lap.

'What's all this? Are you still trying to get round me to stay off school?' he asked.

'Well, yes, but I also just wanted a cuddle. Dad, you don't *really* get on my nerves. I just love you. You know that, don't you?' I whispered into his neck.

'I know. And I love you – lots and lots and lots. And Mum loves you too.'

But not lots and lots and lots. Not enough to stay.

I don't care, I don't care, I don't care.

I chanted the three words over and over again as Dad drove me to school, trying to convince myself it was true. I ran straight to the canteen, lowering my head and hunching up as I passed the teachers' car park, worried in case Miss Hope had come to school early.

I had cornflakes and milk and an apple and orange juice for breakfast. I stirred the cornflakes around until they were an unpleasant sludge in the bottom of the bowl. I nibbled one side of the apple but left most of it. I only had two sips of juice.

I wanted to be left alone, but nearly all the other

children at breakfast club had seen my television interview. They all gathered round me and asked all sorts of silly questions. Even the breakfast-club ladies came and said I'd looked sweet. They wanted to know what the television reporter was really like, and one of them asked where I'd got such a beautiful bridesmaid's dress. She made me write down Marty's mum's name so she could get in touch with her. I was pleased for Marty's mum because it meant more business for her, and a little pleased for myself, because it was fun being the centre of attention.

When Matty got to school, she was all over me too.

'I texted everyone I know to tell them to watch London Local on their iPlayer because my best friend was the star of the show,' she said. 'And Lewis told everyone too. He even told people in the park when we went for a walk on Sunday. And lots of them said they'd seen you. You're *famous*, Tilly!'

'My mum saw me on television,' I said.

'Yes, I'm sure she would have done,' said Matty, slightly awkwardly.

'No, she really did. She came to see me on Sunday,'

'What? *Really?* Oh, Tilly! You're not making it up, are you?' Matty asked.

'No, she really came, Sunday morning. And we had roast chicken for lunch and we were supposed to have banoffee pie but I spilled it so I made fairy cakes instead,' I said.

'So what's the matter?'

'Nothing's the matter. I've got some of the cakes in my lunchbox. You can have one later if you like,' I said.

'Your voice is still all funny, like something bad happened.' Matty put her arm round me. 'Tell me, Tilly.'

I squeezed my eyes shut so I wouldn't start crying again. 'It wasn't the way I wanted it to be,' I said in a shaky little voice.

'Why? Wasn't your mum nice to you?'

'She was ever so nice and gave me lots of cuddles, but . . . she wasn't the way I remembered her. She doesn't even look the same. She's got fat and her hair's black now.'

'Are you sure she really *was* your mum?' asked Matty. 'She looked ever so slim in that photo in your bedroom. And fair.'

'She's dyed her hair. And she's not actually *fat* fat, she's going to have a baby.'

'A baby?' said Matty. 'What? So she and your dad have got back together then?'

'No, it's someone else's baby. Tim. He's her partner now,' I said.

'Oh,' said Matty. 'Poor you. And poor your dad too.'

'Well. He says he doesn't mind.'

'I think he's just saying that,' said Matty, her arms folded, her head on one side, trying to look worldly wise.

'No, I think he likes someone else now,' I said.

'Who?'

'Well, it's someone you know.'

'Really?' Matty wrinkled up her nose. 'Not that Aunty Sue lady, the one who used to fetch you from school?'

'*No!* Don't be daft. Look, promise you won't tell, because it's obviously a secret, but I think Dad's got a crush on Miss Hope,' I whispered.

'*Miss Hope?*'

'Ssh!' I glanced around the playground to see if anyone was within earshot. 'I said, it's a *secret.*'

'But Miss Hope's a teacher.'

'Well, she's not *Dad's* teacher, is she?'

'No, but – well, it's a bit weird. Are you sure?'

'Dad phones her up a lot at night. And when he talks to her, his voice goes different. It's all soft and happy-sounding.'

'Imagine Miss Hope and your dad kissing!' said Matty, and she started making kissing noises and squealing with laughter.

'Do shut up, Matty. It's not funny.'

'It is, it is! I'm not laughing in a mean way – I think it's great. Oh wow, what if they get married? Then you could be their bridesmaid in that pink dress!'

'Yes, well, it's not going to happen. Because I yelled down the phone at Miss Hope last night and told her to go away and leave my dad alone,' I said miserably.

'You didn't!'

'I did.'

'Tilly! So what did she say?'

'I don't know. I just ran upstairs afterwards. Oh, Matty, I don't know what to do now. Do you think she'll be really cross with me?'

'Yes! She'll probably make you stand outside with your hands on your head. She might even Sellotape your mouth up. Or she might find one of those canes from olden times and beat you with it,' said Matty. 'Don't look like that, Tilly, I'm *joking*.

No, I think she'll act all sorrowful and reproachful and say she's very disappointed in you. That's the way she was with me that time I threw the ball at Simon Perkins's head accidentally on purpose.'

'I *hate* it when she's all sorrowful and reproachful,' I said. 'What if she doesn't like me any more?'

'But you don't like her, do you? I thought you yelled at her to go away and stop seeing your dad?'

'Yes, but I don't think I really meant it,' I said.

'Oh, Tilly, you don't half do my head in. I don't get you at all sometimes,' said Matty, exasperated.

'But you *are* still my best friend?'

'Of course I am, you nutter.'

The bell sounded for the start of school.

'Oh help,' I said.

'Come on. It'll be all right, I'm sure. Just give her a big smile and hope for the best,' said Matty as we went in.

I tried to fix a smile on my face, but it went a bit wobbly as we went into the classroom. Miss Hope was there, looking just the same, her hair up, her moon earrings gleaming, her same old navy pinafore and white shirt neat and boring, her shoes flat and sturdy. She was smiling, but not especially at me.

'Good morning, everyone,' she said calmly.

'Good morn-ing, Miss Hope,' we chorused.

She took the register, calling our names. Mine was first on the list.

'Matilda Andrews?' she said. She didn't look at me – she kept her eyes on her register.

'Yes, Miss Hope,' I said, my voice a bit husky, partly from all the crying yesterday, partly from nerves.

Matilda sounded so formal and unfriendly. Though this was what Miss Hope always called me when she was taking the register. She called Matty Matilda too.

The lessons that morning went on for ever and ever. Miss Hope wandered around while we worked on our Anglo-Saxon village projects. She did actually pause and say, 'That's looking good,' to Matty and me as we wove our raffia huts, but then she drifted off and spent a good ten minutes with Cathy and Amanda.

I discussed the situation worriedly with Matty at break time.

'She hates me now. I just know she does,' I said. 'I can tell.'

'Don't be so daft. She's being ever so nice. She *is* nice. I still don't quite get why you yelled at her on the phone. If I didn't have a proper mum, I'd *like* Miss Hope to go out with my dad,' Matty said.

'I *have* got a proper mum,' I said automatically.

'Yes, but she's moved on now, hasn't she? She's going to be someone else's mum too.'

'Imagine! I never thought I'd ever have a sister. I always wanted one,' I said.

'Me too. I'll swop you Lewis for your new sister. Especially as I wouldn't have to see her heaps or share a bedroom with her,' said Matty. 'Lewis snores. Really snores, like a little old man. I feel like putting a clothes peg on his nose.'

'Poor Lewis. You're so mean to him.'

'He's mean to me! He secretly scrubbed all the ink tattoos off Princess Power and dressed her up in Mum's silk scarf with an earring in her hair for a tiara, and started calling her Princess Pretty-Face. So then I got my scissors and unstitched the mouth and eyes on his stupid cuddle bear and called him Blank-Face, and Lewis started howling and told Mum and Dad, and they got really narked with me. It was just a joke to get even with him, that's all. But now I don't get any crisps or chocolate for a whole week, not even a measly little packet of chocolate raisins for my packed lunch. And Mum sewed a much better face on Lewis's bear, with a big smile, and Lewis likes him even more, so he's ever so happy. And I'm in disgrace and starving – I've just got boring old hummus sandwiches and carrot sticks and an apple for lunch.'

'You can have cake. I've got special fairy cakes. Well, the icing melted into the cakes, but they still taste all right.'

It was a relief talking about ordinary silly things like Matty and Lewis having an argument, but all too soon we had to go back into school for lessons. We had Art, and we all looked at this picture of people in a park wearing long dark clothes. They all seemed to be huddled under umbrellas, but then I noticed that one especially pretty lady and her little girl didn't have umbrellas, though they didn't seem to be getting wet. They were staring straight at me.

We talked about the painting for a while, and then we all had to draw and colour our own picture of people in a park with umbrellas. Matty got started straight away, drawing her mum and dad and Lewis and her, all in raincoats and wellie boots, sploshing through the puddles in the park.

She drew a pond beside them, with a pair of ducks.

'And you could do a whole line of ducklings from the pond waddling along behind your family,' I suggested.

'Good idea,' said Matty. 'Why aren't you starting your picture?'

'I'm thinking . . .' I sat still for several minutes, making it up in my head. Then I drew two lines down my paper, dividing it into three.

'What are those lines for?' asked Matty.

'You'll see,' I said. Right at the left-hand side of the page I drew a lot of little people with umbrellas in pouring rain. I also drew another lady and a girl standing side by side, one dark, one fair. They were perfectly dry, smiling in a little patch of sunshine.

'That's good, Tilly. But you haven't used up the page. There's all this big gap here,' said Matty.

'Yes, because it's going to be like a comic strip,' I said. 'I'm telling a story.'

I started on the middle section next. It was much windier and the trees were being blown about crazily. All the people with umbrellas were being carried up into the sky, looking like great black birds. The lady and the little girl were still smiling away, not the slightest bit bothered.

'You're not going to have time to colour it,' said Matty, who had already started doing dark blue sky with lots of little dashes to indicate rain.

'Miss Hope didn't say we had to colour it, she just said do a picture,' I replied.

Then I started the third section. Matty saw me hesitating.

'Hurry up, the bell will go soon.'

'I don't know what to put.'

'Why don't you have the lady and the girl having a picnic? Or feeding the ducks on the pond? Or sitting on a bench together?'

'Mmm,' I said, thinking about it. But my hand started drawing all on its own. It drew the lady up in the air, her long hair flying out, her skirt whirling around her. Great black umbrella wings had grown out of the back of her bodice and carried her away. She didn't seem to mind. She had her head tipped back and she was smiling. She seemed to have forgotten all about the little girl on the ground below.

The bell went for the end of morning school.

'Come on, Tilly,' said Matty, running to collect her dinosaur lunchbox from the back of the classroom.

'I just want to finish this bit,' I said. 'I'll catch up.'

Matty hesitated. 'Oh, come now. We've got to bag the best table together.'

'You save a place for me,' I said, drawing rapidly.

'You know we're not allowed to save places,' said Matty. 'All right then, but don't blame me if Cathy and Amanda get there first.'

She went off in a slight huff. The classroom emptied. Soon there was just Miss Hope at her desk and me. I wished Miss Hope would go off to the staffroom but she stayed where she was. I hated being trapped there with her, but she wasn't even looking at me. So I carried on drawing.

I drew my girl staring up at the lady as she flew away. The girl's mouth was open, as if she were shouting. I drew little black dots for tears down her cheeks. I sat there, staring at my drawing.

I barely noticed Miss Hope standing up and walking over to me. She felt in her pinafore pocket and brought out a clean tissue.

'Here, Tilly,' she said softly.

I realized I was crying a little bit too. I scrubbed at my eyes with the tissue and then blew my nose. I didn't know what to do with the soggy tissue so I tucked it up my sleeve. Miss Hope wasn't looking at me. She was looking at my picture.

'It's very good, Tilly,' she said. 'Do you want to start colouring it now?'

'No. I don't want it to look too bright. Is it all right if I leave it black and white?' I asked.

'Of course it is,' said Miss Hope. 'You're absolutely right. It looks much starker like this.'

'What does stark mean?'

'Severe. Sad.'

'Oh.'

'I think you're sad, Tilly,' said Miss Hope, sitting down beside me on Matty's chair.

'A bit,' I said. I bent my head. 'And does severe mean cross?'

'It can do.'

'Then I was very severe with you last night, on the phone,' I whispered. 'I'm sorry.'

'It's all right. I understand, I truly do.'

'I wasn't really cross with you. It was just that my mum came round yesterday. We had Sunday lunch together, and it should have been lovely, but it wasn't. And Dad wasn't really very friendly to her, and I thought that if perhaps he wasn't friends with you, he might have tried harder and then Mum would have stayed – but I can see that was silly. Mum wouldn't stay, no matter what. She just came because of the bridesmaid thing. I was on television, Miss Hope!'

'I know. I saw you. You and your dress looked lovely,' she said.

'That's why Mum came. She saw me too. I thought she might still be abroad, but she lives in London now. Though it's still quite far away. She says she's going to come and see me lots now.'

'That's good,' said Miss Hope.

'But she might forget,' I said.

'Perhaps,' she said cautiously.

I sighed. Miss Hope patted my shoulder. We sat for a little while in silence.

'Hadn't you better go and have your lunch, Tilly?' Miss Hope suggested.

'Oh, lunch.' I got up and fetched my lunchbox. I unsnapped it. I had a lemon drink, a chicken sandwich, a clementine, and two fairy cakes with dribbly icing and little pink hearts. 'Would you like a fairy cake, Miss Hope?' I said, offering her the box. 'I made them all by myself.'

'I'd love one,' she said. 'But you've only got two. One for Matty and one for you.'

'I don't really want one. And there's more at home anyway. You have it. It's my saying-sorry cake for you,' I said.

'Then I'll say thank you very much,' said Miss Hope, helping herself. She took a bite. 'Mmm, delicious!'

'My friend Mrs Flower is teaching me how to bake. We're going to do cheesecake next, which will be super yummy. When I can make cheesecake, could you come to tea?' I said.

'I'd like that very much,' said Miss Hope. 'But perhaps we'd better check that it's all right with your dad.'

'You know he'd like it too!' I said.

'And would *you* really like it, Tilly?' asked Miss Hope, taking another bite.

'Yes, of course I would,' I said.

'Then that should be fine,' said Miss Hope. 'Perhaps we'll be a little discreet about this, mm?'

I nodded. 'It's a secret,' I promised.

It was definitely a secret and I didn't tell a soul – except for Matty. You tell your best friend forever *all* your secrets. And I didn't tell her at school, where anyone could be eavesdropping. I told her when we were at her house after school, playing Warrior Princesses with Lewis. Little brothers of best friends can hear secrets too.

'Oh wow!' said Matty. 'Then maybe you really will be your dad's bridesmaid!'

'*If* they get married,' I said.

'And you wouldn't mind?'

'I think I'd like it.'

'So your teacher would turn into your mum then?' said Lewis.

'No, because I've got a mum already. Miss Hope would be like a friend-aunty,' I told him.

'If only it didn't mean wearing an awful frilly dress, I'd like to be a bridesmaid too when Miss Hope marries your dad,' said Matty.

'And me,' said Lewis.

'Don't be daft – boys can't be bridesmaids,' said Matty. 'Boys don't wear dresses!'

'Yes they do! Dad read us a story about a boy in a frock. *Two* stories,' said Lewis.

'That's just stories, stupid.' Matty bashed him with her Princess Powerful.

Lewis tried to smother her with his biggest bear. They started rolling around the floor, giggling and squealing.

'Stop fighting, you two. There probably won't be any wedding at all,' I said.

'Do you think your dad's really serious about her?'

'I'm not sure. I *think* so,' I said. 'I'll sound him out tonight.'

So on the way home in the car I told Dad I'd given Miss Hope one of my cakes and that I'd said sorry for shouting at her on the phone.

'That's good,' said Dad.

'She likes my cakes,' I said. 'She wants to come to tea some time when I've made some more.'

'She said that, did she?'

'Well, sort of. I invited her and she said yes.'

'Right,' said Dad.

'That's OK, isn't it?'

'Of course it is.'

'You like Miss Hope, don't you, Dad?' I asked as we parked the car outside our house.

'I like her very much,' said Dad.

'A *lot*?'

'Tilly, quit badgering me,' he said, but he was smiling as we went up the path to our front door.

Dad put his key in the lock and let us in. He put on the kettle and then switched on his iPad. I walked up and down the hall, swishing an imaginary bridesmaid's dress.

'I love weddings,' I said dreamily. 'Dad, are you listening?'

'Mmm,' he said, reading his messages.

'Do you think I'll ever get to be a bridesmaid again?' I asked, hinting heavily.

'I'd say a definite yes to that,' said Dad.

'*Really?* So you're going to marry Miss Hope?'

'No, I didn't say that at all! It's early days yet. Much too soon to think about marriage. Good heavens, we haven't really gone out together properly yet! We'll just have to wait and see,' said Dad.

'But you said I'd definitely get to be a bridesmaid again.'

'I know. Come and look at this message from London Local. Apparently they've been inundated with emails, all wanting to get hold of you. Half the people London seem to want to rent you as their bridesmaid!' said Dad.

There were at least twenty requests for me to choose from! My bridesmaid's dress would be worn to shreds by the time Dad and Miss Hope made up their minds to get married. And I'd have grown a bit too.

So let's end this story with another dress. Not any old dress. Not a checked school dress or a pinafore dress or a party dress or a princess dress. This is a bridesmaid's dress.

But it's not raspberry pink. It's maybe sky-blue silk, patterned with white embroidered daisies, with white petticoats as fluffy as clouds. Or perhaps it's lilac satin, reaching right down to the ground, like a proper evening dress, and I'll wear purple sparkly shoes with real heels. Or perhaps it's a winter wedding and my bridesmaid's dress will be soft red velvet with a little white fur bolero. Whichever I choose, it will definitely be the most beautiful bridesmaid's dress in the world.

Tilly's Wonderful Wedding Facts

The Guinness World Record for the most guests at a wedding stands at 150,000! The guests were hosted by Jayalalitha Jayaram at her son's wedding in Madras, India, in 1995. The record for the biggest bridal party is held by Nisansala and Nalin, a Sri Lankan couple who, on their wedding in 2013, had 126 bridesmaids, 25 best men, 23 flower girls and 20 page boys.

Around 240,000 people attended the Wedding Dresses exhibition at London's Victoria and Albert Museum in 2014 and 2015. The exhibition took two weeks to put in place, and six people were required to install one dress, designed by Norman Hartnell, due to its 5.5m-long train!

It is thought that the tradition of exchanging wedding rings was created by the Ancient Egyptians. Rings are worn on the third finger as people believed that finger contained a blood vessel which went straight to the heart, the loveliest internal organ.

One of the world's most famous gowns is the wedding dress worn by Lady Diana Spencer when she married Charles, Prince of Wales, in 1981. The dress was designed by David and Elizabeth Emanuel, who knew it was going to be a global sensation. They even created a back-up dress which Diana was to wear if details of the main dress had been revealed before the big day.

Queen Victoria is credited with making white the colour of choice for bridal gowns in Europe. The dress she wore to marry Prince Albert in 1840 is now in storage at Kensington Palace. It is not the only item to have survived from her big day – a slice of the huge wedding cake (it weighed about 140kg!), which was boxed as a gift for a guest, is still owned by a London collector, and was displayed at Christie's auction house in 2014!

Make Your Own Wedding Favours!

Unlike Tilly, you may not have a calendar bulging with weddings to attend, but that doesn't mean you can't have all the fun of the party! Follow the instructions below to make wedding-style favours, which you can enjoy whether or not there's a bride and groom in the room!

1. Copy or trace the template onto sheets of stiff paper or card. Cut out carefully with scissors – you might need help from a grown-up – and use a hole punch to make two holes over the dots as indicated. Use pencils, paint or felt pens to decorate your cut-outs any way you like – you may even want to use glitter!

2. When you're happy with your decorations and your cut-outs are completely dry, apply glue to the strip to the left of the dotted line. Making sure there isn't a hole at the bottom, twist your cones into shape, pressing down on the glued strip to seal them.

3. When the glue is completely dry, thread ribbon or string through the holes to make a handle.

4. Fill your cones with delicious treats – sugared
almonds are traditional for wedding favours,
but you can use whatever you like – raisins,
popcorn or gummy sweets! Now all that's left
to do is share the beautifully packaged
favours with your friends!

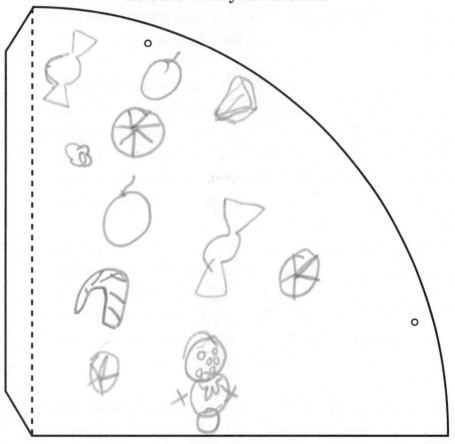

Design Your Own Bridesmaid's Dress

Tilly has designed countless bridesmaid's dresses – and you can too! Trace or decorate the template below to create the bridesmaid's dress of your dreams.

Spot the Difference

There are eight differences between the two pictures below – can you spot them all?

Miss Hope's Quiz

What's Aunty Sue's favourite treat?

cupcakes

What colour are Matty's special
sparkly trainers?

blue

What's the name of Marty's
homemade snake creation?

What flavour cake do Tilly
and her dad take to the lido?

What kind of flowers does
Mr Flowers bring to Iris to say sorry?

Which delicious dessert does Tilly
enjoy at Simon and Matthew's wedding?

What's the name of the school where
Simon is the headteacher?

What does Mandy demand Tilly get
replaced on her bridesmaid's dress?

How long is Tilly's TV interview?

What cake is Tilly going to make for
Miss Hope when she comes round for tea?

Word Search *what a great book*

There are ten wedding-related words hidden in the word search below – can you spot them all?

Z	C	B	B	P	E	U	H	G	O	A	Z	O	E	A
F	Y	O	G	N	G	K	O	L	M	A	N	O	T	D
G	B	U	N	K	P	X	A	H	I	H	H	H	E	Y
M	U	Q	U	F	Z	X	D	C	L	S	R	I	N	G
G	G	U	D	G	E	H	A	Q	W	M	T	D	W	H
G	K	E	Y	X	E	T	W	N	D	O	R	E	J	X
I	M	T	N	D	Q	O	T	I	M	E	X	L	C	I
D	R	S	P	E	F	N	A	I	S	E	C	N	A	D
I	B	S	A	C	C	M	X	S	O	J	V	F	M	I
X	K	B	P	N	S	Q	H	J	A	T	E	Z	R	W
F	H	S	W	E	Z	V	U	T	F	U	L	R	X	J
Z	Q	V	D	O	M	Z	H	Y	H	S	Q	Y	J	Q
W	Z	I	I	U	Q	J	K	H	H	A	S	L	R	U
X	R	U	O	P	P	V	C	G	U	Q	O	K	B	Z
B	C	H	A	M	P	A	G	N	E	F	L	C	O	P

BOUQUET BRIDESMAID CAKE
CHAMPAGNE CONFETTI DANCE
DRESS LIMO RING SHOE

Visit Jacqueline's Fantastic Website

There's a whole Jacqueline Wilson town to explore! You can generate your own special username, customize your online bedroom, test your knowledge of Jacqueline's books with fun quizzes and puzzles, and upload book reviews. There's lots of fun stuff to discover, including competitions, book trailers, and Jacqueline's scrapbook. And if you love writing, visit the special storytelling area!

Plus, you can hear the latest news from Jacqueline in her monthly diary, find out whether she's doing events near you, read her fan-mail replies, and chat to other fans on the message boards!

www.jacquelinewilson.co.uk

Also available

Jacqueline Wilson

ILLUSTRATED BY NICK SHARRATT

The Butterfly Club

Tina has always relied on her sisters. But can she learn to fly alone?

Also available

Also available

Jacqueline Wilson

ILLUSTRATED BY NICK SHARRATT

Cookie

Will Beauty and her mum find their Happy Ever After?